"Uncommon" is an apt title for Willi
accomplished collection of short fiction. '........ ...., ... calm, at the heart of these graceful, gentle stories. Cass provides his readers the space to ponder and reflect along with his mostly male characters who relate as much to their environments as they do other people. His protagonists are largely middle-aged or older, often reticent, quiet observers who are pulled into the lives of others. They sometimes regret actions not taken but at other times seek to right a wrong, to take a risk for those in more vulnerable positions. Pain and hope often cohabit the same narrative. Cass plumbs the complex depths of isolation and loneliness but also underscores the resilience of the human heart. The result is a beautifully realized composite of fictional worlds that resonates with authenticity.
—**Kerry Langan**, author of *My Name Is Your Name & Other Stories, Live Your Life & Other Stories*, and *Only Beautiful & Other Stories*

William Cass writes stories that will break your heart and then stitch it back together. *Uncommon & Other Stories* consists of fourteen small unflinching slices of life. Vividly real people deal with tragedies and regrets, but the stories are leavened with hope, grace, and affirmation. Cass's masterful prose is spare and straight forward, immersing you in each story's world and making you care deeply about the characters and how the story develops.
—**McKie Campbell**, author of *Clean Slate* and *North Coast*

The characters in William Cass's *Uncommon & Other Stories* are mortal beings striving to realize their humanity. In settings of landscape and place, these characters go about the business of finding a self—of compassion, forgiveness, empathy, discernment, and pursuit—that leans toward or consummates the better side of humanity's nature. The stories thus pulse with a verisimilitude within the journey of self as soul, just as Ryan and the elderly Mrs. Wheeler in the opening story, "Uncommon," find unexpected revelations in the depths of their simply living their lives. In the thirteen stories that follow, the characters—Isabel or Haley, Brad or Iris, Stan or Tim or Stuart, Ruth or Drew, Nick or Sam—are testaments to the ongoing search of an interconnected, perceivable, human existence.
—**Sandra Fluck**, *The Write Launch*

UNCOMMON & OTHER STORIES

UNCOMMON

&

OTHER STORIES

WILLIAM CASS

Wising Up Press Collective
Wising Up Press

Wising Up Press
P.O. Box 2122
Decatur, GA 30031-2122
www.universaltable.org

Catalogue-in-Publication data is on file with the Library of Congress.
LCCN: 2022951006

Wising Up ISBN: 978-1-7376940-6-9

For my mom, dad, Grandma Cass . . . and Charlie

CONTENTS

UNCOMMON

It was just before 9:00 a.m.. Ryan had been sitting in his car at the curb for ten minutes after pulling up in front of the house he'd been looking for. His shoulders were still slumped. The place was about what he'd expected, a ramshackle little bungalow surrounded by a dried-out lawn and a low fence badly in need of paint that was missing pickets on each side. An empty bird bath perched in a bed of dying roses in one corner, a few late blooms wilting through their tarnished foliage. Where the front walk met the sidewalk, a crooked mailbox dangled partway open like a stifled yawn.

Ryan waited a little longer, listening to the diminishing tick of his engine, then forced his lanky frame out of the car. He blew out a long breath and made his way up the red brick walk and three short steps to the front door. There was no bell, so he pounded on it twice. He heard shuffling inside, accompanied by an old woman's mumbling voice. Perhaps a minute later, a series of locks were unleashed, and she emerged in the opening. She couldn't have been much more than five feet tall and wore a shabby blue housedress that she clutched at her chest with one hand. In the other, she held a green plastic cup. He could see her skull through her cap of cotton-candy hair. Behind large oval glasses, her eyes darted then narrowed, uneasy and suspicious. Ryan put her in her mid-seventies.

She said, "You the young man who answered my ad?"

Her voice was low-pitched, gravelly. He nodded.

"You're Ryan."

"Right." He saw her frown deepen. "You Mrs. Wheeler?"

"Yes."

They regarded one another while a car alarm sounded nearby, then stopped.

Finally, she said, "And you're trustworthy."

He shrugged. "Hope so."

"You keep yourself clean, bathe regularly?"

He nodded again, then watched her lift the cup to her mouth and spit into it.

"Ever been in trouble with the law?'

"No," he lied. "Never."

She looked him up and down. "You appear healthy enough, all your limbs attached. Why are you available for this job?"

He gave another shrug. "Just got out of the service. Sort of between things right now. Need something to pay the rent for the time being while I figure out what's next."

"Where do you live?"

"I have a little studio. Over on Divinity Street."

"Near the cemetery."

"That's right."

She spat into the cup again. "Live alone?"

He gave another nod.

"Me, too. Guess that's obvious. Health stuff and my age are why I need a bit of assistance."

He kept nodding.

She looked past him, then back up at his eyes. "I used to have a dog. He was good company. But he died, too." She let another moment pass. "You might consider getting a dog if it's allowed where you're living. Nice to have around. Another beating heart, you know?"

"Sure."

She took a turn nodding and spat again. "Okay, then. First, I need you to take me to a doctor's appointment. One quick stop on the way back, and I have to pick up a few things at the pharmacy, too, before we get home; it's just up the street. And I need the latch on my kitchen window fixed and the trash cans brought to the curb for collection tomorrow. Maybe three, four hours total. Can you do those things?"

"I can, yes."

"Wait here, then. I'll be out in a bit."

The door closed slowly. Ryan gave another sigh, then turned around and sat down on the top step. It was cold, an early rime of frost coating the lawn. He zipped his old Army-issue jacket up closer to his chin and pictured himself later going into his corner tavern and telling the big bartender, Jesse, about this. "Yeah," he imagined himself saying, "she's a piece of work, but I need the money." He wouldn't say, "Hard to find anything else on the heels of a Dishonorable Discharge." Without wanting to, his thoughts drifted back to when he'd been escorted out of the base gates at Fort Jackson. After they closed behind him, he'd tried one more time shouting after the guards as they walked away that he'd been framed. He'd bought a few of those drugs, but had never sold any. He clasped his hands together between his legs and rocked a little back and forth.

Ryan stood up when he heard Mrs. Wheeler come through the front door. He watched her go through elaborate steps to re-lock it. She wore a brown overcoat over a tan dress and plain black shoes over black hose. She stuck out the hand that didn't hold the green cup and said, "Here, give me your arm."

Ryan extended the one closest to her, she gripped it, and he helped her slowly down the steps and up the walk into the passenger side of his car. After he got her snapped into the seat belt and was in himself, he started the engine. The heater came on full blast with it. He looked over at her and said, "Where to?"

"1015 Division."

She stared straight ahead, small in the seat, her mouth set hard.

"Okay," he said and pulled away from the curb.

With the start of workday traffic finished, the streets were fairly empty. The mid-October morning continued as overcast as it had begun. They turned onto Division and passed old strip malls and businesses on both sides of the street, nearly bare trees here and there along the sidewalks, traffic lights swaying on wires in the small, cold breeze.

Mrs. Wheeler spat a longer, phlegm-filled wad into the cup, wiped her lips with a tissue, and asked, "What make of car is this?"

"Valiant."

"Old."

He chuckled. "Yeah."

"Parents give it to you?"

"No, they left when I was little."

She jerked her head suddenly his way. "Who raised you then?"

"An aunt. She moved away while I was in the service."

"So, you're alone now."

"I know people." He glanced her way. "Grew up here."

"What high school did you go to?"

"North Central."

From the corner of his eye, he saw her nod. "I taught elementary school a few blocks from there. Second grade." She paused, spat again. "Thirty-three years."

He glanced over at her again, then back to the road. "I went to a different elementary, but I know where that's at. Big, brick building."

He saw her nod again, more slowly this time.

They drove the rest of the way in silence. It only took ten more minutes to reach a series of buildings at the address she'd given him that formed a medical cluster. He parked in front of the one she indicated, helped her out, and she leaned a hand again on his arm. She pointed to the office in front of them. He looked at the sign next to the door, which held several doctors' names under the word "Oncology" and felt his muscles tighten.

"Careful," Mrs. Wheeler said, nudging him forward. "Might be slippery."

After he got her inside and up to the receptionist's window, he found a chair in the waiting area and sat down. The receptionist buzzed Mrs. Wheeler in right away, and Ryan watched her spit, then shuffle through the door that had opened and disappear inside. The waiting room was empty. Except for the tap of the receptionist's fingernails on the keyboard behind her glass screen, it was silent. Ryan found a magazine on the table next to him and began leafing quickly through it, reading nothing. He wished there was something to distinguish the place, but there wasn't: just the sterile walls, the occasional tap on the keyboard, the stillness afterwards, and whatever went on through that door that Mrs. Wheeler had passed through.

She came back out about a half-hour later, spat once into her cup, then nodded towards the exit.

"You need a card with a reminder about your next appointment?" the receptionist called after her.

"No," Mrs. Wheeler mumbled. "I can remember."

Ryan opened the door for her, she took his arm, and he got her settled back in his car. After he'd started the engine, she said, "Head back the way we came. I'll show you where to turn."

Ryan backed out and drove onto Division again. He glanced over and saw that Mrs. Wheeler had resumed her straight-ahead stare, at what, he didn't know. He let a few minutes pass before he asked, "Appointment go all right?"

She shrugged.

"What kind was it? Initial, ongoing, follow-up?"

"Follow-up."

He felt his shoulders loosen. "You finished treatments then?"

He glanced over long enough to see her nod once. He waited another moment, then said, "Those go okay?"

She shrugged again. "So they told me. Won't know for sure until they do another PET scan in a couple months."

He nodded slowly. "If you don't mind me asking, what kind was it?"

She coughed and hacked up another longer, mucus-filled stream into the cup. When she pulled it away, a string of phlegm stayed attached to it from her lips like a dangling spider-web. Her swipe with a tissue to remove it seemed almost angry.

Ryan waited another moment before saying, "I think you were going to tell me the type of cancer you had."

She looked out her side window and shook her head. "Base of tongue," she said. "I never smoked."

"Shucks," Ryan gave a low whistle. "That really sucks."

"Yeah," Mrs. Wheeler muttered. She spat again. Afterwards, she appeared to try to swallow, then grimaced in a way that made Ryan wince. She slapped her hand hard across her thigh and said, "These damn excess secretions have been going on since chemo and radiation ended a month ago. They never stop: 24/7. I'm sick and tired of it. Can't sleep worth a shit."

Ryan stiffened again. "That's awful. Can't they do anything about it?"

Mrs. Wheeler took a slip of paper out of her coat pocket and shook it. "Gave me another new script," she said. "Potassium iodine this time. Said it might help dry them up."

Ryan glanced once more her way, then back at the road, and said, "Sure hope it does."

A few blocks later, she said suddenly, "Turn right at the next light."

"That's my street."

She nodded. Ryan turned on Divinity, and as he slowed through the neighborhood, Mrs. Wheeler said, "Show me where you live."

He passed another few cross-streets, then pointed to a ranch-style house on a little berm with two garages at the end. He said, "I live in that last one."

"The last garage?"

"Has everything I need."

"It's a damn garage."

He shrugged and attempted a sheepish grin. Disbelief filled her face, and he watched her lips draw into a line of disapproval. They drove in silence for several more blocks until Mrs. Wheeler said, "Go in here."

They'd come to the cemetery. Ryan crept along its central gravel lane towards the back while Mrs. Wheeler unlocked her seat belt and pulled her purse onto her lap. She held up her hand just before the lane ended. "This will do," she said. "And I can walk myself. It's just a few steps."

Ryan watched her heave open the door and carry her purse and cup across a short stretch of grass. The frost had burned off, but she still stepped haltingly. She came to two gravestones ten feet or so from the car and stopped in front of them. One was tall and the other short; moss had grown over both, though the smaller one was almost covered with it. Ryan could only make out the "D" of a first name on the larger gravestone. Mrs. Wheeler stood very still, her back to him, a cirrus cloud inching slowly above the treetops beyond her. He couldn't tell if she was praying or crying, though she made no prayer-like gestures and her shoulders weren't shaking.

He'd turned off the engine and hunched his jacket up against the cold. Ryan didn't know if his parents were still alive or buried somewhere themselves; if his aunt knew, she hadn't told him and he'd never thought to ask. As he gazed across the long slopes of gravestones in each direction standing grim and silent, he wondered what he'd do when his aunt died. He realized he'd truly be on his own then, although he'd always felt rejected and resentful. Even when he'd finally happened upon those few equally ostracized guys to hang out with in high school that he'd loosely called friends. They'd first introduced him to drugs. But not one of them was there for him after he'd been arrested while making a buy for the group, and he'd seen none of them since returning from his stint in the service.

A plane flew off above the cloud as silent as the gravestones and disappeared into the distance. He watched Mrs. Wheeler raise her cup slowly and spit into it. Occasionally, the cold breeze lifted the bottom of her coat. Eventually, she opened her purse and took out two tired rose blooms, the stems cut at about three inches each. Ryan recognized the white-pink blossoms curled with brown from the front of her house and thought she'd must have taken time to find the best two remaining. She bent down and set one against each gravestone, not having bothered with any container or even damp tissue and foil around the stems. Then she reached out her fingertips towards the gravestones, turned, and made her careful way back to the car. Ryan got it started and the heater blowing again before she arranged herself inside. He reached over and helped her clasp her seatbelt, then they left the cemetery and drove without speaking until she directed him the last few streets to the pharmacy.

They went through the same basic routine at the pharmacy as they had at the doctor's office. Mrs. Wheeler asked him to get more Kleenex while she waited for the prescription to be filled. He came up beside her with three boxes as the pharmacist was explaining how to administer the new med. She nodded when he finished and said, "I should also have a couple more waiting. clotrimazole lozenges and hydrocodone. Oh, and some two-by-two gauzes and 60 cc syringes, too."

Ryan felt his pulse quicken at the mention of the second med; it wasn't the strongest opioid he knew of, but it would do. The pharmacist retrieved the additional meds and supplies, rang her up, and they were back in the car and heading home a few minutes later. He helped her up to the front step with one hand and carried her bag from the pharmacy in the other. After she finished with the locks, she had him follow her inside into a dim living room with the curtains pulled at all the windows, through a small, similarly darkened dining room, and into a kitchen with an L-shaped counter that was full of light from two windows over the sink. Mrs. Wheeler put her purse on the counter and motioned for him to set the bag there, too. Then she pointed to a toolbox next to the sink.

"That used to be my husband's," she said. "You should be able to find what you need in it. The window that needs fixing is the left one. Won't latch right anymore."

Ryan tried the window's locking mechanism, which caught at the tip of the groove into which it was supposed to slide. "Probably just needs adjusting," he said. "These old windows settle funny after a while."

He jiggled the bottom half of the window, slid it up and down, then selected a screwdriver from the toolbox. While he worked, he heard her spit again, then empty the contents of the bag from the pharmacy.

"What are those meds for?" he asked as casually as he could while he unscrewed one portion of the latch.

"Told you about the new one," she said. He heard her fold the bag and slide it into a lower cupboard. "The lozenges are for a delightful thrush fungus I've developed in my mouth from the accumulation of all the secretions: slimy, tenacious, nasty stuff. The hydrocodone is for the pain in my throat from all the radiation treatments; still hurts like hell in there, but I don't use it much. Scares me."

He nodded as he adjusted the placement of the latch slightly, tried the slide, then re-set it with a screw. While he did, she carried the items from the counter into her bedroom. He swore to himself because he'd hoped to see where she stored the hydrocodone. When she came back, he'd already replaced the screwdriver in the toolbox and was sliding the latch back and forth.

"See," he told her. "Good as new."

She nodded, but didn't smile. Instead, she tried to swallow again, grimaced, and dropped her head, shaking it hard. A short groan escaped her. With her head still lowered, she pointed to the back door. "Trash cans are out there." Her voice seemed rougher. "Bring those to the end of the driveway and you're done for today."

When he came back inside, he found her in the darkened dining room sitting at the table. She still wore her coat, but held her head cradled in one hand, her elbow propped on the table. Her eyes were closed; she looked exhausted. She extended an envelope his way with her free hand. He took it from her and saw money inside.

"That should cover today," she mumbled. "Can you come at the same time tomorrow?"

"Sure," he told her. "You bet."

"Okay, then. Thanks. You can go."

He hesitated, watching her sitting there perfectly still. He said, "You going to be all right?"

The head in her hand gave a slight nod.

"You sure?"

She made the same gesture. He thought about giving her a quick touch of reassurance, but thought better of it. Instead, he walked through the living room and let himself out through the front door.

❧❧ ⚜ ❧❧

Ryan stopped at a fast-food drive-thru on the way home. When he got to his studio, he hung his jacket inside the door, turned on the space heater, and ate standing at the counter with the TV turned low for some noise. The owner had converted the space himself to build the studio, and he'd made a rough go at it. Ryan had spread an old area rug on the concrete floor, found a second-hand pull-out couch, television, and a stand-up lamp along with some linens and basic kitchen supplies at a thrift store, and made it home. There wasn't really a kitchen; just a mini-fridge, small microwave, and two-burner hot plate built into the counter the owner had thrown together in the space where a washer and dryer had been; an industrial-basin sink that had gone with the washer and dryer still stood next to it that he used for sponge baths. The only window was the small one in the side door that served as his entrance. A tiny utility bathroom with no tub or shower was across from the door, and none of the wiring was up to code. The owner lived in the house attached to the garages and was a retired vet who gave him a discount on the rent when he heard that Ryan had been in the Army; Ryan didn't tell him about his discharge.

After he ate, he sat on the couch and booted up his laptop; the owner let him hook into his wi-fi and cable for free. He smoked half a joint, answered a few emails, then played warfare video games for a couple of hours alternating between membership sites he belonged to. He fell asleep about three, his chin in his chest, the games he was playing still active. His head jerked with an occasional dream as he slept.

Ryan awoke with a startle to a room that had already grown murky in the late afternoon's decline. As they often did, his thoughts went immediately to the fellow plebe who'd sold him the dope and then convinced the authorities that Ryan had been the distributor, and stopped himself from grinding his teeth. He chased those memories away and thought instead of Mrs. Wheeler. He wondered what she was doing alone there in that house with her green plastic cup as the late afternoon crept towards evening. He rubbed his chin, shook his head to try to clear it, grabbed his jacket, and walked down the street to his corner tavern.

The place was long and narrow with a pool table in back and a few booths to one side; it was about half-full and as dimly lit as Mrs. Wheeler's house. Ryan found his customary stool at the near end of the bar and exchanged nods with Jesse. The big bartender finished with the customers he was serving, then brought over a draft beer and set it on a coaster in front of Ryan. They exchanged fist bumps, and Jesse watched Ryan take a long sip through the foam. They'd gone to the same high school, but Jesse was a few years older, so they'd been more acquaintances than real friends.

"So." Jesse put his hands flat on the bar. "How goes the battle?"

Ryan tipped his head from side to side. "Not bad."

"You start that new job?"

Ryan nodded.

"And?"

"And." Ryan paused. "And, it's okay. Easy." He took another swallow of beer. "Old lady's recovering from cancer, which I knew nothing about beforehand."

"That so?"

"Yeah," Ryan said. "Lives alone. Kind of sad."

"Why don't you bring her in, buy her a beer?"

Ryan laughed. "Don't think so. She can hardly walk from me to you."

"Remind you of your aunt?"

Ryan frowned and considered the woman, his dead grandmother's sister, who had basically raised him. She'd wanted a warmer year-round climate after he enlisted, so had sold her place quickly and moved into a mobile home park down south. She'd always been abrupt, but supportive and patient, much more so than he deserved.

"Maybe a little," he said. "Hadn't thought of that."

Jesse left to take an order from the other end of the bar, and the place gradually filled with its usual after-work crowd. Ryan drank in fits and starts, nursing three beers and a hot dog until just after seven, then walked home along the empty street. The neighborhood had seen better days and wasn't much different than Mrs. Wheeler's or the one he'd grown up in.

At home, he finished the other half of the joint he'd started, then stretched out on the couch and channel surfed on the television. He fell asleep a little before ten. He awoke briefly fifteen minutes or so later, but didn't bother turning off the TV or pulling out the couch; instead, he just yanked the afghan his aunt had knitted him off the couch's back, wrapped himself in it, turned over, and fell asleep again.

🦇🦇 🕷 🦇🦇

About that same time, Mrs. Wheeler finished her last feed and meds for the day, flushed the extension leading to the G-tube they'd inserted in her stomach before treatments began, threw away the formula cartons, and washed out the syringes and extension at the kitchen sink. She tore off a piece of paper towel and left them on it on the counter to dry. She'd skipped the hydrocodone against her doctor's bedtime recommendations and had given herself a liquid pain reliever instead. The lozenge she'd been sucking on had finally dissolved, so she spat secretions, phlegm, and thrush into the sink, rinsed it, broke the string dangling from her lips with the back of her hand, swore once, and flipped off the ceiling light.

Mrs. Wheeler went into her bedroom. She'd already changed into her flannel nightgown and arranged the cup, Kleenex box, and washcloths on her nightstand, as well as the pile of prop pillows against the bed's headboard. She'd also turned on the humidifier at the foot of her bed earlier so that it had time to fill the room before she tried to sleep. She gave a hopeful sigh, turned off the lamp on the nightstand, climbed under the covers, and settled herself so that she was almost sitting upright against the stack of pillows, the position she found most comfortable given her circumstances. She reached over, clutched the cup in one hand and a washcloth in the other, and sighed again into the darkness. Instinctively, she slid the hand in which she held the washcloth over to the side of the bed where Dale had always slept until his accident ten years earlier. She tried to swallow, grimaced against the pain, then closed her eyes and willed sleep to come.

It was quiet: just the faint sound of the nightstand clock and an occasional passing car in the street. She tried to concentrate on her breathing, keeping her inhales short and her exhales long and extended. The first ten minutes passed deliciously without event, but then she felt the first tickle in the center of her chest. She tried to breathe up to and not over it, but the cough came anyway, and with it, she raised the cup to her lips and spent twenty seconds emptying her lungs, stomach, and mouth of phlegm, mucus, and secretions that were the consistency of Cream of Wheat. That spot in her chest where the tickle began, as well as the lining of her airway above it, had grown raw and tender over the past month, but she tried to reassure herself again with the oncologists' insistence that her excessive secretions were a normal side effect for a patient in her stage of recovery from the particular treatment she'd endured, as was the nasal drainage and drip that she wiped away with the washcloth from the tip of her nose. When she'd asked how long they'd last, she was told it was impossible to say for certain; they might begin their transition to permanent dry mouth any day, or they could persist several months or more. Her salivary glands had basically been attacked and burnt during treatment with daily radiation, and this was their natural reaction to the end of that onslaught.

She spat again, secretions only, into her cup and tried to settle back into the pile of pillows. She'd given up trying to figure out how many hours of sleep she got during a typical night; she guessed perhaps a few total, but it only came in brief, odd snatches of fifteen or twenty minutes at a time before she'd need to clear secretions again and reposition herself. She allowed for two more coughing fits, the second including retching, gagging, and vomiting a little stomach acid into her cup, before climbing out of bed, rinsing the cup and her mouth at the bathroom sink, then scattering the pile of prop pillows to the floor and lying flat on the mattress on her stomach. She took care to be sure the G-tube button wasn't twisted beneath her. It was a position that she found almost untenable, but the only one that slowed the nasal drainage a bit so she could claim those brief snatches of sleep. She awoke sore and stiff after each, and changing sides did little to mitigate her discomfort. She cursed at the irritation the bile in the vomit caused to the array of mouth and throat sores she'd developed during radiation.

Lying there, she tried, like always, to ignore her discomfort and force herself instead to think of pleasant memories of time spent with Dale, and many years before that, the brief period they had together with their son, Tom. But those thoughts were episodic at best, like short stints of calm and repose between another stroke of lightning and tumble of thunder in a storm preceded by the haunting tickle in her chest.

❧❧ ⚜ ❧❧

The next morning, Mrs. Wheeler was waiting in the open front doorway as Ryan came up the walk. She wore the same housecoat and gripped the same cup as the day before and appeared a little more bent to him as she let him inside. She pulled out two chairs at the dining room table, and they sat down. The curtains had been opened a bit, but the room was still dim.

Ryan watched her spit into the cup, then asked, "How was your night?"

The old woman gave a dismissive shrug. "Not great."

"Sorry about that. The new med didn't help?"

"Not so I could tell." She reached suddenly for her right ear, cupped it, and grimaced.

"You okay?"

She shrugged again. She lowered her hand slowly, and when she glanced up at him next, Ryan could see that her eyes had gone watery against the pain.

"That's something new. You call your doctor about it?"

Mrs. Wheeler shook her head. "Not yet. Took a little hydrocodone. Hoping that will help."

Ryan raised himself from his chair. "Should I get you some more?"

"Nah." She made a gesture with her hand like she was shooing away a fly, then slid a blank check across the table to him. He settled back in his chair and saw that it was dated and signed with the merchant filled in, but had no amount inserted. "Want you to concentrate on that front fence today," she told him. "It needs painting and some pickets have to be replaced. Check first in the garage to see what Dale left there that you can still use. Then go to the hardware store on the corner of Sprague and South Pine and buy the rest."

"Dale?"

"My husband. Before he died." She paused. "He was pretty handy."

"Okay," Ryan said. "I can do that." He picked up the check and looked at it. "Won't I need some identification to use this?"

She shook her head and spat again. "No, Dale worked there after he retired. There won't be a problem; the staff all know me."

"What was his job before he retired?"

"Supervisor in the M&O department at the school district where I taught. Redesigned their whole work-order system. Streamlined it." The gaze she gave him looked almost challenging.

Ryan said, "That so?"

In a sudden, swift motion, she grabbed at her ear again and her jaw set hard.

"You sure you don't want me to run you to that doctor again?"

She made the same dismissive gesture with her hand. "No. Time for my morning feed." She pointed. "You passed the garage yesterday when you took out the trash. Bring those cans back in again, too, when they've been emptied."

Ryan nodded, slipped the check into his jacket pocket, and stood up. "That ear hurt on the side you had cancer?"

"Yes."

"You'll let me know if it gets worse?"

Mrs. Wheeler made a last dismissive wave with her hand, less vigorous this time. "Go on with you," she said. "Get to work."

❧❧❧

Mrs. Wheeler finished her morning feed and flush quickly, then went into her bedroom where she sat on the edge of the bed. She clenched her teeth against the pain in her ear and forehead; it had begun near her eardrum during the middle of the night, but had gradually spread outward and higher in each of its successive waves. It came on first as a dull ache, then grew into stabbing spikes so intense she felt blinding flashes behind her eye and thought several times that she was going to pass out. The top of her head on that side had grown too sensitive to touch, and she only put on her glasses when she had to because even those felt heavy on her face. She'd waited until after dawn to try the hydrocodone, but it had done little to mitigate her discomfort, nor had the other over-the-counter meds she'd tried earlier.

She felt another wave beginning and lowered herself to her side. She attempted to breathe evenly against it, but her gasps came more quickly in spite of those efforts, each was accompanied by a short moan that she could not control. She raised her knees up towards her chest until she was almost in a fetal position. As it had more and more recently, the familiar realization of how utterly alone she was crept through her like a shadow. Mrs. Wheeler began to weep silently as she suffered and waited. The first episode had lasted only a few minutes, but this one took almost a half-hour before it began to pass.

❧❧ 🕸 ❧❧

Ryan was pleasantly surprised to find Dale's former garage workshop meticulously organized under the pale light of a tin-shaded bulb: tools arranged by size on a peg board on its back wall with screws, nuts, and bolts mounted there, too, in old jars. Pieces of woodworking projects were cordoned off in sections and labeled at the back of the bench itself: birdhouse, coat rack, lazy susan. It looked like they were all in the process of being built, but there wasn't a speck of dust anywhere. Mrs. Wheeler had replaced Dale's toolbox on one side of the bench and the other held shelves with various paints, stains, and varnishes along with brushes, sandpaper, and such organized by type and grade. Ryan quickly found a nearly-full gallon of exterior white paint and primer combo, as well as the brushes, drop cloths, and other supplies he'd need for painting the fence. He also selected an assortment of potential wood screws from the jars on the peg board, pocketed them, and carried those things along with the toolbox out front.

Ryan surveyed the front of the house. From what little he knew about the man, he thought Dale would be dismayed at the sorry state it had fallen into since his passing. He quickly counted the number of missing pickets, unscrewed and discarded a couple more that were on their last legs, found the correct length wood screw to use for re-attaching, and pulled all the weeds along the bottom of the fence line. Then he got started with the sanding. There had been no rain for several weeks, so the fence's wood was good and dry. The morning was still cold, but the haze burned off and gave way to sun; by the time Ryan had finished sanding the first side, he'd unzipped his jacket all the way, and he'd taken it off altogether before he'd completed the rest of the fence a couple of hours later. Occasionally, he'd seen Mrs. Wheeler peeking at his progress through the living room curtains.

As he was storing the paints and various supplies he'd need next under the elm tree in the yard, Mrs. Wheeler opened the front door and called to him. "I made some lunch. Come eat it. Use the back door. There's a bathroom through my bedroom to clean up."

Ryan went around to the back of the house, sliding the emptied trash cans into their original spots as he did, and dropped in his bag of weeds. He went inside, locked the door to the bathroom, used the toilet and washed up at the sink, then let the water from both faucets continue to run. Mrs. Wheeler's meds and other supplies were stacked neatly where the sink counter met her bedroom wall. The hydrocodone was in the largest bottle at the back. He shook it and found it nearly full. Ryan had only tried opioids a few times, but liked the way they made him feel. He liked it a lot. He knew he'd have to take at least a few long belts for any type of lasting buzz, and figured he could refill the bottle with water to approximate the present amount in it. She'd probably never notice the difference, but then its strength wouldn't cover whatever pain she was feeling, especially the new one in her ear. He opened the bottle's cap, sniffed the contents, then re-screwed it, replaced it where it had been, and looked up. A plain young man with a crooked nose and troubled eyes stared back at him in the mirror. He shook his head, turned off the faucets, and left the bathroom.

Ryan went into the dining room where she'd set a place for him at the table with a bowl of tomato soup, some Saltines, and a glass of milk. She'd changed into sweat pants and a cotton blouse.

"Looks good," Ryan said. "Thanks. Aren't you going to have some?"

"Can't eat by mouth again yet," she told him. "Have to take everything through this."

She lifted the blouse up to the bottom of her bra, and Ryan could see the capped G-tube button backed by a single square of gauze just to the left of her breastbone's bottom. "You get started while it's hot," she said. "I'll join you in a minute."

She went through the kitchen into her bedroom while Ryan sat down at the table, broke the crackers into his soup, stirred it, and began eating. He looked around the room as he did. The wall that joined the kitchen had glass cupboards with a buffet beneath it. Two photographs anchored either end of the buffet, both in frames tarnished by age. In the first, a happy-looking young couple posed arm-in-arm in front of a waterfall, their smiles squinting against the sun. The second was of a boy around seven years of age standing behind the house wearing an oversized baseball uniform and holding a wooden bat with one hand and a fielder's glove in the other; his grin was missing teeth and his eyes were hidden by a too-big cap that covered the tops of his ears.

Mrs. Wheeler came back into the room carrying her feeding supplies and sat down in the chair next to Ryan in front of the buffet. She arranged two cartons of formula, a measuring bowl, an extension tube, a large plastic bottle of water, several syringes, a handful of napkins, and her green cup in front of her. Ryan watched her click the extension into place at her G-tube, twist it so it pointed up at her chin, and pour formula into the measuring bowl. Next, she twisted an empty syringe into the top of the extension, filled it with water, released the extension's clamp, and watched gravity empty the water into her stomach, the skin there clammy-white and wrinkled. She followed this by filling another syringe with formula from the measuring bowl, wiping its tip with a napkin, then using its plunger to slowly empty it into her stomach.

As she repeated the formula process, Ryan tried to only glance at her and to keep eating his soup as naturally as possible, but she met his gaze on one glance and said, "One and a half cartons of this four times a day, plus three liters of water. Hydration, the doctors call it. Some of it after the feed and some at other times. Means I basically have to do this eight times between waking up and going to bed, leaving set intervals between each. Then there are meds that I also have to take periodically through the tube, too, a half-dozen or so at various times throughout the day. Another handful of swallowing exercises I'm supposed to do daily, as well, so I don't lose that ability and the muscles involved don't atrophy. It's basically around the clock . . . more damn things to keep track of than when I was teaching."

"Sounds like." Ryan held his empty spoon above the bowl. "Keeps you busy, I guess."

Mrs. Wheeler gave a small grunt that approximated a derisive chuckle and shook her head. "Suppose so," she mumbled. He watched her spit into her green cup, finger her ear gingerly, then fill another syringe with formula.

They ate together in silence for the next few minutes, Ryan being careful not to slurp the soup. By the time he'd finished and pushed away the bowl, the sun had grown high enough with the partly drawn curtains that the dim room had brightened some. He cleared his throat and decided to take a chance.

"I like those photographs on the buffet." She watched him point. "That one there you and Dale?"

She glanced quickly at the first photograph and nodded. "On our honeymoon. Bridge was at the place we stayed on a reservoir in the mountains. We went back every summer after that until the end. Swam every day." For the first time, Ryan saw her give the hint of a smile. "It was very beautiful. Still is, I suppose."

"I'll bet." Ryan smiled, too.

She nodded and filled a new syringe with formula, but didn't look his way. He waited another few seconds, then said, "And that other one. Who's the little boy?"

A cloud seemed to pass over Mrs. Wheeler's face, and her hand paused on the plunger of the syringe. She kept her eyes averted and said, "Our son. His name was Tom."

It was hard to hear her voice. Ryan watched her resume using the plunger to insert and suck up more formula. To busy himself, he took a sip of milk. A street sweeper passed outside the dining room beyond the ivy-covered fence that separated the deck there from the sidewalk. It made slow, scratching rotations past the house up towards the corner. When the sound of it had all but faded away, Mrs. Wheeler said, "You can just leave those dishes if you're done. Go ahead and get started on that fence again."

Although she wasn't looking, Ryan nodded. He got up from the table. "Thanks again. That was good," he told her. "So, I'll run to that hardware store now. Should be back shortly. Need me to pick you up anything else while I'm gone?"

She shook her head, her eyes studying the syringe as she filled it with new formula.

"Might get a few more things for the front yard while I'm there. That okay?"

She nodded, but appeared distracted. When the syringe was full, she spat phlegm into her cup, rubbed her ear again, then seemed to struggle to secure the syringe's tip into the extension. Ryan left her there with her thoughts and preoccupations and went out the back door into the sun-splashed afternoon.

🦇🦇 🦋 🦇🦇

He'd finished securing the new pickets and painting two sections of the fence shortly before five with the sun hovering just above the roofs of houses across the street. Ryan stored away the supplies neatly in the garage, estimated again the number of old red bricks stacked beneath the workbench, washed out the brushes at a sink like the one in his studio, and set them on rags on the workbench to dry. He went up to the back door and knocked on it. There was no answer. He knocked again, waited another minute, then pushed the door open and called, "Mrs. Wheeler, I'm done for today."

There was no response that he could hear. He frowned, entered the house, closed the door, and called her name again. He was greeted again by silence, so he went through the kitchen into her bedroom where he found her lying on her stomach partly on the bed with her legs dangling off of it. One of her hands still clutched the green cup extended above her head as if in offering, but there was a large pool of secretions on the bedspread that had drained and spread from her mouth and her eyes were squeezed shut. When he got close enough, he could hear her constant and almost inaudible moans; they came with each short breath, and her free hand was cupped partly over her bad ear and partly over her forehead.

Ryan touched her shoulder and asked, "What's wrong? Tell me."

She grimaced, shook her head, and whispered, "It hurts so bad."

"Come on," Ryan said, gripping her under the arm and lifting. "Let's get you to the ER."

In less than a minute, he had her to her feet with her overcoat draped over her shoulders, and several minutes later, he was speeding down the street with her towards the closest hospital. It wasn't much more than a five-minute drive, and when he shouted for help after he pulled up in front of the emergency room entrance, two nurses were there within seconds getting Mrs. Wheeler into a wheelchair. She was whimpering by then, slumped towards her bad side, her hand still cupped in the same manner. Ryan watched them whisk her through automatic doors, then found a place to park, went inside, explained things to the receptionist, and sat down on a hard plastic chair. Ryan glanced at his watch, and the thought crossed his mind that he'd normally be getting his second beer from Jesse around then; since it was a Friday night, he'd usually also be there for several more, hopeful with the larger crowd of women, but he always went home alone.

A doctor in a white coat finally came into the empty ER waiting room a little before nine. He regarded Ryan for a moment, then came over and sat down next to him. "You the guy who brought Mrs. Wheeler in? Ryan?"

"That's right."

"She authorized you as the person we could speak to about what's going on with her. Said she had no one else. Called you her caretaker."

Ryan felt his eyebrows raise. "Okay," he heard himself say. "Sure."

"Well, we did a CT scan and then an MRI on her, and she has a sizable cavity where her cancerous tumor had been, as well as a small fracture in her hyoid bone, so we consulted with her oncologist by phone. It appears that combination has some nerves interacting in a very problematic way, nerves in her throat and to her ear, which can cause a lot of pain, excruciating sometimes. That cavity and bone have not healed completely and need to before this can be resolved. In the meantime, we'll experiment with a combination of nerve and pain meds until we find the right cocktail that can successfully manage her pain for the interim. That might take a little while, so we've already admitted her upstairs."

"For the night."

"At least."

"Can I see her?"

"No point. We've given her IV meds that will basically knock her out until morning, so she can get some sleep. Told us she's hardly slept for weeks." He gave Ryan's knee a quick pat. "Come back tomorrow."

Ryan bit his lip and nodded.

"She's a tough old nut," The doctor gave his knee a last pat. "That's for sure."

Ryan drove home in a daze. When he got there, he made himself a bowl of cereal and ate it in front of a soccer match on television he hardly knew was on. The worst pain Ryan had ever felt was a broken arm when he'd fallen out of a tree as a boy, and that had lasted less than an hour until it had been set at the hospital. Next to that, he'd had strep throat once and an eye infection another time that both hurt a lot. But he could only imagine what Mrs. Wheeler was going through. And that on top of the problems with her secretions and swallowing, the cancer treatments and prolonged recovery. At her age and by herself. He set the cereal bowl on the arm of the couch, put his head back, and was asleep in a matter of minutes.

Getting the right combination of meds to manage Mrs. Wheeler's pain proved to be tricky. But she had the nurse's call button she could use at any time when she could tell a bad episode was starting, and then they'd administer a quick-acting, high-potency opioid through her IV that usually began helping within minutes and promptly put her to sleep. They also administered all of her feeds, hydration, and regular meds for her, so she spent most of her time in grateful slumber.

That's where Ryan found her the next morning when he arrived just after visiting hours began at eight. He pulled a chair to her bedside, watched her sleep for a while, then looked around her room. He regarded the numbers and squiggly lines as they changed on the sat monitor fastened from a pole next to her bed, as well as the wires and probes that led from it under her covers. Sun crept low through the window in the wall beyond the bed, and through it, Ryan could see an exterior stairwell against another part of the hospital. There was a quiet murmur of voices from the hallway and at the nurse's station; otherwise, besides Mrs. Wheeler's soft snores, the muffled quiet seemed almost soothing.

Ryan sat there watching her sleep for nearly an hour until her face began to contort and her exhales became exaggerated. He winced himself watching her shoulders start to twitch; her movements reminded him of an agitated racehorse he'd once seen led into its starting gate. When she started to moan, Ryan searched for the nurse's call button and struggled with it until he got it pushed correctly. The same nurse who had showed him into the room, a young woman in green scrubs, appeared in the doorway a minute or so later, just as Mrs. Wheeler had opened her eyes partway, her face grimacing further and used her gravelly, low voice to plead for help.

The nurse went quickly to the bedside, sorted through a set of labeled syringes on a long lap table there, and inserted one into the port in the IV on the back of the hand closest to where Ryan sat. Mrs. Wheeler's moans grew louder.

After the nurse had finished, she flushed the line, then rubbed Mrs. Wheeler's wrist and said, "That should take care of the pain." She glanced at the clock on the wall. "And, look, that's getting better, lasting longer, closer to when you get your next time-release OxyContin. The doctor has upped that dosage, too, so you may not need many more of these boosts."

The nurse typed something into a computer on a stand next to the sat monitor. Mrs. Wheeler's eyes remained only partly open, but her moans grew gradually softer and further apart. He watched her fiddle with the wand tucked under the pillows by her side, flip a button on it that exposed its tip from a sleeve, suck the secretions from her mouth with it, flip the button again to re-cover the tip, and slide it back beneath her pillows. Finally, she blinked several times, turned her head Ryan's way and gave a startle; she looked almost frightened to Ryan without her glasses. Then the lines in her forehead eased and she said, "You came."

The old woman reached out the hand in which the IV was inserted, and Ryan grasped it gingerly with his own. He smiled. Then, just as suddenly, her eyes closed and her soft snores resumed. He waited a few more seconds before putting her hand back into the bed under the covers. The nurse had turned from the computer stand and had placed the empty syringe away from the others. She looked down at Ryan with kind eyes and said, "You must be her grandson."

He shook his head. "Just a friend."

"That's nice." Her eyes grew warmer. "Really nice."

Ryan nodded, a heat rising behind his ears, and they both looked at Mrs. Wheeler. Someone pushing a cart passed in the hall, and laughter came from the nurse's station. When it was quiet again, Ryan asked, "What happens with her now?"

The nurse shrugged. "She'll sleep. That's mostly what she'll be doing until we get this balance of pain and nerve meds right." She straightened the covers across Mrs. Wheeler's chest. "But that's fine. She needs it. I wouldn't wish what she's going through on my worst enemy."

Ryan nodded and stole a glance at her identification badge. Her name was Vicki, and if he'd seen her in his corner bar, he would have looked twice. They were quiet together until she said, "Well, then." She gave him a small smile, and he watched her leave the room. He stared at where she'd been, then waited another ten minutes, as Mrs. Wheeler's sleep seemed to grow more restful, before leaving himself.

❦❧ ❦❧

When he got to Mrs. Wheeler's house after leaving the hospital, he first finished painting the front fence, which only took another couple of hours. He cleaned the brushes, left them to dry, and filled a wheelbarrow to bring a load of the red bricks from under the workbench along with a spade out front. He used a pair of bricks to measure the entire length of the fence by taking turns placing them along its bottom as he crawled along next to it. Ryan made sure he had enough bricks, used one as a guide under a portion of the fence where the gap was particularly high, then began spading out a continuous gully in the grass that was the depth of a brick under the fence's pickets so that they could be placed short-end to short-end under it and keep weeds from inhibiting it again. He used a putty knife and a flat-head screwdriver, as well as his hands, to break the sections of turf away and to even the gully so it would have a consistent depth. Then he began carefully placing the bricks end-to-end under the fence as intended until they resembled a lawn-high pathway of their own mirroring the front walk. It took some time and detailed digging here and there to get them to all line up completely flat.

When he'd finished, he stood off on the sidewalk, put his hands on his hips, and admired his work; he thought that Dale would like the way the new bricks under the fence tied in with the walkway. The sun had already reached the roofs across the street; he'd completely forgotten about lunch. He heard a rustle from the house next door and glanced over to see a man in the nearest upstairs window slide it closed. He was staring down at Ryan with what looked like a faint smile in his close-cropped beard. When Ryan felt his forehead knit, the man gave him a thumbs-up, then disappeared into the house.

✒ ⚜ ✒

Very early the next morning, Mrs. Wheeler lay on her back looking out the window of her hospital room. A pale pink line mingled with the gray of dawn over the stairwell there. Late the afternoon before, the attending physician had told her that they'd settled on a medication combination that had about the best results they could expect to achieve. Mrs. Wheeler would have a regular course of nerve, steroid, and time-release OxyContin that would form her base coverage, as well Percocet, a faster-acting opioid than the OxyContin, that she could crush and administer through her G-tube every four hours for breakthrough pain; in an emergency, two tabs could be given if one wasn't sufficient.

"But, when an episode like that begins, you won't be capable of administering the med yourself." The attending physician paused then; his arms folded across his chest. "You'll be in too much pain. There will be other times, too, when managing your feeds and such will be too much for you right now. Is there someone who can stay with you to help with those things? That young man perhaps, your caretaker."

"Well, I don't know," Mrs. Wheeler said. "Maybe he could. If he'll do such a thing."

The attending physician gave her a smile meant to be encouraging. "We'll ask him."

Mrs. Wheeler slept then, as she had most of the night. But she was awake now in the perfect stillness of the early morning thinking about things. She suctioned her mouth and let the wand fall to her side. She didn't know what the alternatives would be should Ryan not be willing to stay with her. She didn't want to think about them.

❦

She was asleep again when Ryan came again a few hours later. He resumed his spot in the chair at her bedside and watched her snore softly. She was still alone in the room, and it was quiet, almost peaceful. One of her feet, in hospital slipper-socks and not reaching much past the middle of the bed, had come loose from the covers; Ryan reached over and covered it, straightening the bottom of her gown as he did. In the pertinent information section on the wall-mounted whiteboard across from the foot of the bed, he was pleased to see that Vicki's name had been written in as Mrs. Wheeler's day nurse again. His own name was written there, too, as "Family/PIC" along with his cell phone number.

The same attending physician as the previous night came into the room on rounds a little before nine. He greeted Ryan warmly and quickly summarized Mrs. Wheeler's circumstances in terms of discharge home. When the attending physician asked Ryan if he could stay with her, he didn't answer right away. Instead, he stared past him at the open doorway.

"It wouldn't have to be all day and all night," the attending physician said. "But certainly overnight to start with and close enough to respond in, say, ten minutes otherwise. And it won't be forever." He paused. "Or it shouldn't be."

Ryan heard himself mumble, "I don't know."

"We'll train you on everything you need to know, how to administer the meds and the rest. There's not all that much to it."

Vicki entered the room then carrying a handful of syringes. Her eyes met Ryan's and softened.

He looked from her to the attending physician and nodded once.

"I guess I can do that." He shrugged. "I mean, why not?"

"Great," the attending physician said. "Vicki here will teach you all you need to know. Vicki, this young man is going to take care of Mrs. Wheeler after she's discharged. Can you show him how to measure meds and so forth?"

"I'll be happy to." She held up the syringes in her hand. "In fact, I can do that right now."

"Good," the attending physician said. He turned back to Ryan. "So, we'll want to observe her throughout most of today, be sure the med regimen we have her on is maintaining well, that there are no setbacks. And we want to be sure to send you home with adequate meds and supplies from our pharmacy; that always takes a while. I'd say discharge should be around four o'clock or thereabouts. There will be paperwork and instructions we'll give you that will tell you just what to do, and you can always call us if there are any problems."

Ryan's nod was hesitant. He wasn't sure he would have agreed to things if Vicki hadn't walked in the room when she did. But he had, so that was it. He nodded again with a bit more vigor, they did the same, and the attending physician left the room. Vicki set the syringes on the lap table, smiled at him, and said, "Well, let's get started. First, I guess I'll show you how to crush and mix the tab meds with water."

She did that. Each time she prepped and administered a med, Ryan mimicked her actions with the next one. Vicki showed him how to measure out Mrs. Wheeler's formula and flush the tube, as well as the schedule for all that was needed to be done throughout the day; they'd intentionally arranged it so that no meds or feeds needed to be given overnight in order to keep Mrs. Wheeler's sleep as uninterrupted as possible. She showed him how to reposition her in bed and how to shampoo her hair with a special pre-packaged cloth; Mrs. Wheeler slept through both. By the time they finished, the sun was beaming sideways through the room's window and the hallway outside was bustling with activity.

"You should be set to go now," Vicki said. "You could do my job."

"Hardly."

"Well, I think it's wonderful what you're doing." She paused, smiled. "It's uncommon."

Ryan felt the same sort of warmth crawl up his neck as when he'd first met her. He said, "Uncommon. I don't think so."

"It is. Believe me."

He did his best to give a dismissive shrug. "So, what happens until discharge?"

"Nothing new really. She'll mostly sleep. We'll take good care of her until then."

"Maybe I'll go grab some clothes and stuff from my place then. Bring them over to Mrs. Wheeler's. Take care of a few things there."

"Sure." She smiled again. "Come back around four and she should be ready to leave."

Ryan nodded, though he didn't really want to go. "You'll still be on shift then?"

"I will."

"Good." He nodded a few times. "Okay, then. See you later."

❧❧ ❦ ❧❧

It only took Ryan a few minutes at his place to pack some toiletries, his laptop, and a few clothes in a small duffel bag, tuck it behind his car seat, and drive over to Mrs. Wheeler's. He stopped at a deli on the way and brought a sandwich and a soda over for lunch. From the garage, he brought out the rest of the things he needed for the front yard, then ate on the front step, considering the order he wanted to follow to complete his projects. When he finished, he threw away his trash and started on the roses. After graduating from high school, he'd enrolled briefly in vocational college and had taken a gardening class along with general science and novice carpentry. He'd dropped out after his arrest and enlisted in the Army not long after having his charges dropped in lieu of community service.

From the gardening class, he remembered well enough the steps for seasonal pruning of roses and carefully made those diagonal cuts, dropping the excess foliage in a bucket, and leaving the few remaining blooms that seemed salvageable in case Mrs. Wheeler wanted them. Next, he dug around their roots, replacing old earth with new fertilizer and potting soil, then soaked them well with a garden hose he found on the side of the house, scrubbed out the bird bath, and filled that. As he worked, he thought about Mrs. Wheeler and what lay ahead. He thought about his life as he'd led it so far. He thought about Vicki.

After he finished with the roses and bird bath, Ryan adjusted all the sprinklers so they covered the lawn and roses, then raked up old, dry lawn and spread new rye grass seed for the winter, using the back of a rake to mix it with top soil. Although he knew it wouldn't present much of a barrier, he surrounded the new lawn with stakes and string about a foot high, and gave it a good soak with the sprinklers. Last, he re-set the mailbox post so that it was straight, packed earth tight around its base, and oiled its hinges so it opened and closed easily. As he was removing the mail from inside it, he heard the window close again upstairs at the house next door. When he looked up, the same man was staring down at him, nodding slowly. He had friendly eyes and wore a maroon chamois shirt tucked into jeans. Like before, he raised a thumb towards Ryan and smiled. Ryan wasn't sure what to do, so did the same in return. Then the man was gone, and a breeze scraped the tip of a tree branch against the window where he'd been.

Ryan checked his watch. It was just after three-thirty, the afternoon's light already falling. He quickly stored the supplies and Mrs. Wheeler's mail in the garage and drove back to the hospital. She was sitting in a portable wheelchair when he came into the room, wearing the clothes he'd brought her in, free of wires and probes, her glasses a little crooked and one side of her hair flatter than the other. Their eyes met, and Mrs. Wheeler's filled with a tentative hopefulness.

"So," she said to him quietly. "You certain you're up for this?"

He nodded, keeping his own voice low. "Sure. If you are."

Vicki came into the room then carrying two large plastic sacks. She looked back and forth between the two of them and smiled. "Everything you need is in these," she said. "Meds in this one." She lifted a sack. "Other supplies along with the discharge paperwork in the other. I'll go over the meds first, then the supplies and paperwork, you'll both sign, and then you're on your way."

She reviewed the meds carefully, showing them each bottle and its instruction label before replacing it in the sack. Ryan noted the flexibility given with the OxyContin and Percocet, and that there was a month's supply with several refills available for each. He'd exclusively be the one administering them, so Mrs. Wheeler would have virtually no idea how much was left in either one. Ryan could easily poach off both and refill them when needed. It was as if an unexpected gift had plopped down suddenly into his lap, but he puzzled over why he didn't feel the exhilaration he thought he would.

When Vicki finished with the meds, she moved on to the supplies and discharge paperwork, then asked if they had any questions. Neither did, so they each signed where indicated, and she handed the bags to Ryan. "All right, then. Why don't you take those sacks and drive your car around to the front entrance? One of our CNAs will take Mrs. Wheeler down in the wheelchair and meet you there."

"That's it?" Ryan asked.

"Pretty much, yes."

"We just leave?" Mrs. Wheeler said. "Head home?"

"You'll do fine. Hope you're feeling better soon." Vicki paused. "Maybe our paths will cross again."

Her eyes moved from Mrs. Wheeler to Ryan. He swallowed, took the bags from her, and heard himself say, "I'll go get the car."

The two of them didn't say much on the drive home. Ryan asked Mrs. Wheeler if she was sure she'd gotten all her personal belongings from the hospital, and she said she was. Mrs. Wheeler buttoned up her overcoat and said it seemed like it had gotten colder. Ryan mentioned that he'd already packed a few clothes and things from his place.

They sat in complete silence at a long train crossing until Mrs. Wheeler spat twice into her cup, then said, "Our dog was named Jake. He was a stray that Dale found poking around in our alley one morning." Ryan glanced over at her when she sniffed a little laugh at the memory. "Part of his right ear had been bitten off, we assumed, in a fight with another dog, and he had a limp that went away after we'd cared for him a few weeks. He liked to sit up on Dale's lap at night while we watched television; Dale would scratch the top of his head. After Dale died, Jake didn't understand what had happened, where he'd gone . . . he kept nosing around, whining at me, you know. Eventually, he began crawling up in my lap while I watched television alone. I know I shouldn't have, but I let him sleep at the end of our bed, on Dale's side." She smiled as the last of the train passed and the crossing bar slowly raised. "I spoiled him," she said. "I did. But he was a good companion. I really missed him when he was gone. The house was so quiet afterwards, it seemed to scream."

Ryan nodded when she glanced over at him. The cars in front of them started moving again. They drove the rest of the way to the house without speaking. The streetlights blinked on as Ryan helped her out of the car at the curb and collected the sacks and his duffel bag. While he did, she studied the front of the house in the wash of pale light: the fence, the bricks under it, the lawn, the roses, and the rest. When Ryan came over next to her grasping the sacks and his duffel bag in one hand, she shook her head with a pleased frown, looked up at him and asked, "When on earth did you do all this?"

"While you were admitted." He extended his free arm. "Here."

She shook her head, then grasped his arm, and they made their slow way up the walk, the steps, and inside. The thermostat must have been pre-set because the house was warm. He turned on the lamp next to the living room couch that also lit part of the dining room and came back for her.

"No," she said. "This way."

She took his arm again, led him behind the couch, and opened a door there. When she flipped on the room's ceiling light, the first few strains of a familiar circus song accompanied it.

"Dale did that somehow," Mrs. Wheeler said. "Tom loved it. This was his bedroom. You'll sleep here."

Ryan gazed round the room. It looked as if the boy still occupied it. Books lined the shelves, airplane models perched on top of the bureau, and a solar system mobile dangled from fishing line at various spots from the ceiling. The twin bedspread was adorned with logos of Major League baseball teams, a small bathrobe still hung from the back of the closet door, and two red sneakers were just visible under the bed, one mud-stained and tipped on its side. Her hand was still on his arm, but its grip had tightened. He set his duffel bag on the bed.

"How old was he . . . " Ryan paused, then started again. "When he . . . "

"Nine," Mrs. Wheeler said quietly. "He was nine."

She led him through the rest of the room and the bathroom that adjoined it into her own bedroom. She turned on her bedside lamp, took off her coat and laid it on the far side of the bed. Ryan regarded the stack of washcloths on her nightstand along with the box of Kleenex and the carefully stacked pillows against the headboard.

"Well," she said. "Since we just got home, I suppose I should play it safe and get up in bed. Rest a bit." She looked at the clock on the nightstand. "But I'm not getting in my nightgown yet. Too early for that. I plan to get up for my next feed and to make you dinner. I plan to start living again."

"Good for you," Ryan said. He set the sack with the supplies and discharge paperwork next to her coat.

"Listen." She seemed to hesitate. "There's some room in those top two bureau drawers in Tom's room for your things. I finally cleared them out not long ago."

Ryan nodded slowly. "Okay, I'll just go unload my stuff then." He lifted the sack he still held. "And these meds, too, if that's all right."

"All right. And I'll get myself up on this bed." She took a step in that direction, then stopped suddenly. "Oh, say, I forgot to tell you something. My next door neighbor called me on my cell at the hospital while you were coming to get me. His name is Hugh, and we've been neighbors a long time. He's a good guy; took Dale on after retirement to work at the hardware store you went to. He owns that and runs his own home repair business out of it, too. Says he watched you in the front yard and wants to hire you on his crew. Liked your work, I guess."

Ryan felt his eyes widen and shifted the sack at his side. He said, "You serious?"

"Yes. And he pays a decent, competitive wage and provides health benefits, too; Dale was surprised by that. I explained what you were doing for me, and he's happy to have you start whenever I'm on my feet again and then work around whatever jobs I may have for you afterwards. Like I said, he's a good guy. He says just stop by whenever you have the chance, and you can work out the details together."

Ryan tried to hide his excitement. "That right?"

"It is. Apparently, one of the young men on his crew is leaving soon to start chef school. Can you imagine going from home repair to becoming a chef?" She shook her head. "I guess life has a way of sorting itself out."

Ryan nodded again. "I guess so."

"Well, go unload that stuff, and I'll get up in bed. Take a little rest."

Ryan left her there and went through the bathroom, closing her door behind him, and into Tom's bedroom. But he didn't open the bureau drawers. Instead, he looked over the room more closely. Sports posters adorned the walls and a carefully labeled rock collection was propped up on the bookcase in boxes behind glass. What looked like the same baseball bat and mitt from the photograph in the dining room leaned against the side of a desk which was spread with dusty baseball cards, their wrappers still ripped partially around a few as if they hadn't all been completely viewed. Through the window behind the desk and a sparse hedge dividing the houses, Ryan could see Hugh next door in his living room. He sat between a woman and a young girl on a couch, and they were all hunched over the coffee table in front of them. At first, Ryan couldn't figure out what they were doing, and then he realized they were working on a jigsaw puzzle together, something he'd often done with his aunt when he was young. Ryan watched the girl fit a piece into the puzzle and Hugh clap.

He whispered to himself, "You could go over now and introduce yourself, see about those work details." Watching the three of them together, he shook his head. "But that can wait. No hurry there; they're not going anywhere."

Ryan stepped back into the bathroom and turned on the light. He stood completely still in the room's white glare gazing down at a crack that meandered through several of the tiles. The crack ran back behind the toilet where it disappeared, and he immediately began considering the options involved in fixing it. Finally, he roused himself and unloaded the remaining sack, arranging the new meds on the opposite side of the sink. He paused when he came to the large OxyContin and Percocet bottles, shaking them, then opening each. He thought, I could take a handful of both right now and no one would know. What the hell, he thought, I could have some hydrocodone for dessert, too. Then he looked in the mirror again and found the same familiar, troubled eyes staring back at him, but ones that held something new in them, something like he'd seen in Mrs. Wheeler's when he'd come to get her at the hospital.

He heard the old woman cough and spit in her bedroom. "Or you could bring in her mail," he whispered quietly. "Maybe read to her whatever is difficult without her glasses. See if she might have a jigsaw puzzle we could work on together." He paused again. "But that would disturb her rest; that can wait, too."

He went back into Tom's bedroom and sat in the desk chair, its small surface hard and worn smooth. His thoughts shifted suddenly to Vicki, and he whispered to himself, "Or maybe you could find out when her shifts end and wait one night by the hospital exit for her. You don't want to scare her, though. Just say you were in the area and wondered how she was doing. Wanted to say hello, see if she might want to go for coffee or something, maybe take a walk. Ryan shook his head and thought, it's not impossible. Unlikely perhaps, but not impossible. You don't know. Anything might happen . . . anything at all.

LONG AGO, WHEN I WAS YOUNG

When I was seventeen, I used to like to go up to the Maryknoll Seminary in the hills above Los Altos, California. I can't remember how I discovered it exactly; perhaps I just noticed its old, mission-style buildings nestled among oak and eucalyptus trees from the freeway down below. My family had moved up to that area at the start of my senior year, my first attending a public school, where new friendships were all but nonexistent. As a result, I spent a fair amount of my free time on my own exploring places like that. Mostly, I just wandered the grounds, admiring the striking vistas overlooking what wasn't yet known as Silicon Valley or hiking the trails that meandered off into the vast nature reserve behind the property. There never seemed to be many people around, so even back then in the early 70s, seminary enrollment must have already been on the decline. Occasionally, I'd see a priest or brother on preoccupied strolls of their own, black-robed and solemn in that manner I'd grown so familiar with during my many years surviving a Catholic education until it was curtailed by my abrupt dismissal at the end of the prior semester.

Strangely, I never came upon a lone seminarian there until late on an early-winter afternoon when I heard the strains of a cello being played in one of the garden courtyards bordering the dormitory. The melody was haunting, spare but lovely, so I followed it until I saw its source a handful of yards away through the branches of a cypress tree: a boy about my age sat on a stone bench in a black cassock with the instrument between his knees. His eyes were closed and his head bent to his musical endeavor; when he drew his bow in a long note across the strings, his chin followed suit. He wore the same style of plain, plastic glasses that I'd seen on some of the older clerics, and a slight spray of acne riddled his forehead where a loose curl of black hair danced with his movements. He was surrounded by foliage of every shade of green through which dust drifted in shafts of descending sunlight.

Suddenly, the music took on a lilting quality, his head lifted skyward, and I felt a kind of heat behind my eyes at how alone the boy seemed. As alone, I realized, as I felt myself. Just as suddenly, the music halted, he sighed, then packed away his instrument in its case, and stood up. Like me, he was of medium stature, but even skinnier, almost frail-looking. I watched him adjust the red sash around his narrow waist, then heft the case to his hip and start up the pathway near where I stood. As he approached, I stepped out onto the same cinder path and cleared my throat. He stopped short of me and looked my way with no expression at all.

"Sorry if I startled you," I said. "But I heard you playing over there and just wanted to say it was beautiful."

"Thanks." His tone was as inexpressive as his face. The case lowered at his side.

I asked, "Do you study music?"

"Used to." He gave a small shrug. "Not since I came here."

"How long has that been?"

His answer was immediate. "Three years. Almost three-and-a-half now, actually."

"Since answering your calling."

The boy's mouth closed tight. He shrugged again.

I nodded slowly. "So, you've just been playing, learning on your own since then? Practicing or whatever out here."

"Pretty much. Can't play in the buildings . . . no noise allowed." He paused, pushed his glasses up higher on his nose, then said, "What are you doing here?"

"Walking around." I gestured towards the rear of the property. "Some nice trails back there."

"I know."

He nodded himself, uncomfortably it seemed. A hawk called and flew off over the treetops behind him.

"Well," he said and hoisted the case back to his hip. With his free hand, he fingered the crucifix that dangled from his neck; his bottom lip quivered as if he was about to cry.

"Take care," I said and stepped out of his way to the edge of the path.

He passed by me and I watched him go off towards a doorway that stood ajar at the end of the dormitory. His footsteps crunched lightly on the cinder until he entered its long, shadowy hallway, opened the third door to the left, and closed it soundlessly behind him.

My dismissal from the all-boys Catholic high school in Los Angeles I last attended was not a formal expulsion, nor did it involve any notorious or glamorous transgression. Instead, I'd written a series of editorials for its student newspaper that last semester questioning the school's dress code, its admission policy not allowing girls, its over-emphasis on sports, courses that I felt were arcane and meaningless, and calling for a mandatory community service requirement for graduation. When my family relocated that summer, I'd planned to stay in Los Angeles with a friend so I could finish my senior year there, but Father Phil, the principal and newspaper advisor, simply told my parents he thought it was in everyone's best interest if I moved on, too.

My new public high school was five times the size of my old one with established and seemingly impenetrable social circles, especially for someone like me entering as a senior already timid and reticent by nature. It didn't have a student newspaper, which ruled out that option even if I had wanted to continue the pursuit. So, I remained basically invisible, did reasonably well in classes where I only spoke when called upon, located a convalescent hospital nearby where I could continue my weekend volunteer work feeding elderly patients and writing letters for them, and found places with pastoral settings like the seminary where I could wander in the solitary fashion to which I quickly grew accustomed.

I continued to look for the cello-playing seminarian on my subsequent visits there, but didn't hear his music come from that garden courtyard again until several weeks later. The boy had just stopped playing when I reached my hidden spot behind the branches of the cypress tree.

The cello was still tipped against one knee, but he bent down and exchanged the bow with a small book he took from inside the case. Its faded green binding and diminutive size made it clear the book was very old. He opened it on his free thigh, tilted it up towards his gaze, and ruffled through its pages, settling on ones in its middle. As I watched, I found my eyebrows knit because the expression on his face eased, his shoulders fell, and he seemed to caress the interior of those pages with his fingertips. The bell in the chapel's steeple chimed slowly five times while he continued in that manner. At the tolls' conclusion, he closed the book, lifted it to his lips, kissed the cover, then replaced it in the case along with the cello and closed the lid.

I watched him carry it again across the cinder path and through the dormitory's open doorway, but this time, he didn't stop at the third door on the left. Instead, he continued down the hallway to the end and entered what appeared to be a library of some sort; the large room protruded from the rest of the building, and walls of books were visible through its tall windows. I walked along another path parallel to the dormitory and thick with shrubbery until I came abreast of one of those windows. Through it, the library appeared to be empty except for the boy. I watched him remove the book from his cello case, climb a rolling ladder to a top shelf fifteen or so feet off the floor, and place it carefully in a gap in its precise middle, where it was dwarfed among other books. He seemed to smooth its spine before he descended the ladder, lifted the case, and left the library. A few moments later, I saw a light go on in the window of the room three doors to the left of the hallway's courtyard entrance, and then a curtain was pulled across it. I stood frowning and staring at that sprawling, silent building for several minutes before continuing my walk full of questions and with no particular destination in mind.

⟶ ✦ ⟵

I first noticed Isabel Santos in my chemistry class at the very start of the school year. I was struck immediately by her soft brown hair, doe-like eyes, and olive skin; I thought she was beautiful. I was also attracted to a quiet tenderness about her that seemed almost yearning. The teacher in that class posted our weekly test scores on a bulletin board inside the classroom door, and although hers were always highest, she paired herself up as lab partners with an overweight girl whose scores were consistently the opposite, a student I'd heard others refer to derisively as a "band geek." Without being asked, she also stayed after class each day to help the teacher put away lab supplies.

I continued to admire Isabel from afar whenever I came upon her at school, but could never muster the nerve to speak to her. My years at an all-boys school had afforded me absolutely no experience with girls, and my shyness exacerbated my abject hesitancy. I didn't realize she lived in the same neighborhood as me until a month or so after we moved in when I was bringing our trash cans to the curb for pickup late one evening and saw her walking her dog on the sidewalk across the street. Our house's open garage lit the driveway down to where I halted abruptly upon seeing her, holding the can suspended. She passed under a streetlamp and looked my way with what seemed like a small smile. She moved back into the darkness, her big golden retriever tugging at its leash, while I stood frozen, staring after her. A warm, tingling flush had spread up through me.

The next night, I waited upstairs and knelt in the dark by my bedroom window at the front of the house. At about the same time as the previous evening, I saw Isabel walking her dog again on the sidewalk across the street. As she moved in and out of the streetlamp's yellow glare, I caught my breath because she seemed to be looking steadily across at our house. My mother kept an assortment of potted plants on our front porch, so each night after that, I used the excuse of watering them at that time so I could wait with mounting anticipation for her to pass under the streetlamp with her dog, offer her small smile, then move off into the darkness again while I stood flushed and tingling with the hose dribbling aimlessly from my hand.

I regularly began my visits to the seminary with a walk towards the garden courtyard listening and hoping for the strains of the cello. I was greeted with it from time to time, but in no predictable pattern. When I was, I recalled the end of my first interaction with the boy, his forlorn expression and trembling lip, so remained hidden behind the cypress tree to avoid disturbing him again, watching and marveling at the stark beauty of the music. Almost always when he finished, he would exchange the bow with the small green book in the case. Without exception, he would then open it to the middle and caress the interior of those pages while his countenance and posture softened. A minute or two would pass before he'd kiss the book's cover, then close it back into the case with his cello. Next, he'd bring it back to the library where he'd replace it carefully it in its elevated, central position, brush its spine, then return to his dormitory room and close the curtain over his window.

I didn't become well-acquainted with most of the staff at the convalescent hospital where I volunteered, but one of the older nurses on the non-ambulatory unit where I spent the majority of my time engaged with me more than the rest. She asked me how I'd come to help out there, about my studies and plans for the future, and shared affectionate stories about some of the patients we both worked with. When I was trying to coax news from a patient to put into a letter or cajoling one to eat a bit more, I sometimes found her regarding me from across the room or down the hall with what seemed like bemused interest.

One Saturday afternoon when we'd both finished feeding lunch to patients in their wheelchairs at the same common room table, she turned to me and said, "You know, I have a niece who attends the same school as you. She's also a senior: Isabel Santos." She paused. "She says she knows who you are."

I felt myself stiffen as I took off the bib from the old woman I'd been feeding and heard myself say, "No kidding."

"Yes, and I've told her about you helping here. I think she's impressed; she volunteers, too, at an animal shelter. I believe the two of you have a lot in common, actually. Maybe you'll have the chance to get acquainted."

When I glanced her way, her eyes held that same bemused quality, but it was not unkind. I managed a shrug and said, "Maybe. Who knows?"

Without looking at her more, I stood, used the toe of my shoe to release the brake on the back of the old woman's wheelchair, and began pushing her back to her room.

❦❦ ❦❦

With the deepening of winter, daylight grew shorter, and my walks at the seminary necessarily ended earlier. I was usually back at my parents' car in the chapel parking lot not long after five and sometimes as I was leaving, I saw smatterings of seminarians, never more than a dozen or so, making their way into the chapel for what I assumed were evening prayers. When I did, I always looked hard for the boy who played the cello, but it was impossible to distinguish him from the others in their identical cassocks moving through the corridor columns and into the dim vestibule that I knew held that distinctive smell of incense and candle wax, something forever imprinted on my memory.

One evening, while I searched unsuccessfully for him among the seminarians entering the chapel, a groundskeeper pushing a wheelbarrow approached me where I stood leaning against my car.

He said, "You can't park here."

I fixed him with a puzzled glare and said, "What?"

"You'll need to leave. Now." His voice rose. "This lot is for staff and seminarians only."

Another voice said, "It's all right." We both turned towards the sidewalk that separated the chapel from the parking lot. The boy who played the cello stood there, his face in shadows. He pivoted to the groundskeeper and said, "He's a friend of mine."

Then the boy turned around and walked toward the chapel steps. The groundskeeper gave a muttered grumble, hoisted his wheelbarrow, and left in the opposite direction. I remained where I was, watching the boy make his way into the chapel. The temperature had begun to drop, and I pulled up my sweatshirt's hood against the chill. A few moments later from inside the sanctuary, I heard a single older male voice chant in Latin followed by a chorus of younger male voices in response. I could see nothing beyond the chapel's darkened opening except the faint flicker of candlelight from deep inside where I knew the altar must have been.

❧ ✾ ❧

The long winter dragged on, as did the tortured choreography I maintained with Isabel Santos. Each day that passed without our speaking made the notion of it seem more and more impossible. Like a gear stuck in place hardening imperceptibly over time or an unused muscle atrophying little by little into irreversible immobility. Our clumsy, silent evening exchanges across the street from one another continued with an increasing ache like I'd never felt before. Occasionally, I'd find her glancing my way across the classroom or somewhere on campus, and I'd return the same for a fleeting moment, then quickly turn away trying to affect indifference and willing away the color flooding up behind my ears.

Once, when she was walking through the school cafeteria ahead of me, a scarf fell out of her backpack, and I felt a rush of opportunity at the thought of retrieving it for her, but another younger student beat me to it. I stopped still in my tracks, crestfallen, watching in deflated astonishment as he handed it back to her with without even breaking stride.

Another time, both of our lab partners were absent in chemistry class. My excitement surged at the thought of partnering with Isabel for the day's experiment, and she must have felt similarly because she began moving my way when the teacher told the class to get started, but then he assigned another student to work with her and said he'd partner with me himself. His simple directions felt like a stab. When he asked me if something was wrong, it was all I could do to shake my head.

Throughout the spring, the desire to speak to Isabel became greater and greater as did the tormenting unlikelihood of it ever happening. Two magnets trying to reach themselves together. A sought-after ship inching further and further from the pier.

🙢🙠 🙡 🙢🙠

Spring finally made its grudging entry to the seminary grounds, first with crocus shoots, then nodding daffodils, and finally, bursting buds on trees. I blamed the rain that fell most of March for the long stretch of time without hearing the cello's strains from the courtyard garden, but when it remained silent after a few weeks of dry, bright weather, I grew disappointed. A couple of weeks later, curiosity replaced disappointment, and a week or two after that, curiosity became concern. From my spot behind the cypress tree, I often peered into the darkened hallway of the dormitory or walked along the path where the curtain remained closed over the boy's window, but didn't chance entering the hallway myself until late one afternoon in mid-May.

The long corridor was empty and all its doors closed except the third one on the left. I moved as silently as I could across the linoleum floor until I stood in front of the boy's room. It was empty, too, so completely, it appeared utterly hollow. An uncovered mattress on a twin-bed frame, a small desk and bureau, a closet behind the door, and the curtained window, perhaps seven by ten feet of austere bareness in murky half-light. Inside me, something seemed to crumble and fall. I shook my head. Perhaps there had been enough space under the bed for his cello case; if not, I wasn't sure where the boy would have stored it while the room was still his.

A numbness filled me as I considered the empty space for several more moments before hurrying down the hall into the library. It was empty as well, musty-smelling and more cavernous than it appeared from outside. A few long wooden tables with matching chairs sat still on the floor with tall windows interrupting bookshelves on three sides. I pushed the ladder to the middle of the one across from the door, climbed it to the top, and found the small, green book in its spot at the precise center. It was a volume of poems by Alexander Pope. I pulled it out and opened it to its middle where I found a tiny, square space cut out of a swath of interior pages. It looked like it had been sliced away carefully with something like a scalpel leaving a cavity a little larger than an inch wide and a half inch deep. Large enough, perhaps, to hold a small photograph, a locket, or a bound tuft of hair. Whatever it had concealed was gone now, like the boy. As I'd watched him do many times, I ran my fingers across it, the thin pages at the depression wrinkled and faded with age. I looked out the window where I could see the stone bench in the courtyard garden where he had played with such longing and made more tiny shakes of my head. Then I climbed back down with the book, took it with me back to my car, and drove home with it.

⋙ ⚶ ⋘

It wasn't until the week before graduation that I brought the book to school in my backpack. At the end of chemistry class, I lingered pretending to finish scribbling a formula on the chalkboard into my notebook while I waited for Isabel Santos to carry the trays of test tubes she'd collected into the lab storage room. When she disappeared inside it, I walked quickly over to her own backpack perched on the stool where she'd been sitting. I opened it, kissed the book's cover, slipped it inside her backpack, and left the classroom.

That night, she paused as she came under the streetlamp across the street with her dog, then just stood there staring at me. I let the hose I held fall to my side and did the same in return, my heart thundering away. A siren whined off somewhere in the distance. We remained like that until the sound of it had died away completely and her dog finally pulled her off into the night's darkness again.

Isabel didn't come to our graduation ceremony. When her name was called on stage and she didn't walk across it to get her diploma, I heard a boy seated in the row behind me tell another that she'd already gone east to start an early-summer study program at the college where she would become an official student in September.

⋙ ⚶ ⋘

All of that happened a long time ago now, back when I was still a teenaged kid. One who, in those days, was pretty lost and just trying to find his way. Which I eventually did, I guess. I started college myself that fall in San Francisco, studied psychology, and secured a social work internship at the local children's hospital that eventually led to a permanent position in their NICU once I finished my graduate degree. I lived with a woman in the city there for a long time who eventually moved on to someone else, but I cherished the many fine years we'd had together. I gradually gained enough of a reputation at work that, just before I turned thirty-five, I was promoted to the role of supervising all social workers at the hospital.

Shortly after that appointment, I saw Isabel Santos again one morning while I was taking the city bus to work late after a dentist appointment. I was sitting mid-span beside a window, and the bus had paused at a traffic light not far from Union Square. I leaned into the window, my fingertips raising themselves to my mouth when, out of nowhere, there she was standing on the corner waiting for the crosswalk signal. One of her hands gripped a tourist map against the handle of a baby stroller and the other that of the man next to her; my eyes went immediately to the wedding bands on their fingers. She looked older but the same, lovely and composed. She and the man were laughing together over something. Her head turned slowly my way, our eyes met, hers widened, and while her smile dimmed, part of it remained. She lifted her hand in a sort of wave, I did the same, then like the seminarian those many years ago, her bottom lip began to quiver. The light changed, the bus shifted into gear, and it eased away with the traffic. As Isabel Santos slipped from view, I lowered myself back in my seat. I wasn't sure what I felt in that moment, but I knew loss was among the emotions. Loss over irretrievable opportunity, loss over what might have been, loss over youth's passage, over things unsaid and undone.

I never saw the boy from the seminary again. I looked for him in photos I came across of cello players in magazines and periodicals, during the few chamber music performances and symphonies I attended in person, or when I walked the grounds at the seminary on visits home to see my parents. I wasn't sure I would recognize an older version of him without the glasses, the acne, the curl of hair across his forehead, but I thought I would. There was something unique and unforgettable about his face, his eyes, his measured movements. I wished him the best. I still thought of him from time to time, more often than I might have expected. I wondered about why he'd left the seminary or if he returned, what he'd kept in that book, as I also wondered what Isabel Santos had done with it after she found it in her backpack, what it had suggested to her.

As I say, these things happened a long time ago now, when I was young and had very little understanding of them. Truth be told, looking out my window this afternoon at sailboats tacking across the bay with middle age firmly behind me, I don't believe I have very much more understanding, if any, of them today. Now, as I enter this final chapter of life, I'm struck at how much of it has been made up of encounters and events like those—many random and seemingly small, some involving choices or control and others not—and how their meaning remains mysterious, indelible, confounding, fervent.

HACIENDA TRANQUILA

My wife, Gwen, and I started our B&B-type hacienda after I took early retirement at the public health clinic where I worked. I'd been the lead pediatric psychologist there for more than three decades by then and had just had enough of grant applications, annual budget cuts, and increasing accountability mandates. Gwen was still content enough with her hospice nursing position, so we had her ongoing income in addition to my pension. Our two adult sons were living on their own, which made our family home needlessly large, so we sold it and used the profit to buy and renovate the hacienda property that we'd ridden by and speculated about for many years.

The place was unusually large by central Phoenix standards. It sat on a full acre of completely overgrown land with an old, mud-adobe main house, a decrepit casita behind, plenty of dead lawn, and an empty pool in a back corner. To say it needed work was an understatement. But the brother of my clinic's receptionist turned out to be a handyman-extraordinaire who'd just moved here from the Dominican Republic and was happy to live in the casita while he did the entire renovation, contracting laborers as he needed them. My wife and I got an extended six-month escrow on the sale of our old home, all of which was needed to complete the project. When it was finally finished and we moved in, we were astounded by how beautiful it was inside and out: refreshingly unique and distinctive, a sprawling oasis within a few stone throws of restaurants, bars, and shops.

The main house could be divided into two separate living sections. Gwen and I lived in the high-ceilinged rear portion with its expansive kitchen/dining/great room, loft, and bedroom suite. Two bedrooms, a bath, and studio-like space formed the front portion and connected to ours through a hallway door leading into our dining area. We left that door open when our sons were visiting and using the bedrooms, but otherwise, kept it closed and rented out the front.

The renovated back casita also had two bedrooms, bath, kitchen, and living area. Both units had their own patios, as well as access to the long, lattice-covered outdoor living space off our great room with its fountain and rustic banquet-style table. All the patios had grills, chimineas, and Adirondack chairs, which were also situated here and there in shaded seating areas elsewhere on the property. Dripping bougainvillea abounded, as did wide stretches of flood-irrigated green grass, lush landscaping, trimmed trees, and potted plants and flowers. The decking around the pool had all been repaved, and we'd converted a storage shed between the main house and the casita to provide shared access to a washer/dryer, extra linens and towels, a couple of bicycles, and outdoor games like bocce ball and croquet. The adobe wall that surrounded the property, refinished like the buildings, had been extended to a height of seven-feet to give a sense of seclusion and privacy.

While not a B&B in strict terms, we did offer guests the options of having rudimentary morning breakfast or late-afternoon wine and snack baskets left by their front doors for an additional fee. We advertised the place on Vrbo and Airbnb featuring the entire property as a potential venue for weddings, family reunions, and business retreats, as well as traditional rentals for the two units separately. We called the place "Hacienda Tranquila" and managed bookings for nearly a hundred nights that first year, almost doubling that annual number regularly afterwards. While we did host a handful of larger gatherings each year, the vast majority of the bookings were of the traditional variety in the two units for a week or so, mostly from fall to spring.

With Gwen still working fulltime, most of the responsibilities for running the place understandably fell to me. So, in a matter of months, I went from a longtime public health worker to essentially becoming an innkeeper. Aside from hiring companies to maintain the grounds and pool, I handled all remaining duties myself. At first, I thrived in doing so, basking in the excitement of burgeoning entrepreneurship and guiding our vision into life. But by the third year, some of the sheen of the enterprise had worn off. We'd grown a bit weary of always sharing walls and spaces with people we didn't know, constantly responding to their questions and queries, needing to be available to run home at the drop of a hat when guests called to say they couldn't get the coffeemaker to work, and rarely being able to travel anywhere ourselves. As time went on, Gwen and I found that we had less time together than when we'd both been working, and property management frequently dominated our conversations.

For the most part, though, things at the place went along for us reasonably well, and we settled into a rhythm and routine. Of course, we did have some bookings that proved troublesome or irksome—last minute cancellations, more guests arriving than originally agreed upon, requests that sometimes became excessive or irrational, irritable and condescending personalities. But none prepared us for the guests who came to stay during the spring of our fourth year there.

Chris Palmer booked the casita for a five-night stretch spanning an early-March weekend for himself and his daughter, Haley. He contacted me by phone and explained that they were coming primarily to attend the wedding of a young woman who'd once been Haley's longtime nanny, but also planned to enjoy some other warm-weather activities outside of the wedding-related events. He was flying in from Seattle, and Haley from Colorado where she was a college student. His ex-wife would be renting a place of her own nearby —some outrageously expensive hotel, he supposed—and then they'd share their daughter while there. His voice took on a crisp edge when he got to that last part.

He and Haley arrived in a rental car about four-thirty on a Thursday afternoon. He was perhaps fifteen years younger than me and still good-looking in a weathered way, with a hint of paunch, intentional stubble, and eyes that hovered somewhere between cocky and uneasy. Haley appeared quiet and reserved, almost distant. I gave them my standard explanation and tour of the property, then showed them their casita. As far as I could tell, they seemed satisfied with the accommodations. Chris remained with me on the casita's patio while Haley brought her rolling suitcase inside. He set a grocery bag he was carrying on the umbrella table, took out a six-pack of beer, and offered me one. I shook my head and watched him twist the top off a bottle and take a long swallow.

He wiped his lips afterwards and said, "This is quite a place. How long have you had it?"

"Few years."

"Does it do all right? I mean, stay pretty full?"

"We manage."

He nodded, and I watched his gaze sweep across the grounds. I asked, "What do you do up in Seattle?"

"Marketing. Software."

I nodded myself, watched him take another healthy gulp, and asked, "Nice to get out of all that rain?"

He shrugged, then said, "I guess, sure." He turned his head and narrowed his eyes towards the front of the property. "You need some type of code or something to open those big gates out there, right? Only way to drive back here?"

I nodded again.

"So, my ex would only be able to pick up our daughter and drop her off outside that walkway entrance you brought us through, that correct?"

I nodded once more.

"Good."

He pinched his mouth together, gave me a little bottle salute, picked up his grocery bag, and went inside the casita.

Shortly after that, just before Gwen got home from work, I saw the two of them splashing and laughing in the pool. Afterwards, they played a version of bocce ball together; whenever I glanced their way, Chris seemed to have a bottle of beer nearby. A little later, they knocked on the back door while I was fixing a chicken Caesar salad in the kitchen, and Gwen gave them a few restaurant recommendations within walking distance for dinner. They went on their way, and we settled down to our own meal outside on the banquet table. The sun had set, the air had cooled, the fountain made its small splash; it was the blue hour, my favorite part of the day.

Gwen poured us each a glass of chilled wine while I served the salad. We touched glasses, sipped, and she said, "Our new guests seem okay."

I shrugged, took a bite of salad, and watched her move hers around on her plate.

I asked, "Tough day?"

"Oh, you know. A six-year-old passed today." She stopped moving her fork. "That young . . . it still gets to me."

I looked at her in a way I hoped suggested empathy. Gwen had worked for even longer than I had in her position and dealt with things I could hardly imagine. Situations I knew I wouldn't be able to handle with even a fraction of the grace she did. I admired her.

"Well," I said and put my hand on her wrist. "Tomorrow's Friday, at least."

She worked four ten-hour weekly shifts and had Fridays off. Her eyes brightened a little. She lifted her wine and said, "Here, here."

We touched glasses again, sipped, and turned our attention back to our salads.

Gwen checked in our next guest for the front unit the following afternoon while I was in back starting a load of laundry. Chris and his daughter were stretched out on chaise lounges by the pool after riding bikes when I heard Gwen pass by our outside banquet table giving the new guest our regular spiel. I gave a little wave and smile as they passed me on their way to the pool. When they were a few steps away, Chris sat up straight on his chaise and the woman froze. I watched him sit perfectly still, his mouth agape. Then he muttered, "No fucking way . . . Brenda?"

Haley rose slowly and cried, "Mom!"

She scampered over and folded her mother into a hug, to which the woman responded with mild reciprocation without taking her eyes off Chris. She was a few years younger than him, but her attractiveness, like his, had tilted a little past its prime. The hint of a smirk clouded her face. Gwen and I looked back and forth between them until Brenda finally said, "Well, isn't this something? What are the chances?"

"You?" Chris pointed. "That front unit?"

She nodded slowly and, it seemed, almost gleefully. His expression hardened. Their daughter had lowered her eyes, and I stepped out onto the lawn. Chris' next words were directed at me and came out like a bark. He said, "Completely unacceptable."

I showed him my palms. "Sorry," I told him. "She just made a regular email booking. Different last name. I knew nothing about your connection."

I watched him shake his head. His hands had balled into fists at his sides. I said, "You're both adults. Trusting you can work this out." I gestured with my chin to Gwen. "Come on, honey. Let's go inside and give them some time."

Gwen didn't need to be coaxed. I followed her through the French doors leading into the great room, closed them after us, then gave a soft whistle.

"Yeah," Gwen said. She shook her head. "Who would have thunk?"

An hour or so afterwards, we heard Brenda talking with Haley in the front unit, as well as some drawers being opened and closed in the second, smaller bedroom near our adjoining door, so she and Chris must have worked out some kind of arrangement. A while later, the place went silent, and a car crunched out of our small gravel lot beyond the gate.

When I went out back to change the laundry, I found Chris sitting at his umbrella table. He pursed his lips and gave me a beer bottle salute like the previous afternoon, but this one lacked gusto. Another full six-pack was on the table with two empties already returned to their slots.

"Hey, there, neighbor," he said, tipping his beer. "One of these has your name on it."

He didn't wait for me to accept or decline, but just opened a bottle and slid it over in front of the chair next to him. I searched quickly for an excuse to leave, but could think of none, so reluctantly sat down. He watched me take a swig.

"There you go," he said.

"Thanks." I set the bottle back on the table. "So, looks like you two sorted things out."

"I wouldn't go that far. It was her night with Haley. By prior mutual agreement. Arranged over a series of several-word texts." He gave a little grunt. "Our preferred mode of communication."

"Okay."

He finished what was left in his bottle, opened a new one, then asked, "You and your wife happily married?"

"No complaints."

"Good for you." He took a swallow. "I was, too. For a long time, anyway. Until I made one stupid indiscretion last June—had never strayed before, not once—then made the mistake of telling Brenda about it. Couldn't stand the guilt. Honesty and all that." He spun the bottle on his thigh. "She hit the roof, threw me out, filed for divorce five days later." He snapped his fingers. "Twenty-three years of marriage gone like that."

Silence followed. To fill it, I said, "Shucks. Sorry."

"Yeah, well, it didn't take her long to bounce back. Saw photos within a month on her Facebook of her getting all cuddly with two different guys. She blocked me after that, so who knows how many more . . . plenty, probably."

I watched him take another pull from his bottle. The light was falling towards the blue hour again, but it didn't hold its usual allure for me. Chris had begun tapping his foot. He stared off towards the pool with a concentration that made him scowl.

"I can't stand to be around her," he said suddenly. "Drives me crazy." He looked back at me. "Batshit crazy, you know?"

I raised my eyebrows and said, "Sure."

His toe-tapping grew more rapid, as did the bottle spinning on his thigh. He slouched back in his chair.

"Listen," I said. "I've got to take something out of the oven." It wasn't true, but I stood and lifted the bottle. "I'll bring this with me."

If he heard me, he gave no indication of it; he was scowling out towards the pool again. Without looking at me, he asked, "They leave?"

It was clear enough who he meant, so I said, "Drove off somewhere, yeah."

"Went to the meet & greet for out-of-town wedding guests. At some country club, before tonight's rehearsal dinner. That's a party I'll damn well skip."

"Understandable, I guess."

He gave another one of his huffed snorts. The tapping and spinning continued.

"Okay, then," I told him. "I'll see you later."

I didn't bother stopping to change the laundry on the way back to the house.

Brenda had ordered a breakfast basket for the next morning and was already sitting in an Adirondack chair on her patio when I brought it over. Her kimono-like robe hung loosely around her, and she held a mug of steaming coffee between her knees. She smiled at me as I set the basket beside her chair.

"Yum," she said. "Smells good."

"Just some blueberry muffins, yoghurt, and juice. Nothing fancy."

"You bake the muffins yourself?"

"I did."

"Haven't met many men who bake." Her smile lingered. "I like that."

Up closer in the harsh morning light, I could see tiny lines at the corners of her mouth and eyes. She took a sip of coffee, but kept her gaze on me. She said, "This is a lovely property you have."

"Thanks."

She pointed to the widest stretch of lawn. "That wouldn't be a bad place for a wedding."

"We've hosted a few there."

"Chris and I got married at a winery on Bainbridge Island. That's in

Puget Sound across from Seattle." She cradled the mug under her chin, its steam drifting. "Beautiful, sunny day . . . rare. He looked very handsome."

"Sounds pretty wonderful."

"Long time ago."

Her smile had become strained. A couple of branches of bougainvillea against the wall behind her needed trimming. She tucked a strand of hair behind her ear. Her left eyelid had begun to twitch slightly.

I asked, "Sleep all right?"

She nodded.

"Anything else you need?"

"No." Her smile had regained some of its composure. "Nothing. Nothing at all."

I nodded, turned, and left.

🦋

Mid-morning, before it got too hot or crowded, Gwen and I went for our regular Saturday hike up the Quartz Ridge trail. Like usual, I followed. I noted how, like mine, her legs and torso had thickened considerably over the years. She kept her graying hair, long and flowing years earlier, in a non-fussy bob. We'd met during college at an outdoor music festival we'd gone to with mutual friends, and I first noticed her when she declined the joint being passed around as I had. I somehow got up the nerve to talk with her afterwards around the bonfire where we'd all scattered sleeping bags. We got married during our senior year, and she still wore the same style of rimless glasses as she had then, never caring to try contacts.

After the hike, we dawdled over lunch at an outdoor café we liked, talking mostly about our sons. They'd both stayed in their college towns after graduating. The older one was a speech therapist in Tucson, who we were fairly certain was going to propose soon to his girlfriend, an occupational therapist at the same hospital, of whom we were very fond. Our younger son was a middle school teacher in Flagstaff who went off backpacking somewhere new across the globe every summer; Gwen and I wished we had done something like that at his age. We were proud of them both.

When we finished lunch, we made a lengthy Costco run. It was almost three by time we got back to the hacienda, and both rental cars were gone, so we guessed our guests had all headed off to the wedding. I thought I remembered Chris telling me it was a mid-afternoon affair. I was glad we weren't around to see their exiting choreography or how they'd shared the day until that point.

I grilled salmon and asparagus for dinner, then Gwen and I curled up on the couch together and watched a movie. She went into bed to read about nine, while I moved up to my desk in the loft to check our property email account for potential new bookings. My laptop was still powering up when I heard a car park out front and saw Chris pass by below on his way back to the casita, his tie undone and his shirt tails out of his trousers. About ten minutes later, a knock came at the back door. When I went down and opened it, Chris stood under the overhead light clutching the handles of two rolling suitcases. He was dressed the same, but the tie was gone. His eyes were bloodshot.

He slid one of the suitcases my way and said, "Can you put this in the bedroom Haley is using up front? She's supposed to be staying with me tonight because we have a tee time early tomorrow, but I'm leaving and don't want her sleeping back there alone."

I felt my brow pucker. "What's going on?"

His jaw set hard. "I'm leaving. Changed my flight to a midnight red-eye." He shook his head. "Can't take this anymore. Nope, can't. Won't."

"Something happen at the wedding?"

"Wedding wasn't the problem. Haley went and sat with me, then drove to the reception with her mother where they were at a separate table. Fine, those were our arrangements. But then I had to watch Brenda flirt with half-a-dozen different guys. Never once looked my way. After the dancing got going, she kicked off her heels and joined a conga line with the wedding party, arms around some guy's waist half her age, another one grabbing her from behind, her swinging her ass . . . that was it for me." He gave one of his snorts, then said, "Here."

He extended Haley's suitcase handle my way. I took it from him.

"I left her a note at the casita," he said, "but maybe you can leave their front door unlocked for her. Just in case."

"Sure," I told him. "I can do that."

He gave one short, stiff nod and a last troubled glance, then grabbed his own suitcase and left. I remained where I was until I heard his car pull away.

Gwen's voice was halting when it came from a few feet behind me. "What was that all about?"

"Regret," I said and turned around. "Sadness and bitterness and regret."

I looked at her standing there in her rumpled cotton nightgown with its hummingbird pattern. I couldn't remember the last time we'd been intimate. But we still fell asleep each night in bed with my arm around her and her head on my chest.

"I love you, you know," I said.

"I know." Her face softened. "You, too."

I nodded, then pulled Haley's suitcase across our great room. I went through to Brenda's unit, set it in the smaller bedroom, and unlocked their front door like Chris had asked.

❦❦ ❦ ❦❦

I was still at my computer an hour or so later when I heard another car pull into the lot out front. I swiveled in my chair and watched through the window as Haley got out of a taxi there and started back towards the casita on the cinder walkway. Perhaps five minutes passed before her footsteps retraced themselves more slowly, and I heard the front door of her mother's unit open and close. Sink taps turned on and off; a toilet flushed. The loft had open windows directly above those in the smaller bedroom, so I didn't have to strain to hear her get into bed and start to cry. I powered down my computer, shut its lid, turned off my desk lamp, listened to her in the darkness for a little longer, then made my way down to bed myself.

❦❦ ❦ ❦❦

Around two in the morning, I was standing at the kitchen sink after getting up for a glass of water and was startled by a loud crack that sounded like a gunshot being fired from the front unit, followed by a woman's scream. I hurried through the dining area's adjoining door and followed Haley down the short hallway to the open doorway of the master bedroom. Brenda and a tall, dark-haired man had propped themselves up on the mattress that had fallen through the bed's frame. Both sides and the foot of the frame had collapsed onto the floor like a toppled house of cards; only the frame's head remained in place against the wall. I stood just behind Haley, whose hand had clapped over her mouth. Enough light came through the muslin curtain from the eave lamp outside to display Brenda and the man's nakedness; she yanked a sheet over their middles.

We stared at one another until Brenda muttered, "The bed. It broke."

"Mom." Hayley's voice was hardly more than a hiss. "What the hell? For

Christ's sake, he's a goddamn groomsman."

"You're supposed to be sleeping at your dad's."

"He left."

The man ran his hand through his disheveled hair, then across his chin. He looked towards the window like he was trying to find something there.

Hayley had begun shaking her head furiously. She pushed past me, ran down the hall, and slammed the door to her room. I watched Brenda's shoulders slump. She made a few shakes of her own head, then looked up at me and said, "I'll pay for the damage."

I heard myself say, "Let's worry about that in the morning."

I paused briefly at Haley's bedroom, but heard nothing inside. I closed the adjoining door to the unit softly behind me, then stood still in moonlight that streamed through our great room's high, pitched windows. I heard the front door of their unit open and close and a pair of footsteps head out through the entrance, cross the parking lot, then die away. Outside, the fountain gurgled quietly. I could just see a partial moon off above the treetops at the rear of the property, a yellow slice of it already beginning its descent towards a new day. Whether it was waxing or waning, I had no idea.

I waited until Gwen awoke the next morning to tell her what had happened. She said nothing, just shook her head in response, so I got up and started preparations in the kitchen. I wasn't surprised to find no one on the front unit's patio when I brought over their breakfast basket at eight. I set it where I had the previous morning just outside the door next to the Adirondack chair. Then I went back to the casita; it took me about an hour to clean it and get its laundry going.

When I went out front again with hand clippers to cut the stray bougainvillea branches, I found Haley sitting in the Adirondack chair staring at the lawn. The breakfast basket hadn't been touched. She turned slowly and looked up at me.

"Sorry to disturb you." I showed her the clippers. "Just wanted to trim that overgrown bougainvillea a little."

"It's beautiful," she told me. "Very healthy. So is that red yucca and desert rose . . . tough to grow."

"You know something about plants."

"I'm a botany major. Want to become a horticulturist."

"That what your mom does?"

"No, she's an interior designer."

"Making your own path."

"Hope to, yes."

I nodded, then extended the clippers towards the bush behind her. "I'll be quick. Just those two branches sticking out."

She didn't watch me as I snipped. I held the cut portions with my fingertips away from the thorns and watched her stare out at the lawn again, her face completely impassive.

I said, "There's some breakfast in that basket there."

She gave a nod, but didn't move.

"Not hungry?'

She made no reply. For the first time, I saw that she had her father's forehead and her mother's thin nose. I said, "Anything I can bring you? Ice tea, soda."

"A new life," she said without looking at me. "New parents."

"Afraid I can't help you there." I hesitated before saying, "I know they care about you."

"Sure." Haley folded her small hands together in her lap, then said, "We're leaving, too. My mom and I. She got on her cell phone a little while ago and booked us into a resort up in Sedona for our last two nights here. Made us reservations for spa treatments and some fancy massages where they use hot stones. Says I'll love all the red rock." She looked my way. "She's trying to make things up to me for last night. That's what she does. She also wrote you a check for the busted bed. Put it on top of that little journal on the table in the entry where guests write things about their stay. I don't think we'll be writing anything." I watched her rock her head back and forth, considering. "Actually, maybe I will. I might write: fuck everything."

I'd seen plenty of girls over the years like her, younger versions of course, but heading in a similar direction. She was staring back out at the lawn when I said, "Hey, things will straighten out for you, get better, you'll see. You're practically on your own now. Have a whole, big, wonderful life ahead of you to do with whatever you want."

She gave a little snort-like laugh not unlike her father's, but without dismissiveness. She managed a small smile and said, "Thanks."

"You bet."

With my free hand, I patted her shoulder. I carried the stray branches back to our yard waste container, then went to take the casita's laundry out of the dryer and remake its beds.

᷾ ᷾ ᷾

Gwen had breakfast set out for us outside on the banquet table when I got back to the main house: bagels, cream cheese, cantaloupe slices, tomato juice. I thanked her, sat down in the latticed shadows, and we started eating.

After a few minutes, she said, "Our guests in the front checked-out early, too. The woman said she left us payment for the bed. Said to let her know if it's not enough."

I nodded and looked over at her in her sleeveless blouse that was missing a button near the top. It was unusually warm, already near eighty. A film of sweat had formed at her hairline.

"So," she continued, "we have both units empty and paid for the next two days and the place entirely to ourselves. When was the last time that happened?"

I smiled and shrugged. Her blue-gray eyes behind the glasses hadn't changed since the day I met her; they were gentle, thoughtful, tender. I thought it was probably time to think about selling the hacienda and moving into something smaller; maybe a little townhouse where no upkeep at all was involved. I was pretty sure Gwen felt the same, but that was a discussion, like how to replace the front unit's bed, that could wait.

I put down my silverware and asked, "More importantly, when was the last time we skinny dipped?"

"What?" Her forehead wrinkled, but those eyes danced a bit.

I reached over, took off her glasses, and set them on the table. I stood up, kicked off my sandals, and stripped off my shirt. I reached for her hand. She gave a little giggle, but rose and did the same. Our jeans and underwear went next. Then we ran across the grass together holding hands, as awkwardly as anyone of our age and girth would, and jumped in the pool. As we did, we shouted in unison at the top of our lungs.

SOMETHING LIKE THAT

 After I got my administrative credential, I was hired to be one of the assistant principals at the high school where I'd been a PE teacher and girls' basketball coach. My new position involved a variety of site and district-level duties, but one I hadn't expected to face so early on occurred in mid-November when my supervisor, our school principal, told me I needed to take her place on an expulsion hearing panel. She barged into my office shortly before dismissal and apologized for the short notice, but said she'd just gotten a call that her young son had broken his arm in a playground accident. She'd cleared my taking her place at the hearing with the head of the panel, a cold, gruff man named Roy Miller who was the Assistant Superintendent of Student Services. She told me it would start in a half hour, then hurried out of my office as quickly as she'd entered it.

 I sat for several moments afterward staring at where she'd been, a slow wave of dread crawling up through me. I knew about that expulsion case because one of our school's other assistant principals had initially handled the incident. It involved a student on our boys' basketball team and its coach with whom I'd worked for many years. Our practice courts and locker rooms had been right next to one another. I'd long cringed at the way he berated his players, the shouts, the cursing; I'd even heard he'd sometimes put his hands on them. The boy being brought up for expulsion, a senior and star player named Brad Holland, had slugged him during practice the week before and broken his nose. The other assistant principal said Brad had told him he'd just lost it after all the coach's abuse. "That may have been the case, but the kid crossed a line," my colleague said and then chuckled. "Suppose you could say this expulsion is a slam dunk."

 I got to the conference room adjoining the district office boardroom where the hearing was to be held a little more than twenty minutes later.

Roy and the other two admins on the panel, the Human Resources Director and a principal at a neighboring high school, were already seated around its rectangular table. Both men were longtime and highly-regarded administrators who'd been part of the interview team that had selected me for my new position. I'd just turned thirty-two, and they all had three decades on me. We mumbled greetings, then Roy pointed to an empty chair. He told me to close the door first, which I did, before obediently taking the vacant seat. Roy began by reviewing the case's essential ingredients with us; they were basically the same as what my colleague had told me. He then gave us copies of the district's Discipline Action Guide, which all students and parents had to sign during registration, with an asterisk next to the related guidance that read: "Although administrators have some discretion, expulsion will generally be recommended for these offenses." A bulleted list followed, the last of which was "assault or battery upon any school employee"(Education Code Section 48915 [a]).

After we'd read it and looked back up, Roy said, "Trusting you'll agree this particular case is pretty straightforward. No real gray area." From the corner of my eye, I saw the other two admins nod. "So, this is how it will go," Roy continued. "We'll introduce ourselves, and I'll explain who you are on the panel and that your decision on the case must be unanimous and is final, no appeals permitted." He lifted the Discipline Action Guide. "Everyone will have a copy of this, which I'll read aloud, and then I'll very briefly present the district's case for expulsion. Next, the student or his parent, if he has one with him, can say whatever they like in defense. After that, we leave the room and wait in the hallway so the three of you can confer. That shouldn't take long given the circumstances here. When you're done, you come get us, we sit back down, and one of you states your collective decision. Then we all go on our merry ways." He straightened his neck. "Any questions?"

The principal said, "None."

The HR Director stood up. "Let's get this over with."

The boardroom was arranged with two long tables facing each other separated by a half-dozen feet. Three chairs were behind one, and four were behind the other nearest to the doors. At the far end of that table, Brad and a squat, stocky woman I assumed to be his mother were seated with their backs to us. They turned and watched us as we entered. Brad was dressed in dark pants with a dark shirt and tie, his long, lean frame draped over the chair and his eyes following us as the other two admins and I made our way to the seats at the empty table; I took the one in the middle. Roy settled himself into the chair at the end of their table, cleared his throat, and introductions were made; as suspected, the woman with Brad said she was Mrs. Holland, his mother. Then Roy started the proceedings.

When he slid copies of the Discipline Action Guide to Brad and his mother, she frowned deeply. As Roy read, I watched her reach under the table and pat Brad's leg. He folded his arms and stared at the carpet. I didn't know him well, but he'd been in an off-season weightlifting class I'd taught a couple of years earlier and hadn't seemed like a bad kid. Quiet, pretty reserved, a hard worker; he'd been recruited at a small college nearby where I'd played myself. A kid with a bright future and loads of potential. When Roy got to the part about assault and battery, Brad shook his head slowly back and forth.

Next, Roy made his case for expulsion. True to his word, he was short and to-the-point. I took notes as he spoke; the other two admins sat motionless next to me. When he finished, he asked if Brad or his mother had anything to say.

"I do," Mrs. Holland said and stood up. "You can't expel my son. What he did wasn't right, but he was forced into it. That coach berated him and those other players like you wouldn't believe . . . just pushed and pushed and pushed. Brad had more than three years of it, the resentment of it, the unfairness building and building. So, when that coach called him vulgar names at that practice, his spittle spraying in Brad's face, my son, well, just snapped." She paused, looked down at Brad with his folded arms and dour expression, then at each of us. "So, please, extend his suspension, add on community service, anything, but don't kick him out of school. He graduates in six months and has a college basketball scholarship waiting for him that will go up in smoke if he's expelled. You can't rob him of that for a single provoked mistake."

Mrs. Holland sat back down. Roy let a few seconds pass before he said, "I'll just remind the panel again that this student punched his coach, a school employee, in the face and broke his nose."

"That son-of-a-bitch got what he deserved," Brad hissed. He'd raised his head and sat up straight, his eyes narrowed. "You don't know the half of it. Brought a skirt to practice for whoever lost a rebounding drill to wear. Shoved our point guard into a locker after we lost a game because he turned the ball over too much. Told me during that practice I was the first faggot he'd ever made a captain."

"That's hearsay," Roy said. "And not pertinent to the incident being considered." He waved his Discipline Action Guide. "Punched his coach. Broke his nose."

"I think we've heard enough," the HR Director said.

The principal nodded. "I agree."

"Fine," Roy said. "The three of us will wait in the hallway while you confer."

When he stood up, Brad and his mother followed suit. Before turning to leave, Brad leveled each of us with a glare. Before his gaze reached me, I had trained my eyes on the notes I was pretending to study. My eyes remained there until I heard the boardroom doors click shut behind them.

After they left, several moments of silence went by before the HR Director said, "So, I'm ready to vote. Guilty as charged."

The principal nodded again. "That coach sounds like a piece of work, but I vote the same. A student simply can't punch a school employee."

They both turned and looked at me until the HR Director finally said, "Well?"

"I don't know." I'd hoped to sound stronger, but I could barely get the words out. Nausea rose from my belly. I knew that by morning our decision and my complicity in it would be common knowledge across the district. And my future administrative career would certainly be affected by my hand in this decision, one way or another. I had many years of work ahead of me; my wife and I had just stretched our budget to buy our first home on the heels of my higher salary.

"Listen, son," the HR Director said to me. "There's strong precedent to consider here. Think about what this decision says to the next student who gets pissed off at a teacher or another staff member."

"He's right," the principal said. "No question about it."

They each looked at me with set jaws. My temples pounded. The silence in the room seemed deafening.

Finally, I nodded once and muttered, "Okay, sure."

The HR Director clapped me on the back. "Good," he said. "I'll go get them."

I didn't look up when they were all seated at their table again and the HR Director delivered our decision, but I heard Brad grunt and his mother begin to cry. I continued to stare down at my notes while everyone gathered their things and left the room. Brad and his mother were the last to leave.

Afterwards, I sat alone in the dwindling, late afternoon, traffic whispering past in the street outside.

⋙ ⋘

When my wife got home from work an hour or so later, she found me sitting in the gathering darkness at the dining room table, an opened bottle of wine in front of me and a glass of it in my hand. The table wasn't set and no meal had been started; whoever got home first always did those things.

She stopped a few feet away and said, "Hi there."

"Hey."

She came over next to me, gave the wine bottle a shake, and said, "Got a little head of steam going. Must have been quite a day."

I shrugged.

"What happened?"

"Hard to explain."

"Involve a kid?"

I nodded. "A boy." I managed to hold her gaze. "I fucked up with him. Made a lousy decision."

She nodded slowly herself. The look she gave me reminded me of the one she'd fixed me with during her speech at our wedding rehearsal dinner when she said what she admired most about me was my integrity. The knot in my stomach seized. She squeezed my shoulder and said, "You'll make it right."

I lowered my eyes. "Don't see how."

"You'll think of something."

Neither of us said anything then while a car ground its gears as it passed in the street. She waited until the sound of it was gone to say, "Well, how about frozen pizza for dinner. That sound okay?"

"Sure."

I still hadn't looked back up at her. She squeezed my shoulder again and went into the kitchen.

⋙ ⋘

I tried to chase away thoughts of the expulsion hearing, but didn't sleep much that night. Things weren't much better the next morning when I heard the boys' basketball coach crowing to other teachers about the expulsion decision in the staff lounge. Worse yet, later that afternoon, I passed the gym on my way to the parking lot and heard him hollering at his players in practice.

I'd left work as early as possible and stopped at a bar near our house on my way home, something I never did unless I was joining other staff members for an occasional TGIF. The place was narrow, low lit, and mostly empty, just as I was feeling. I took a stool on the far end, nursed a vodka cranberry, and thought about things. I couldn't shake the sound of Mrs. Holland's first choked sob after the HR Director had delivered our decision or the look in Brad's eyes as he'd made his tortured outburst beforehand. I thought about when I'd been a small boy and had let a classmate be punished for stealing a sweater from the coatrack when I knew another student, the class bully, had done it. I'd kept silent then, too; I hadn't had the courage to speak up. I slumped forward, my eyes shut tight.

❦❦ ❦ ❦❦

Over the next few weeks, I regularly checked the log our secretary kept whenever records were requested for a student transferring to a different high school, but Brad's name never appeared on it. I also called a few alternative high schools in the area where he could have completed his GED, but he hadn't enrolled in any of them either. Thanksgiving and Christmas breaks provided distractions that kept me from thinking as often about him and the expulsion, but those thoughts were never far away, like muted clouds always lurking. I pushed harder and longer on my morning runs, but that didn't help much. Sometimes, my wife found me lying awake next to her in bed late at night and asked if I was still thinking about that kid; when I just rolled over and didn't answer, she'd wrap her arm around me and snuggle close.

❦❦ ❦ ❦❦

I did my best not to let any lingering preoccupations about Brad affect my work at school. I was in charge of all our standardized testing, which ratcheted up in February, so the challenge of coordinating that, as well the data analysis sessions that followed each test, largely preoccupied my mind until the end of the school year. Ours was the only site in the district with no testing compliance violations. I'd always been good at organizing things of that nature and analyzing data, areas key to what made me successful as a basketball coach. I guess senior administration took notice, too, because they appointed me as the temporary replacement for the district's Assessment Coordinator when she left on maternity leave in June. That meant working through the summer, which I was happy to do to stay busy, as well as extra pay, which pleased my wife.

When the new school year began, the Assessment Coordinator decided to resign in order to stay home with her new baby, and her position became permanently mine. A jump from assistant principal directly to the district office was almost unheard of, so a lot of kudos came my way. I admit that I did bask a bit in the comforting waters of professional validation. But I shuddered when Roy Miller stopped in to congratulate me on the permanent appointment saying he knew from the start that I was destined for big things. Like I also did when, driving home from work, I sometimes saw a bicycle with a tall seat and handlebars like the one Brad used to ride leaning up against an abandoned building in a shady part of town. Or, when a small boy from up the street walked by the front of our house wearing a sweater almost identical to the one that had been stolen from that classroom of my youth.

Just before Thanksgiving break, not quite a year to the day of the expulsion hearing, when I was returning a shopping cart to its rack in a grocery store parking lot, my blood turned cold as a woman's voice behind me said, "I'll take that if you're done with it."

I turned slowly, and Mrs. Holland's eyes rose to meet my own. They narrowed like her son's had at the hearing, and I watched her go rigid. She said, "You."

I heard myself say, "How's Brad?"

"Awful, after what you people did to him." She was breathing quickly through her nose, her chest rising and falling. "Gone to hell, if you want to know the truth."

"I hoped he'd finish school somewhere else. Maybe play ball at a JC."

"Never went to class again, never picked up another basketball. Was just lost, got in with a bad crowd, started using." Her eyes had widened and her bottom lip began trembling. "He's at Caron now, thanks to you."

I was familiar with the name of the rehab center; I'd known a few other students who'd ended up there over the years. An image flitted across my mind of Brad hitting the free throw that iced the section championship during his junior year, followed by the swarm of teammates mobbing him afterwards as time expired and the din of cheers from the stands. The stiffness evaporated from Mrs. Holland, and her shoulders sagged. A bitter grief overcame me.

"I'm sorry," I said. "For whatever it's worth, I've felt awful ever since that hearing. I made a terrible mistake. I shouldn't have voted for expulsion. But I didn't speak up, didn't have the guts. I'm so sorry. So very, very sorry."

Along with anger, something new filled Mrs. Holland's eyes, some combination of weariness, resignation, hopelessness. "Try telling that to Brad," she said, her voice barely audible. Then she walked past me towards the store, leaving the cart I still gripped behind her.

❦ ❦ ❦

It took me a week to gather the nerve to go the rehab center. My wife and I were on our way to meet some friends near it for dinner, and I told her I just had to run inside for a minute. I ignored her curious frown as I parked at the curb in front of the building and left the car.

I wasn't even sure Brad would still be there, but when I asked the receptionist, she said she'd let him know he had a visitor. She pointed to a little room to her right. A small table filled most of it. I sat in the chair facing the door and rubbed my forehead. Music played faintly somewhere through the walls.

A few minutes later, Brad appeared in the open doorway and stopped. We looked at each other for several seconds, his face expressionless. Finally, he said, "What do you want?"

I pulled back the chair next to me, but he shook his head. I swallowed once, then said, "I came to apologize. I shouldn't have voted to have you expelled. I've felt horrible about it every day since."

Nothing in his face changed. He was wearing jeans, a baggy shirt, and the same high-top sneakers that had been issued to all the school's basketball players. He looked like he'd lost weight. His eyes stayed on mine, but he remained silent.

I asked, "How're you doing? Here, I mean."

He scowled. I nodded slowly, then took out some folded papers from my sport coat pocket and pushed them across the table in his direction.

He looked from the papers to me and said, "What are those?"

"The district next to ours has started a new online continuation program. I went over your records with the director, and he thinks you can get enough credits to graduate in a few months if you work at it hard enough. I registered you. Didn't need your mother's signature because you're eighteen now. I'm guessing you have some free time here and access to a computer, so you could start right away." I pointed to the papers. "The username and password are there on top."

He looked down at the papers again and shook his head.

"And I talked to the coach at the college that offered you a scholarship. He's actually an old friend of mine; we were teammates there. I explained things to him, including the expulsion hearing, how it should have gone down. He says there'd be a spot for you on the team in the fall if you get your diploma, finish rehab, stay clean."

Brad stood very still in the doorway staring at me. "Why are you doing this?"

"Because I screwed up and you got screwed up because of it. Because that old coach of yours is an asshole and shouldn't be working with kids. Because I owe you. Because I want to see you do well."

"Big guilt trip, huh?"

I hesitated, then said, "Something like that, I guess."

He took a turn at nodding slowly, then reached over and picked up the registration papers. I watched him roll them into a tube, and then he was gone. The music had stopped. I looked out the room's window where darkening clouds stretched towards the setting sun over the treetops. It looked like it might rain. I hoped it would and that would help wash things away.

After I got back in the car and had started the engine, I could feel my wife's eyes steady on me.

She said, "Take care of everything?"

I looked over at her and shrugged.

She glanced by me towards the rehab center, then back. "That the boy you've been worried about?"

My nod was short.

"Things better?"

I shrugged again. "Hope so."

"Listen." She paused and put her hand on mine. "I'm sure you did your best . . ."

Her voice trailed off. She shrugged herself. I tried to smile, but it felt feeble. So, instead, I brought the back of her hand to my lips and kissed it.

INCONCEIVABLE

A bee stung the bottom of my foot one morning in late June while I was paying bills. Right beneath the third toe. A big bumblebee. How it got under the desk in my study, I have no idea. Initially, I felt a prick, and then a sharp pain followed. I jumped out of my chair thinking that perhaps it had been a spider or red ants. But there was the bumblebee, lying on its side beneath the chair, waving its fragile legs.

I ended its misery with the squish of an envelope, dropped it in the wastebasket, and then began to sweat, an anxiousness spreading up through my chest. The reason for this was that I'd been determined to be allergic to bee sting many years earlier when I was a teenager. The first instance occurred when I was stung on a golf course and broke out all over in hives. My mother had me lie in a bath of cold water and Epsom salts, and gave me Benadryl; after an hour or so, the reaction eased. The second happened when I was working on a construction crew for a summer job in college. I was jackhammering a patch of blacktop, and a bee flew into my mouth and stung the back of it. I spat it out. The inside of my throat immediately began to swell, and my breathing constricted. The crew foreman drove me to an Urgent Care nearby. By the time I got there, hives had begun again, and I was laboring just to breathe shallowly through my nose. The doctor gave me a cortisone shot and calamine lotion for the hives. He had me wait in the examining room while he saw to other patients long enough to be sure the swelling in my throat had decreased and my airway had cleared. When they had, the foreman drove me home while another laborer followed in my car. But it scared me. And I stayed scared of bees from then on. Much later, after epi-pens were common, a girlfriend suggested that I get and carry one, but I never bothered doing that.

Somehow, more than twenty-five years had passed without further bee incidents. So, I was unsure how my body would react to the bumblebee. I'd heard that allergies could change over time, but I had no way of knowing if that had been the case for me. And I wasn't sure what the potency of a bumblebee's sting was in comparison to other bees. The ache under my toes had intensified a bit and spread to the top of my foot, but I felt no itching yet, and my breathing seemed fine. I decided to drive down to the emergency department at our town's little hospital and sit in their waiting room in case the reaction worsened; if it did, I could pursue immediate care there, and if it lessened, I could just leave.

I wore flip-flops and limped a little entering the tiny waiting room. There were only four other people inside: two border patrol agents and two young men who appeared to be of Mexican descent sitting forlornly across from them. One of the young men was taller than the other and his sneakers had no laces; he had a bandage wrapped around his left wrist and kept his head turned towards the windows. The other held an icepack over the bridge of his nose. They both wore jeans with untucked shirts and slumped in their chairs. Their faces and hair were scarred with sweat and dirt. The agents sat directly across from each of them, arms folded, murmuring over something that made them laugh. They wore identical uniforms, but the shorter, older one also had a ball cap with a border patrol insignia on the front. They had thick matching belts around their waists with holsters at each hip that held radios and pistols.

I sat down away from them and around a corner from the sliding glass window where the receptionist was at her desk. Her head was down when I entered, and I don't think she noticed me as I came in. There was a magazine about parenting on the next chair, so I picked that up and started flipping through it, glancing over on occasion at the foursome across from me. The top of my foot had begun to throb dully and a couple of the toes had swollen up a bit, but that was all.

After a while, I heard the window slide at the receptionist's desk, and she called out a Spanish surname. The agent closest to her stood up, reached across to the young man with the bandage, and led him by the elbow of his good arm around the corner out of sight from me to the window. They were almost the same height.

I heard the receptionist say, "This one has a problem with his arm?"

"Yes," the agent said.

"Sustained how?"

"They fell while fleeing from the back of a truck in the secondary inspection area at the Tijuana-San Diego border crossing. They'd been hiding under a tarp and some painting supplies. I think that one over there may have a broken nose."

"Both undocumented then."

"Yes."

There was a long pause before I heard her say, "So, you're going to get them patched up and then deport them."

"That's the basic plan. Yes, ma'am."

"What's the problem with his arm?"

I heard the agent say, "Show her." There was the sound of the bandage being unwrapped. "He's had some sort of recent surgery," the agent said. "See the incision?"

"All right," she said. A buzzer sounded at the door next to me that led to the examining rooms. "You can go in."

The agent led the young man by the same elbow, the bandage now dangling from his injured wrist. When the agent opened the door, the buzzing stopped. He nodded the young man into the opening. The young man looked over at me as he entered the hallway, and I tried to give a small, encouraging smile, but his expression remained grim. I wondered about how he had come to choose those particular shoes for what they'd planned to do earlier that morning.

Perhaps ten minutes passed before the same procedure was repeated for the second young man and the agent with the cap. They were buzzed through in exactly the same manner. Then I was alone in the waiting room. The pain in my foot remained about the same, and I heard a television that was mounted high on the wall on the other side playing a channel of continuous news. The volume was turned low, but as I flipped through the magazine, I was aware of reports on terrorism, stalled legislation on gun control and immigration, an encouraging jobs report, and a possible hurricane approaching the East coast.

After about a half hour, a woman in maroon scrubs came through the entrance. She stopped and looked at me. I recognized her vaguely and thought she was probably the parent of a kid who'd been in one of the recreation programs I coordinated at the town's community center.

"Well," she said. "Hello there. Are you all right?"

I explained to her why I was in the waiting room. She nodded when I'd finished and asked, "How does it feel now?"

"Not bad." I wriggled the toes on the foot that had been stung. "Better actually."

"That's good." She nodded some more. "Well, just ask for help if you need it. Nice to see you."

"You, too." I nodded as well and watched her lift an identification badge attached to a lanyard around her neck up to the panel on the door that led to the examining room hallway. The same buzz as before followed, and she opened it. It closed slowly behind her.

After she left, I wriggled my toes some more and reached down to feel the swelling on top of my foot. The ache had diminished a bit and the slight itch I felt seemed to have more to do with that ring of swelling lessening than with anything more alarming. I looked outside the windows at a mid-morning full of sunshine and blue, cloudless sky over the housetops across the street.

I waited another twenty minutes or so while the pain continued to decline before leaving. I'd parked my car as close to the entrance as possible and saw that it was across and down a little from the border patrol van, which I hadn't noticed when I came in. I'd just started the engine and rolled down the windows to cool the interior when the agents and the young men came out of two double doors that opened directly into the examining room hallway. They walked in the same pairs, led identically by elbows to the back of the van, which the taller agent opened. The young man with the wrist injury had a new bandage wrapped around it and a soft blue splint of some kind over that. The other young man had gauze sticking out of both of his nostrils and held a different size of icepack against one side of his nose; it seemed as if patches under both of his eyes had blackened a little where they met the bridge of his nose.

The agent with the ball cap climbed up into the back of the van first, then the shorter of the two young men, and last, the taller one. They all fastened seat belts on padded benches facing each other while the other agent spoke into his radio. I watched the taller young man's eyes pass me and fix on something to my left. I followed his gaze and saw a young Mexican woman standing in the shadow of a tree holding a baby boy against one hip. She kissed the fingers on her free hand, extended them towards the young man, and he did the same in response. He seemed to make an attempt to rise and move in her direction before his companion pulled him back by his shirt tail onto his spot on the bench.

The taller agent locked both the van's back doors. He shook the handles, went around to the driver's side, and started the engine. I watched the van pull slowly away out of the parking lot and drive up the street towards the highway. I wondered how the young man had contacted the woman. He wasn't handcuffed, so perhaps he'd managed a cell phone call or text. Or maybe one of the agents had simply agreed to do that for him.

When I looked back at her, I saw that she'd begun to cry softly. Her baby pawed at her cheeks, and she took his tiny hand in hers. She hoisted him to her shoulder, straining a tear there in her blouse, and I watched her slink away with him around the corner of the building. A kind of ache spread inside of me, as it had earlier that morning after the bee sting, but different. I found myself wishing that I'd lifted that struggling bumblebee onto the envelope and set it outside to go about its own affairs. It may have lived; I had no way of knowing for sure.

A few seconds later, I backed out myself and started for home. I drove several blocks before making a sudden U-turn and heading back to the hospital. I thought perhaps I could offer the woman and her baby a ride somewhere or at least see if she needed some kind of help. I drove slowly along the side of the building where they'd gone and searched in all directions, but didn't see them anywhere. I made a complete lap around the hospital block, but still couldn't find them. They were gone, off to their new reality; I'd missed my chance. I pulled to the curb and chastised myself for not acting sooner. I thought about benignly flipping through a parenting magazine with lives hanging in the balance beside me. Or listening to television news reports and engaging in idle conversation about a bee sting while destinies were being determined and altered a few feet away. In that moment, those dichotomies seemed to me utterly inconceivable. My eyes made a final search of the surrounding area before I shook my head and headed home for good.

IF YOU TREAT THEM RIGHT

Iris bought the place shortly before she retired after thirty-seven years on the grounds crew at Northern Arizona University. It was only twenty miles south of Flagstaff, but a couple of thousand feet lower in elevation, so heavy snow was infrequent and the coldest temperatures less severe. Besides being drawn by the more temperate winter climate, she'd loved the surrounding piñon-juniper woodland, the raised bed garden, and the greenhouse. Although the place needed work and what was advertised as a house could really only be called a glorified cabin, it suited her. She felt at peace there.

Iris was a loner by nature. After starting work at the university, she'd quickly developed a penchant for dealing with struggling flora, a niche that allowed her comparative solitude; she routinely refused opportunities for advancement in the department in order to avoid the additional interactions they would require. Because of her gruff manner and self-induced isolation, there was no ceremony or recognition attached to her retirement, hardly a farewell or acknowledgment of any kind.

Aside from a futon and a desk she bought for the house's little second bedroom, she simply arranged all her furniture, myriad potted plants, and other belongings exactly as she'd grown accustomed to having them in her old apartment and spent most of her energy outside on the garden and greenhouse. She moved in early September and within days had functioning drip irrigation and composting systems in the garden with vegetables, herbs, and flowers flourishing by the end of that month. The greenhouse took longer to repair. She ran a water line to it, replaced some rotted framing, inserted new high-quality plexi-glass, and built hotbeds to improve heat retention in colder months. By late October, she began using it to cultivate seedlings, a variety of succulents, and a few orchids on its newly latticed shelves. She spent a good portion of her remaining time reading on her back deck, playing online chess, or hiking nearby red-rock trails through swaths of Ponderosa pines, aspens, and Douglas firs. Iris was sixty-six years old, squat and solid, and wore her silver hair like a bathing cap.

The nearest dwelling to hers was a rusting mobile home thirty or so yards away through a spray of juniper bushes. She'd never seen a soul there and was glad to consider it abandoned until she arose early one morning in mid-December to find a beat-up sedan and a pickup truck parked haphazardly in front of it. Iris stood at her kitchen window and watched as a thin man in a denim jacket emerged from the trailer, ran a hand through his scraggly hair and beard, stumbled down the steps, and climbed into the pickup. A woman followed him onto the front steps clutching a terrycloth robe to her chest with one hand. The woman's dishwater-blonde hair was tied into an untidy knot at the top of her head, and even at that distance, Iris could see shadows under her eyes and in the hollows of her cheeks. The man sped off in the pickup spraying red gravel while the woman took a pack of cigarettes from her robe pocket, lit one with a plastic lighter, and blew out two long streams of smoke from her nostrils. Iris watched her pick at a scab on her cheek. The woman inhaled and exhaled again, then went back inside, the outer screen door slapping shut behind her. Iris winced at the sound and watched the woman's cigarette smoke disappear into the clear blush of late dawn.

🐦🌷🐦

Iris didn't see the woman again until later that afternoon while turning her compost pile after adding kitchen scraps to it. The pile was at the far end of the garden, a little beyond the greenhouse, half-again closer to their shared property line, so Iris could see her more clearly. She was still wearing the robe, her hair unchanged and another cigarette burning between her fingers, but a small boy now stood next to her beside the sedan's open back door. Dressed in ripped jeans, V-necked shirt, a navy-blue nylon coat, he stared at Iris under a mass of brown curls with big eyes of the same color. His mother lifted a box of pots and pans from the back seat of the car, then shoved its door closed with her hip. She stuck the cigarette between her lips, squinted, and nodded once at Iris. A covey of quail skittered between them among the junipers. Before the woman could see the reluctant nod Iris gave her in return, she'd headed towards the trailer, but the boy saw it and raised two fingers slowly in reply. Iris nodded again and watched the boy's eyes grow even larger before he scurried after his mother inside.

Iris stood very still in their wake. She thought the boy might be eight or nine years old. Something in his appearance seemed waifish, forlorn, and in spite of her misgivings, her heart clutched a bit. On the small breeze, the junipers' familiar, dusty tang gradually replaced the lingering smell of the woman's cigarette. The quail covey had moved closer, but Iris didn't turn and try to find it in the tangle of gray-green branches.

❦

When she heard the pickup rumble back in front of the trailer next door later that afternoon, Iris was in the greenhouse watering carrots and bibb lettuce that she'd transferred from starter trays to a hot bed. The pickup's engine heaved to a stop, its door creaked open and closed, and stillness resumed. The day's last light had already started its descent, so Iris couldn't see well through the junipers, but heard the trailer's screen door open and the woman's plaintive voice call, "Got the sugar?" The man's huffed ascent followed, then his footsteps stirred the thin gravel, and the screen door clapped shut again. Iris stood as still as she had earlier, this time frowning deeply, her ankles warm from the small, propane space heater under the shelf. She shook her head—tiny, repeated, unconscious shakes—and slowly lowered the watering can to the shelf.

❦

In the days that followed, Iris observed a pattern emerge next door. She'd hear the pickup rumble off about the same time each morning and also saw the boy leave the trailer an hour or so later, his bookbag straining his thin shoulders, heading down their driveway towards the school bus stop up the road. She rarely saw the woman afterwards during the day; if she did, Iris was usually startled to find her standing on their front steps smoking and staring at her without the least bit of pretense or self-consciousness; the rare nods they exchanged were marginal and succinct. The pickup's rumble returned in the evenings, followed by the same strained exchange between the woman and the man. Many nights, late, Iris heard them shouting at each other in the trailer.

The boy was the one she saw most frequently. He began pausing to look over at her house on his way to the bus stop each morning, and did the same in the afternoons when he came home. He shuffled as he walked, kicking up red dust and small stones in his path. She often saw him kneeling in the junipers separating their properties watching her as she worked in the garden or the greenhouse.

One afternoon while she was adjusting the garden's drip irrigation, she turned suddenly towards where he was hiding and barked, "I can see you, you know."

The boy didn't speak, but seemed to retreat deeper into the bushes' speckled shadows. Iris lifted a hand in his direction. "What do you want, anyway?"

The boy seemed rooted to the spot, his eyes like a small, startled animal's. A hint of approaching snow hung in the air, and his foggy breaths crept through the branches. It was so still Iris could hear the trickle of the tiny creek down the ravine behind her house.

She said, "I don't need trouble. From you or your folks." She realized that her voice had lost its sharp tone, deflated somehow like the air leaving a balloon. She stood up and slipped her hands into the pouch of her sweatshirt. "All right, then," she said. "You best get inside where it's warm."

The boy made no movement or reply whatsoever, so Iris walked slowly to the back deck, crossed it, and opened the kitchen door. Before going inside, she glanced at where the boy had been, but he'd disappeared. Just the empty junipers remained, bracketed by the red earth and endless sky.

❧ ❧ ❧

Later that night, the regular shouting from next door erupted in earnest, reaching levels she hadn't heard before. After a while, a sudden whack of the trailer's screen door was followed by another in close succession, then the pickup's engine grumbling to life.

The woman shouted, "And don't come back!"

"I won't," the man growled. "Count on it!"

The truck door slammed, the screen door did the same, and the pickup tore down their driveway. Its gears shifted quickly as it gained speed up the road until the sound of it had died away completely in the vast still night.

Iris rolled over on her back and stared up into the inky blackness. She pulled her comforter to her chin. A soft hiss came from the fireplace's dying embers in the living room. There were no other sounds. She made tiny shakes of her head again and nibbled at her lower lip. It took more than an hour for sleep to finally overtake her.

Iris was startled awake several hours later by the siren of an ambulance screaming up the driveway next door. Just as abruptly, it stopped. She hurried out from under the covers to the bedroom window where she could see its rotating light flashing through the bushes and hear the chaotic sounds of paramedics going in and out of the trailer, the clatter of a stretcher being maneuvered up the steps, and clipped phrases she could distinguish between voices over a receiver that included "apparent overdose . . . unconscious," "female—mid-thirties," "initiating immediate transport." She raised her hand to her chest and shook her head again. The commotion continued for another handful of minutes, then the siren pierced the night again, and the ambulance roared away down the driveway and off towards Flagstaff. It took a long time for the sound of it to die away. Iris lowered herself onto the bed and pulled the bunched comforter over her. She glanced at the clock on her nightstand: 4:52. She lay there for perhaps twenty minutes before giving up on sleep, rising, and pulling on slippers and a sweatshirt over her nightgown. She went into the living room, got the fire going again, and put the kettle on for tea. Her stern reflection stared back at her in the kitchen window.

"I didn't move here for this," she said to it. "I didn't."

It wasn't until Iris had been seated on the couch in front of the fireplace and was halfway through her tea that she considered the boy. As she did, she went stiff. He must have gone with the ambulance, she thought. Or else, with all the commotion, I just didn't hear the father came back in his truck and take him. Either of those, she thought, or something like it.

But a slow clamminess crept over her, and she moved to the window that had the best view of the junipers along the property line. The faintest etch of milky light hovered low in the eastern sky and was just enough to reveal a portion of the trailer through the bushes: dark, still, silent. Iris rubbed her forehead, gave more shakes of her head, then finally kicked off her slippers and pulled on her work boots. Leaving the house, she shuddered at the sudden, bitter chill and trotted through the thin dusting of snow that had fallen overnight towards a gap in the junipers.

Iris passed the sedan, climbed the trailer's steps, and pounded on the screen door, rattling its frame. No movement or sound came from inside, and outside, just the lonely, distant hoot of an owl. She peered through the door's murky window and saw a lopsided couch with a collection of drug paraphernalia on the side where one cushion was missing. No lamps, chairs, television, or pictures on the walls. She banged harder on the door; more silence replied. Iris walked around the exterior of the trailer, but was too short to see inside any more of the windows, though she paused to bang on the siding several times with no response. When she returned to the front, she peered inside the sedan which held only fast-food debris, several discarded envelopes addressed to the same woman's name, and on the back seat, a child's rubber boot. Iris heaved a sigh and retraced her steps in the snow with a coyote's tinny yelp echoing off beyond the neighboring arroyo.

"That boy's gone," she said to herself. "But someone's taken him. He's safe. He has to be."

When she was inside the house again, she took a long, hot shower, then turned on the radio to a news station for the background distraction it provided. She stoked the fire, fixed herself another cup of tea along with a bowl of granola, and switched between several chess matches she had going online as the morning gradually brightened, sun cresting the trees and creeping across her floorboards.

A little after nine, Iris shut down her computer and looked outside. Except in the deepest shadows, all the snow had already melted. Flecks of dust danced in the sunlight and she recognized the distinctive chip of a Western Meadowlark off towards the ravine, a sound she loved. She thought with hopeful anticipation about her temperamental Phalaenopsis orchid that had hinted at a first bloom the previous day. Iris turned off the radio, left through the back door, and crossed the path to her greenhouse.

She stopped short of its door, cracked ajar, and frowned; she was sure she'd left it closed. And her frown deepened when warmth from the space heater greeted her as she entered. After she crouched down and closed its dial, she recoiled. The boy from next door lay sleeping on his side next to it under the latticed shelf that held her orchids. His mouth was in a perfect oval and he was wrapped in a dirty blanket adorned with dinosaurs, his bookbag crumpled under his head for a pillow. A dozen or so of her baby carrots had been plucked from the hot bed, their scrawny, worm-like fruit gone, only their tassels left and strewn on the ground near his face. Iris sucked in air, shook her head. Several moments passed while she watched the boy's steady, even breathing before she reached over and shook his shoulder.

His eyes snapped open and met hers. He pushed himself up on one elbow and said, "She told me to come over here." He paused. "If anything happened to her."

"Your mom?"

The boy nodded.

"Where's your dad?"

His eyes narrowed. "He ain't my dad."

"Why didn't you go with the ambulance?"

"I hid when I heard it coming."

"Didn't you call for it?"

He shook his head. "She did." The boy adjusted his weight. "I came here after it was gone."

"Why didn't you stay put?"

He screwed up his face. "Got no heat. Nothing to eat."

The tiny shakes of her head had begun. They continued while the two of them stared at each other. Several more meadowlarks chipped out in the sun-drenched brush. The boy sat up, and the blanket fell from his shoulders. He was wearing his coat, zipped askew.

Iris gave a last shake of her head and brushed away the carrot tassels. "Come on, then," she said. "Let's get you in the house and fed proper."

The boy crawled out from under the shelf. He grabbed his bookbag and blanket and followed her back to the house. He stopped just inside the door and Iris watched his eyes sweep its interior, take in the sprawling assortment of plants in their clay pots, his mouth opening into the same oval it had been while sleeping. His gaze settled onto the fireplace where low flames licked the logs.

Iris said, "Go on. Sit on the couch there."

The boy did as he was told, his feet barely reaching the floor. Iris stirred the fire and added a log. The flames grew and so did the fire's warmth. The boy inched towards it on the couch and held out his hands.

"You like oatmeal?"

He nodded. She did the same. The fire cracked loudly, and he flinched. Iris felt herself frown before going into the kitchen to make his breakfast.

~~~ ✿ ~~~

She sat on the opposite end of the couch and watched him eat. She'd poured him a glass of orange juice and quartered an apple along with the oatmeal. He ate and drank quickly with studied concentration.

Iris waited until he'd finished to say, "Don't you have school?"

He shook his head. "Winter break. Christmas vacation."

She watched him stare into the fire, holding his hands out to it again.

"And your mom told you to come here."

He nodded and looked over at her with his big eyes. "Said she didn't want me to go into the system again."

Something inside of her dropped, then hardened. Memories.

More quietly, she said, "This happened before, then."

The boy looked back at the fire. "Couple times, yeah."

Iris waited a moment before she said, "Drugs?"

He nodded again. A breeze rose suddenly rattling the dry leaves on a pair of aspens just outside the living room window. Without warning, it halted, and the room grew quiet again except for the soft crackle of the fire. The boy stared hard at it.

"What's your name?"

"Caleb."

"I'm Iris."

He gave a short nod, not looking at her.

"When's the last time you had a bath?"

He shrugged.

"Well, let's get you into one." She looked at his dirty coat and jeans, his stained shirt. "You need a change of clothes."

"Got some." He patted the bookbag next to him.

"Then go on and pick out the cleanest you got left, and I'll wash the rest."

He turned and regarded her with curiosity. "You'll do that?"

Iris stood up. "Come on. I'll show you where the bathroom is." She hesitated. "And a room where you can put your stuff."

☙☙ ❀ ☙☙

While he was in the tub, she started his laundry, including the thinly padded coat. It was hard to imagine that any of it had ever been cleaned before. Then she stood at the kitchen window and looked at the portion of the trailer she could see through the brush: silent, still, dark.

"Who knows what happened to her," Iris whispered to herself. "She could be dead for all I know."

Iris shook her head, then used a lowered voice to call the hospital in Flagstaff and inquire about the status of an ER patient by the name of the woman she'd seen on the envelopes. The hospital refused to give her any information because of confidentiality restrictions and the fact that she wasn't next of kin. She tried to explain that she had the woman's son, but got nowhere with that additional information. She ended the call, dropped the phone on the counter with a clatter, and closed her eyes. From the bathroom, she could hear the boy swishing water in the tub, quietly singing some tune she didn't recognize.

A little later, he came out fully dressed, his mass of curls only partly dried, and stood in front of her in the middle of the kitchen like he was awaiting inspection. The clothes he wore were only marginally cleaner than his others.

She said, "Feel better?"

He shrugged, then nodded.

"When I stumbled upon you, I was about to do some work in my greenhouse."

Caleb hesitated before saying, "Okay."

"You interested in plants, growing things?"

He shrugged again. "I like science and stuff."

"Good. You can help me, then." She took one of her thick sweatshirts from where she'd placed it on the counter. "I'm washing your coat, so put this on. It's one of mine, but I'm not all that much taller than you." She watched him look from the sweatshirt to her face. "Go on. Raise up those arms."

He did, and she slipped the sweatshirt over him and rolled up the cuffs. It fell to below his knees. She took one of her knit caps off the counter and tugged it on crooked so it covered his ears.

"Your hair's still damp, so that will keep your head warm. Keep you from catching cold." They looked at each other. "Let's go," she said. "Day's not getting any longer."

Inside the greenhouse, she switched the space heater to low because the interior had already warmed considerably. She began by checking the water trays on the shelf beneath the orchids: they were all less than a quarter full. She slid one out, and said, "Fill this. Then replace it and fill the rest."

"What for?"

"Creates humidity." She pinched off the dry leaf tip of an orchid. "These need that to grow."

"Don't you have to put water right on them?"

"Not much." Iris poked through the straw moss she'd arranged around the orchid's stalk. "Just enough to stay damp. These are fine right now." She handed him the empty tray. "Use that spigot over there."

Caleb followed her directions while Iris wiped bits of mildew from a few orchid leaves. She inspected the Phalaenopsis closely, found the bloom cresting, and turned the pot more fully towards the southern light. By then, Caleb had replaced the trays and stood watching her.

He asked, "Why you doing that?"

"It's getting ready to bloom."

"Where?"

"See this bud?" She tilted one his way. "It'll open soon into a flower."

His big eyes grew wide. "Pretty?"

She nodded.

"What color?"

"Purple, mostly. Purple and a little white. Other buds will follow, a whole string of them. Hopefully."

"If you treat them right."

She looked at him and nodded again.

"I'd like to see that."

"Maybe you will."

He looked around the greenhouse. "What else can I do?"

"The bottom two rows of windows need cleaning."

He wrinkled up his nose, and she tried to hide her smile. Iris handed him a spray bottle of apple cider vinegar mixed with water and a cloth.

"Spray and wipe. Simple." She pointed. "I'll be working on those hot boxes."

He nodded. Iris moved to the other side of the greenhouse near the space heater and fiddled with her hot beds for a while, but kept glancing at the boy whose brow was furrowed into concentration with his work. As she did, she allowed a smile to pucker her lips.

🦅 🪷 🦅

Iris got his things going in the dryer, then made them toasted cheese sandwiches and pickle chips for lunch. They sat at the dining table and ate in silence while Caleb's eyes swept the interior until he said, "Where'd you learn so much about plants?"

Iris chewed and swallowed without haste before answering. "Began a long time ago. When I was about seventeen."

"How?"

She breathed deeply several times, her eyes on his, then said, "My last foster mom got me started. My only good one. Before she died and I went off on my own."

The boy had been about to take a bite of his sandwich, but lowered it to his plate. "You had foster parents, too?"

"I did." She paused. "A bunch."

His eyes had widened again. "No kidding."

She shook her head while he cocked his. They looked at each other for several seconds. Iris finally took her last bite of sandwich, pushed her plate away, and said, "How about hikes . . . you like those?"

"You mean taking walks?"

"Yep."

"Haven't done it much."

"Well, I generally take one after lunch. Not too far, just down one of the trails and back. Look around, see what I can see." She glanced outside. "Nice afternoon, warmed up now. How about if you and me do that?"

Caleb shrugged.

Iris reached behind her and pulled a well-worn field guide off the nearest bookcase. She began flipping through it and folding down the corners of pages. "I'll give you this to carry. We'll make a game out of it . . . see how many of these species you can identify as we go. I'll put a miniature marshmallow in your hot chocolate afterwards for each one you can find."

The boy gave a gap-toothed grin.

Iris forced her face into a frown. "You finish that meal first. Go on now. Eat up."

⨯⨯⨯

The afternoon sky had turned cloudless, expansive, robin's-egg blue, with the crisp, white light that always stirred something deep inside of her. Iris led him down the ravine and along the creek bed for the better part of a mile. He grew more excited with each item he found from the field guide. When she suggested turning around, he prodded her on so he could look for more. The light fell further in stages, liquid shadows from the willow trees along the creek bed growing longer across the red earth. Iris could taste moisture on the unusually warm breeze blowing up from the south against the cooling air.

By the time they returned back up the path to the house, he'd identified everything in the turned-down pages and the sun was just visible above heavy-bellied clouds that had accumulated low over the western ridge. While

Caleb stopped in the greenhouse to check on the orchid's bloom, she watched a distant line of birds scratch the upper edge of the clouds heading south. Iris looked over at the trailer, which stood unchanged, silent and dark through the stand of junipers, and a hollowness filled her.

She heard the boy leave the greenhouse, turned to him, and asked, "Anything?"

He shook his head. "Not really. Few new buds starting to open, but no flowers yet."

"Be patient. They'll come." She walked over to him. "Let's go. Time for grub."

She reheated stew and biscuits for dinner while he watered her houseplants. Iris stopped filling the kettle for his hot chocolate and shook her head when she heard him humming as he worked. How can he do that, she thought, with the life he's led? With his mother wherever she is, how can he sing in the tub? How is that possible?

She had tea with their meal while he lingered over his hot chocolate, counting each marshmallow before he slurped it down. Afterwards, he dried the dishes she washed and helped her put them away. Complete darkness had surrounded the house, the lamplight within soft and warm with the roaring fire.

Iris hung his dish towel over the edge of the sink and put her hands on her hips. "So," she said. "I always sit by the fire and read after dinner. You have any books in that bag of yours."

He shook his head.

"You like reading?"

He lowered his eyes. "I'm not very good at it."

"That's all right. I'll read to you. I think I have a few books stored away from when I was your age. About a boy like you named Tom Swift who likes science and has a flying ship. That sound all right?"

"Sure."

He sat close to her on the couch, completely still and silent, while she read. From the corner of her eye, she saw his small mouth tighten over troublesome passages, then ease again when they resolved themselves. After a half hour, she felt the side of his head lower against her upper arm. In another ten minutes, his breathing had steadied and deepened into sleep. Iris stopped reading, set the book in her lap, watched the fire, and listened to his puffed snores. She thought more about his circumstances, his mother, the man who'd driven away. She thought about her own life, the entirety of it, the things that had brought her to that moment in that place.

When the fire had almost burned out, Iris heard the first mumble of thunder off to the south. By the sound of it, she estimated that any precipitation was at least an hour away, if it came at all instead of fading out altogether. A winter thunderstorm was pretty rare at their elevation, but when she'd gone outside earlier for more firewood, she'd been struck by the sudden slide in temperature and the heavier taste of moisture in the air.

Iris waited for the last flicker of flame before she rose and carried Caleb into the spare bedroom. He didn't awaken when she lay him on the futon or slid a pillow under his head, took off his sneakers, and tucked three heavy woolen blankets around him. For several more minutes, she stood in the doorway watching him sleep and considering the day's events before leaving the door open and getting into her nightgown.

Iris lay propped in bed and tried without success to concentrate on an organic gardening manual before setting it on her nightstand and turning off the lamp. Claps of thunder had grown steadily closer and occasional flashes of lightening began blinking through the thin curtains over her window. She listened and watched.

An enormous lightning flash eventually illuminated the entire room, and a loud clap of thunder followed with its barrel-roll. A moment later, she heard Caleb's footsteps scampering down the hall into her room. She could distinguish his figure in the darkness at her bedside but not his face.

She said, "It's nothing. Just rain coming."

"I'm scared."

In another longer flash of lightening, she saw his eyes stretch wide and his body jerk at the roll of thunder that followed.

"Here," she said and pulled back her covers.

Iris scooted over in bed and he clambered into the warm space she'd left. The first few drops splattered the rooftop. Iris pulled the comforter up over him and smoothed his curls.

"Shh," she said. "You're fine."

The rain fell harder, peppering the roof, and the sudden dusty smell of it off the red dirt stirred the back of her nose. Iris continued to gently stroke the boy's head as the thunder and lightning crept off to the north. The rain fell steadily for another forty minutes, then stopped as if a faucet had been turned off. By then, Caleb had long been asleep, his purr-like snores ruffling the darkness. Iris let her hand fall from his head to his shoulder. She left it there while she fell asleep, too.

⋙ ❀ ⋘

Iris awoke first to a meadowlark, then to the sound of a car door opening and closing next door. Her eyes opened to dawn's muffled, gray light leaking through the window's curtains. She looked over at Caleb; he lay facing her, hugging himself, snoring softly through his nose. She inched out of bed, but the boy didn't stir. She pulled her sweatshirt over her nightgown and tiptoed to the living room window. Through the junipers, she saw a taxi idling in front of the trailer. Her heart tightened in her chest.

Iris didn't bother tying her work boots. She closed her front door quietly behind her and moved quickly through the gap in the bushes. The exhaust from the taxi bounced off the red gravel; its driver didn't even glance up from his cell phone when she passed it and climbed the steps to the trailer. The screen door was closed, but the inner one was open, and Caleb's mother sat staring open-mouthed at Iris from where she perched on the edge of the couch. One of her hands clutched an open duffel bag stuffed with clothes, and the other held a hair dryer suspended above it.

Iris opened the screen door and stepped inside. The interior was cold, dank. The woman's eyes held hers for a long, breathless moment until she finally asked, "Is he with you?"

Iris nodded.

The woman's shoulders fell in a combination of relief and resignation. She continued staring directly at Iris, but had begun to weep, her face caving into itself. She dropped the hair dryer into the bag, balled her hand into a fist, and brought it to her lips. The corner of a scab on her face had opened: a tiny smudge of scarlet in the flat, dull light.

Iris watched the woman cry while the taxi idled outside and the same meadowlark chipped twice more at intervals. The woman shut her eyes tight, opened them again, then said, "I'm sick, you know." She wiped snot from the end of her nose. "I need help, and I'm going to a place where I can get it." She sniffed loudly. "And this time I'm going to make it work." She set her jaw, though her brimming eyes seemed to plead. "It's going to take time, though. A month, maybe more."

Iris nodded again.

"I can't pay you." The woman's voice had become almost a whisper. "I got no money."

Iris said, "Doesn't matter." They looked at each other until Iris stepped back, held the screen door open, and said, "Go."

The woman nodded slowly herself, then looked away. She used the back of her hand to swipe at her face again, then jerked the bag's zipper closed, stood, and pushed past Iris outside. She got into the taxi and didn't look back at the trailer as the driver made a three-point turn, drove down the driveway, and turned onto the road. The sun was just cresting the treetops there, steam rising off the wet pavement at the driveway's end. The air held a fresh, after-rain smell. Iris waited a few moments before closing the trailer's doors and descending the steps.

When she came through the gap in the junipers, she saw the greenhouse's door ajar. Inside it, Caleb stood with his back to her bent over the orchid shelf. She stopped still in her tracks, then approached slowly and eased inside. He'd pulled on the sweatshirt he'd borrowed from her, but was barefoot, and his head was tilted over the Phalaenopsis's new blooms. He was delicately fingering the largest one, which had unfolded completely into a burst of purple.

He turned to her without surprise and said, "They are pretty. Even prettier than I thought they'd be."

There was sleep at the corners of his eyes and something else there, too. She said, "Your mom came back."

His even gaze remained. "I saw."

Iris nodded. "She's going where she can get some help."

"Rehab." The boy's small lips tightened into a practiced dash.

"That's right." Iris paused. "For now, you'll stay with me."

His mouth loosened; his eyes brightened. He nodded, too, then turned and poked his finger down through moss around the orchid's stalk. He said, "I think this needs water."

Another blanket of mist was rising off the garden in the gathering sunlight. Iris lifted the watering can off the shelf next to her and gave it a shake. It made a slight, sloshing sound.

She said, "Plenty in here. Don't overdo."

Caleb nodded again. She handed him the watering can and watched him concentrate as he tipped it over the pot's rim, a fraction of an inch at a time. Iris allowed herself another small smile.

She asked, "You ever play chess?"

He shook his head, but kept his attention on his task.

"Maybe I can teach you later."

"Okay," the boy said. "Sure."

He used his finger to test the orchid's soil beneath its bed of moss, nodded once more, and set the watering can aside into a rhombus of sun. He sighed. The meadowlark chipped again. From off in another direction, a second one answered it.

SWAP AND SHOP

Like every Saturday morning from October to April, Stan listened to
Swap and Shop while he split wood for the week. He kept the old radio in a
corner of the woodshed near the chopping block and ran an extension cord
to an outside outlet on the log cabin. Priest Lake was nestled up at the top
of the Idaho panhandle against the Canadian border, and the radio station
in Coeur D'Alene was ninety miles away, so the reception was sometimes a
little scratchy. While he listened, he quartered rounds from dead tamaracks
he'd found and felled during the summer along one of the fire roads in the
surrounding mountains; it took him about an hour to chop enough wood
for the following seven days. He liked the steadiness of the exercise, the
peaceful lap of the lake on the pebbly shore a dozen yards away, the satisfying
accumulation of V-shaped logs, the symmetry of the growing stack in the
spreading morning light, and the varied descriptions of things people wanted
to buy, sell, or trade on the radio. He looked forward to it all week.

Stan always split slowly. He was alone there—his wife had left him
five years before—and he was in no hurry to finish. He often chuckled over
the exchanges on the radio. Stan liked the way the host never passed any
judgment over what the callers had to say, however ludicrous or bizarre.
With his easy demeanor, the host simply repeated their essential words, then
emphasized the digits of their telephone numbers twice in conclusion. As he
did, Stan pictured him writing the information down on a legal pad under his
suspended microphone. He liked the folksy tenor of the host's voice, its drawl
hinting somehow of Southern roots. He pictured the host to be about his
age, early sixties, with short slate-gray hair like his own and a similar affection
for untucked flannel shirts, jeans, and worn ball caps. But the truth was he'd
never met or seen a photo of the host, so that visual notion of him was born
entirely, Stan supposed, of some vague inner wish. The host sounded like
someone Stan would have liked to have had as a friend. He didn't have any of
those here; they were all back in Portland.

Stan had been at the cabin full-time for three years, since retiring early from a career as an environmental engineer. His ex-wife had agreed to let him have the cabin in the divorce even though it had been in her family for several generations and she was the last of the lot. The truth was she agreed to just about anything he asked for during their lawyers' negotiations; she was already living with her lover across the country at the time and just wanted things over and done with. She and Stan had spent a good portion of every summer together at the cabin before she left. But he'd always been fonder of it, something they'd both long recognized, and they had no children she could have passed it on to.

That Saturday, the first of December, was one of cold, white light. The rounds Stan placed on the chopping block were only about a foot in diameter and came from an impossibly tall tam he'd come across during one of his scouting rides on the three-wheeler in June. He thought back to spotting its tip above the other trees twenty or so yards off the dirt road near the Horton Ridge lookout. He'd gone back to the cabin immediately, returned in the truck with his chainsaw and other gear, and set it down perfectly through a gap in the trees diagonal to the road. Then he'd cut the rounds and hauled them out into the truck's bed; it took two trips up and back from the cabin to get them all. The wood was tight and hard, splitting cleanly with his sharpened axe, the perfume-like scent from it wafting in the clean air after each swing.

That morning's callers on the radio were a typically varied group. Most were selling things: vehicles, farm equipment, furniture, pets, property. Some were hoping to find work like caregiving or babysitting, or looking to buy mostly odd items: a forklift, a Wurlitzer spinnet piano, Pekin ducks, a gas-powered leaf blower, fresh brown eggs. Fewer were wanting to swap things: an entertainment center for a bicycle with at least three speeds, a collection of arrowheads for a 10-horse outboard motor. Stan chopped deliberately without interruption while he listened until he stopped abruptly during a woman's call who said she had a hospital bed she wanted off her hands.

"A hospital bed," the host repeated.

"That's right. Don't need it anymore with my husband passing on."

A moment of soft static followed, then the host said, "I'm sorry."

Stan heard the woman exhale on her side of the line. Another moment went by before she said, "Yeah."

"All right," the host said. "Any special details about the bed?"

"It works real well; didn't use it very long. Sides click up and down. Motorized, so you can incline the head. On wheels."

"Almost new," the host repeated. "Adjustable side rails, motorized incline, wheels. And what price are you asking for it?"

"I don't know."

"You're not sure."

"I'd just as soon give it away to someone who needs it."

The host paused again. Stan had lowered the axe to his side. He felt his forehead furrow. A flock of late migrating geese called as they flew south overhead towards Spokane.

Finally, the host said, "All right. Cost: free."

Stan pictured each of them on their sides of the call: the host with his headset and microphone, his pen poised over his legal pad; the woman standing perhaps in her yellow kitchen using an old wall phone with a coiled cord, the same dusty, white light Stan was staring at streaming through her lank curtains, the empty house cavernous around her. Like the host, she sounded about his age.

"Can I have your number, please?" the host asked. "Give it to me slowly."

She did. The host repeated it twice, then brought the call to a close like he always did. "And this item will be up on our station's website for one month or until a transaction is completed."

"Thank you," the woman said.

"You're very welcome," the host told her.

Stan heard the click on her end of the line. The host took another call right away, but Stan wasn't listening. He sat down on the chopping block, the partial round there falling softly into the sawdust. The image of the woman caller had suddenly been replaced by one of his ex-wife the evening she'd left. She'd been perched in her coat on the edge of their couch when he came through the front door, her suitcase at her feet. She told him that she didn't love him anymore, that she'd met someone else, that she was leaving. He felt like he'd been hit by a tank; he'd never suspected a thing. When he reached to embrace her as she stood, she shrugged under his arms with her suitcase and was gone. That was the last time he ever saw her. The flock of geese called again further away, but he didn't notice that either.

Stan waited until after lunch to check the radio station's website on his laptop. He found the posting about the hospital bed quickly. It included a black-and-white photo of the bed in what appeared to be a wood-paneled room. Its head was inclined and the near set of side rails was lowered. A framed painting hung centered above it on the wall. There were no blankets or pillows on it, just the bare mattress in a clear plastic sleeve. And at the head of the bed looking into the camera with a blank gaze was the woman he assumed was the caller. She was younger than Stan had imagined, mid-fifties, attractive, a little heavyset with shoulder-length hair and eyes that were kind but worn. He recognized the weariness in those eyes. He touched her face on the screen.

The other information the host had summarized was recorded, too. Stan moved his cursor over the phone number and watched it blink there for several minutes as he felt his heart and breathing quicken. Finally, he picked up his phone and dialed the number.

The same woman's voice answered, "Hello?"

Stan steadied himself, then said, "I'm calling about the item you listed on *Swap and Shop* this morning." He paused. "The hospital bed."

"Yes."

"I was wondering if it's still available."

"It is. It's yours if you want it."

"Okay."

"Do you have a truck?"

"I do, yes."

"Good. Where are you coming from?"

"Priest Lake."

"Pretty place." She paused, too. "My husband and I used to drive up and fish there sometimes. At the outlet of the Dickensheet."

"That's a nice spot."

"It was." A long moment passed with only static on the line until she said, "I live just outside Coeur d'Alene. When can you come and get it?"

"Now, if it's convenient."

"That would be great. I really can't stand to look at it anymore."

After she gave him directions, Stan said, "I should be there in a couple hours."

"I'm Marge, by the way."

"Stan." He closed his eyes and pinched the bridge of his nose. "Okay, Marge. See you soon."

🙢🙠 🙡 🙢🙠

Before he left, Stan tucked in his flannel shirt under his fleece-lined canvas jacket, wet and smoothed his hair, and left his cap on the kitchen counter. There weren't any other vehicles on East Shore Road as he drove along it; most of the other lake cabins were only used during the summer or warm-weather holidays. The few deciduous trees on both sides of the road stood bare among the jumble of pines and firs and tams. Sundance Peak was still lit with sun to his left, but by the time he reached the T at the gas station/restaurant in Coolin, it had already begun its descent across the lake towards the Selkirk Range. He started down Route 57, which was like a tunnel among the trees in the descending light, crossed the Dickensheet, and drove another thirty minutes before the brown stubbled fields began north of the hamlet of Priest River. They were interrupted only by an occasional big spool of forgotten hay or strand of rolling irrigation pipes. The stretch south on Route 41 was more of the same, except the farms were larger and most of those long, wide fields were still black from the late summer burn-off. The light fell further as he drove, and darkening clouds had begun gathering to the northeast. Somewhere near the halfway mark to the interstate he found himself practicing ways to invite Marge to the lake to go fishing, but then chased those thoughts away. He put on a CD of classical music and tried instead not to think about anything.

At Post Falls, he got on the interstate going east. The off ramp that led to Marge's place came up not long afterwards. Stan followed the series of turns she had explained through a neighborhood of older pre-fab homes that differed from one another only in color. Her house stood on a little rise at the end of a cul-de-sac. Stan pulled into the driveway, turned off the ignition, and climbed out of the cab.

An auburn-haired woman came out of the front door onto the top of three steps and raised a hand to him. "You must be Stan," she said. "I'm Marge."

Stan came up to her and they shook hands, a warmth spreading through him as they did. Marge wore a mauve turtleneck sweater, black leggings, and moccasins. She gave him a small smile that folded the tiny wrinkles at the corners of her green eyes, and something crumbled a little inside him.

"Come on in," she said. "I'll show you the bed."

She led him through a living room, past a kitchen, and down a hallway into a small room with the cheap wood paneling he recognized from the photo on the website. The bed stood in its spot against the wall under a painting he could now distinguish as an original of Lake Coeur d'Alene near where it met the Spokane River. It was well done.

Marge walked up to the bed and placed a palm on the plastic-covered bare mattress. The side rail had been raised and the head of the bed was flat. Stan came up beside her, nodding. He lifted the control dangling on a chord from the side rail.

"That works fine," Marge said. "Want me to plug it in so you can see?"

"No," Stan said. "I trust you." He returned the control to the side rail, looked at the painting, and said, "Nice picture."

She regarded it briefly, then said, "My husband painted it."

Stan nodded some more. "So, you said on the radio that he'd used this bed."

She lowered her eyes to the mattress and he watched her lips press closed. "He did."

"Sorry for your loss. How long ago?"

She looked at him evenly. "Five months. He had stomach cancer that wasn't diagnosed until it was late stage. He went pretty quickly."

"That's tough."

She nodded. "I'm a nurse, so I could take care of him until the end. Didn't need hospice."

They looked more at each other. It was warm in the room. He heard a radio playing softly from the kitchen: a report about grain prices. Stan imagined Marge and him in his skiff with their lines in the water off one of the islands, Kalispell or maybe Eight Mile. Standing there together, he thought about saying, "I know something about loss, too." But he didn't.

"Well." Her eyebrows raised. "We could disassemble it or try bringing it out to your truck the way it is. Save some time, if we could."

"Sure," Stan said. "Worth a try."

"My boyfriend can help. He just got home from work."

Stan felt his own eyebrows raise, a slow, coldness crawling up his spine as he watched her turn her head and call, "Gary, can you give us a hand?"

A big man appeared in the doorway. He had a brown beard and was dressed in a khaki National Forest worker's uniform. He smiled at Stan, his eyes alert and friendly. He said, "Sure thing."

"The mattress is light," Marge told them. "I'll take that out. If you each take an end of the frame, I think you can turn it on its side and walk it around the doorways."

Their choreography went exactly as planned, though Stan moved in a kind of numb fog. They set the frame on top of the mattress in his truck bed, legs up, then tied a tarp Stan had brought over it, tossing a rope back and forth to cinch it secure.

Stan found his way to the driver side door and said, "Can I pay you something for it?"

Marge shook her head. "No, just put it good use."

Stan felt himself nodding and stared at the two of them standing side by side a few feet away at the edge of the driveway. He got in the truck and backed out into the street. When he glanced back at them, they had their arms around each other's waists. Marge raised a hand to him like she had when he'd arrived. He did his best to return the gesture, then drove away.

It began to snow before he reached Post Falls: fat, crazy flakes that danced in his headlights. Stan didn't play any music on the way back, but he kept the heater on high. Somewhere near where Route 41 met the 57, he pounded the steering wheel with the heel of his hand and howled. He did it twice more before Priest River, but was silent afterwards.

By the time Stan reached the cabin, it had long gone completely dark. The snow had stopped. He stored the mattress up against the far wall of the woodshed, slid the frame onto the ground on its wheels, and rolled it to the same spot. He tipped it on its side against the mattress, then covered both with the tarp and went into the cabin. He didn't turn on any lights. It was pitch black, cold. There were enough glowing embers left in the woodstove to get a new fire going quickly. He took the whiskey bottle out of the cupboard, opened it, and took a long pull. Then he sat down on the floorboards against the foot of the couch, watched the fire burn in the darkness, and drank.

❧ ❦ ☙

A real blizzard blew up later during the night that lasted well into the following week. When it finally broke, Stan went snow-shoeing most days down the path along the lake as far as Hunt Creek and back. Once, he came upon a depression in the needles on the leeward side of a hallowed tam where a deer had bedded down and left scat. It wasn't cold enough yet for the lake's shallows to freeze over, so most mornings he still saw the pile driver from Cavanaugh Bay motor by slowly a hundred or so yards out heading to someone or other's dock for repairs, and then motor back again in dwindling light about four o'clock.

Stan tried to find things to do to keep busy in the cabin. He sharpened his axe and chainsaw. He attempted to read. He did a couple of jigsaw puzzles. He watched DVDs of old musicals that he and his ex-wife had accumulated over the years. Often, he just sat staring out the window across the lake at the opposite shore a half-mile away; the tiny buildings of Hills Resort there just visible and closed up for the winter, as still and barren as he felt inside. Most days, he was able to avoid reaching for the whiskey bottle until the weak winter sun had descended completely behind the Selkirk Range, the octaves of towering mountains there deepening from dark green to charcoal-gray to black as they grew more distant. At night, sleep was even harder to come by than usual.

Stan still split wood and listened to *Swap and Shop* each Saturday morning. He looked forward more than ever to hearing the host's quiet, thoughtful interactions with callers and paused sometimes as the host concluded a call to swallow over a hardness in his throat. He waited until the Saturday before Christmas when he'd finished the week's wood chopping to call the show. He only had to wait on hold a few minutes before he heard the host's familiar voice say, "Hello, you're on *Swap and Shop*. What would you like to buy, sell, or trade?"

Stan was sitting at his dining table gazing out at the flat lake, the dark mountains, the cold, gray sky. He said, "I have a hospital bed."

"A hospital bed?"

"Yes."

"To sell or trade?"

"To give away to anyone who needs it."

The host paused. "You know we had another one of those not too long ago."

Stan didn't respond. He watched a float plane pass low in the sky on the far side of the lake heading north. It was too far away to hear. Wisps of snow blew sideways.

"Caller?" the host said. "Are you still there?"

Stan cleared his throat and said, "I am, yes."

"Any special details you want to share about the bed?"

Stan gave him the same basic information Marge had, but added, "The mattress has a plastic cover."

The host summarized those elements and asked for Stan's phone number. He repeated it slowly twice and told listeners that the item would be on the station's website for one month or until a transaction was completed. Then he asked Stan, "Anything else?"

"I'm wondering," Stan said slowly. "Do you have a name?"

Another pause followed before the host said, "It's Paul, actually."

"Paul," Stan repeated. "You sound like a nice guy, Paul. I like the friendly way you deal with callers. I like the sound of your voice. I think a lot of listeners do."

"Well," Paul said. "Thanks, I guess."

"You're welcome," Stan told him. His own voice caught. "Take care."

He hung up. The float plane had advanced further up the lake towards Chimney Rock. Stan wondered where it was heading in that weather. Maybe to the upper lake, though it seemed too cold for a picnic or camping. Maybe it was just out for a ride, looking things over before returning somewhere warm. A place where someone else was waiting. Who knew? People did things, went places for any number of reasons, many of which were never completely clear.

MAKE YOUR OWN BED

Tim had gotten up early. The trailer was still. He lifted the corner of the bedroom curtain with his finger and looked outside: it was snowing again, hard. Only the week after Christmas, and already the heaviest winter snowfall on record for that part of the Cascade Range. He dressed, walked down the short hallway, plugged in the Christmas tree lights, and started breakfast.

Austin woke up next. He came in carrying the new stuffed elephant that had been poking out of his stocking, holding it by the ear. He sat on the edge of the couch and looked at the tree, his eyes full of sleep. Tim poured pancake batter into small circles in the greased skillet.

"Hey, bub," he said.

Austin rubbed his nose and asked, "When do we have to take it down?"

"No special time. We usually wait until the first of the year and make a bonfire out back. You remember last year?"

The boy shook his head and looked for the first time at his father. His brown hair was mussed and his mouth drooped like his mother's.

"That's all right," Tim said. "You weren't even three yet. You'll like it. We can roast marshmallows."

"Like when we go camping?"

"Sort of. Go snuggle your mom. Breakfast's about ready."

He padded off in his footed pajamas. Tim turned the radio on low. The weather report said that even heavier snow was expected throughout the day across the region. He flipped pancakes with the spatula, then slid them with the rest onto the plate he was keeping warm in the oven. He poured more batter into the skillet and looked outside again. He watched the snow fall in big flakes over the rusted storage shed out back and breathed as slowly as he could. The snow had almost covered the tires that he'd left leaning against the shed when he'd changed them out on his truck for the winter.

His wife came down the hall holding Austin's hand. She was a big woman who'd kept getting bigger after giving birth. Her bathrobe strained its cord, and her strawberry-blonde hair was cinched in a short ponytail. They both sat on stools at the counter where Tim had set places. He and his wife looked at each other.

She said, "To what do we owe this honor?"

He was holding the spatula like a baton. "Can't I make breakfast for my family?"

"Sure," she nodded. "Sure you can. Absolutely."

It was the same tone she'd begun using with him soon after he'd gotten laid off at the mill in August. She'd used it especially and often after they'd begun to rely on her meager weekday lunch shift down at the river lodge. She looked outside and said, "See you got your woolies on. Going for a hike?"

"A buddy I was in the service with called yesterday. He's coming up from Yakima to go snowmobiling. Asked if I might want to go along. I told him I thought it would be all right."

She was still looking outside. "Called while I was at work yesterday?"

"That's right."

"But you didn't think to tell me about it until now."

"Right again."

She shook her head slowly. Without looking at Tim, she reached across the counter for her cigarettes and lit one. Then she pushed off the stool and said, "I'm going to take a shower. Please call if you're going to be late for dinner."

Tim watched the back of her go down the hall. Then he brought over the pancakes, and he and Austin ate without talking.

🙦🙦 🙰 🙦🙦

Danny had told Tim he'd leave early from his parents' place in Yakima where he'd been crashing so they could get started by nine. They'd arranged to meet at a turnoff from the two-lane that led down to the river. Tim had his truck parked there back under some trees. But Danny was late, so he ran the heater every now and then to try to stay warm but not waste gas. No other cars were at the turnoff; very few vehicles went by at all. It was just too nasty out. He wished he'd brought a thermos of coffee, but he'd wanted to get out away from home as quickly as possible so hadn't bothered.

Danny didn't show up until almost ten o'clock. He was pulling the snowmobile that his father had brought with them in the family's move from Duluth on a trailer behind his truck. Tim walked over, and Danny pushed the passenger door open for him. The heat from inside hit him full on, and so did the smell of reefer.

"Man," Danny said, "I'm sorry. This damn weather. I got stuck behind three wrecks, and I left before six."

"Doesn't matter," Tim said.

"Well," Danny asked, "you jacked or what? Could we have picked a better day than this?"

Tim shook his head. Danny had an old Tom Petty CD playing in the dashboard. He nodded his head to the music's beat. They'd spent some time together at Camp Pendleton, then later at Parris Island, but to say Tim knew Danny well would have been a stretch.

"All right," Tim said and pointed. "If we're going to do this, let's go."

They drove without talking towards the river. It seemed funny to Tim that they should find nothing to say after so long apart and given what they were planning. Danny drummed his thumbs on the steering wheel. They passed no one during the five minutes it took to reach the big curve down to the Y. To the left the road led quickly to the bridge that crossed the river to the lodge, but they headed to the right onto a narrower, unpaved track. The lodge kept the road to the left plowed back to the two-lane, but the long stretch to the right was unmaintained and, in meaningful snow, unnavigable for any regular vehicle. Tim had Danny turn immediately into a dead-end turnout where they parked.

They didn't speak as they unhitched the snowmobile and slid it off the trailer. Danny took a Flexible Flyer sled with wooden slat sides out from under the shell of his truck and hooked it to the back of the snowmobile. He put a flashlight, a tire iron, a small fishing tackle box of tools, and an empty meal-sized Tupperware container into a burlap sack, wrapped that in a green garbage sack, and bungee-corded the whole thing inside the sled.

"That's it?" Tim asked.

"Yep," Danny nodded. "That's it."

He took two helmets out of the back of the truck and handed one to Tim. They yanked them over their knit caps and pulled their ski gloves tight. In a muffled voice, Danny said, "Ready, Red Rider?"

He climbed onto the snowmobile and tried three times to start it with the choke engaged until it finally caught, coughing. Tim got on behind him, gave directions, and they started on new snow down the unplowed road.

Danny couldn't go very fast because of the swirling flurries, but he went more aggressively than was safe. Tim kept his head turned to the side and watched for the river. For a while, there were only the trees and bushes fleeing by. Then they crossed Cougar Creek, and the river emerged on the left a few hundred yards away, gray-blue and tumbling, with the mountains spreading off beyond its opposite shore. A kind of gentle flush spread over him, as it always did, watching it unfold. They passed the incline leading to the sandbar where his father had first taken him fishing when he wasn't much older than Austin. Then they crossed Roaring Creek and he shivered again for a different reason because he saw the line of newer cabins along the curving shore where the river widened into bay-like inlet. Tim looked for smoke from any of the chimneys, but saw none and realized suddenly how badly he'd hoped to see some.

Danny slowed the snowmobile to a stop and turned his head back. Tim couldn't see his eyes through the cloudy shield, but his mustache was crusted with ice and his mouth grinned.

He said, "This smooth, or what?"

"It's pretty smooth."

"We could take a damn chandelier out and not break a crystal, it's so smooth. Jesus H. Did we pick a perfect day, or what?"

Tim just nodded.

"So, where do we start?"

"Up past that next bend. There's a long drive to the left that leads to all these cabins."

Danny grinned and whistled. Tim followed his gaze down towards the line of cabins.

"Nice places," Danny said. "What are there, fifteen or so along here?"

"About."

"And you're sure that Captain guy lives far enough up the road?"

"The Colonel. And yes." Tim pointed. "He lives way the hell up upriver."

He'd worked summers during high school and a couple years afterwards for the Colonel installing and servicing septic tanks. He knew that only the Colonel wintered along this stretch of river, retired now to his small cabin well past the campground more than two miles away. Plus, the old guy would never be out in this weather.

Danny gunned the engine, shifted, and they rounded the next bend, then turned down the drive leading to the cabins. Tim tapped him on the shoulder and pointed to a woodshed above the initial cabin. Danny pulled under its corrugated tin roof next to a neatly stacked pile of cut wood and cut the engine. They climbed off the snowmobile and took off their helmets.

Danny looked at Tim and shook his head. "Hell, we don't even need the damn tarp on top. If we looked a little harder, we could probably find a damn garage with a space heater. This is too easy. Even if somebody wanted to follow us, was intent on it, the snow would cover our tracks like that." He tried to snap his gloved fingers.

Tim shrugged. "So far, so good, I guess."

"Damn straight."

Danny unhooked the sled and they started down between the trees to the first cabin, which was like a small log lodge with dark green shutters. At the back door, Danny didn't hesitate. He simply took out the tire iron, shoved it in the door jam, and pulled hard back and forth until the wood splintered and the lock gave way.

Watching him, Tim thought of that muggy evening on a bluff near Beaufort, South Carolina, where they'd first talked about doing this. It was late after a day of daring one another with girls on the beach. They were drinking beer and looking at the stars over the ocean. Danny had told him about how he and a cousin had broken into some places at a resort lake in Minnesota just before they'd graduated from high school and Danny's dad moved his family west. Seven little cabins in a row, Danny said, maybe an hour total; they'd only been interested in cash. Tim had told Danny about the river, which Danny had never visited even though he'd lived in Yakima for two years before enlisting and it was only a couple hundred miles away. As they drank more beer, the idea somehow evolved into a winter scheme; Danny said he knew some guys in Yakima who'd pay well for jewelry, silverware, credit cards, things like that.

The two of them got sent different places after Parris Island and lost touch. Tim had all but forgotten about their talk until the day before when, out of the blue and after four years, he answered the telephone and heard Danny's voice. He'd been out of work going on five months by then with no prospects in sight. And his wife had her attitude. He thought it wouldn't be hard to dole out any money he got a bit at a time. And if she became curious and started asking questions, he could say that, after snowmobiling, he'd won it while playing poker at one of the bars along the highway with his old Army pal and some of his cronies who'd come along.

So, with his heart hammering, Tim followed Danny into that empty, cold cabin with its pine walls and its still new smell and looked through the bathrooms and living room while Danny searched the bedrooms. Tim found an old Rolex watch with a chip in its face, and Danny discovered three paper-clipped fifty-dollar bills under some socks. They put both in the Tupperware container, then Tim trudged behind Danny through the snow to the next cabin as he pulled the sled behind him.

After that, there was nothing to prevent them from going on. Since noise and stealth were not factors, Danny continued to use the crowbar with regard to neither. Although the electricity was turned off in most of the cabins, there was plenty of natural light from outside to search by. And it was too cold not to wear gloves, so leaving fingerprints wasn't a concern.

They moved through the first few cabins quickly and with some urgency, but gradually slowed their pace and began searching each cabin unhurriedly. In one, Tim came upon Danny in a bedroom with his face buried in a pair of woman's underwear; in another, he came downstairs to find him knocking back a slug from a bottle of Chivas. He began to pause himself over occasional photographs: families grilling on back decks, holding strings of fish, canoeing on the river, children growing up on dim hallway walls from one picture to another. He recognized a number of people vaguely from his days working with the Colonel. He came across one snapshot in a standing frame of an older man he'd once helped change a tire on the side of a road and was almost certain the woman in another had been the valedictorian in his younger brother's high school class.

They did better than Tim thought they would at finding things of value: a few checkbooks and credit cards, a set of antique silver in its original cherry wood box, a laptop computer, and several hundred dollars in cash, which Danny kept adding to a roll in the zippered pocket of his ski pants. The Tupperware container grew better than half full of jewelry.

They came upon two things at the end that Tim would later regret. The first was a Husqvarna chainsaw sitting next to the backdoor of the last cabin. It looked as if it had never been used, but when he squatted down next to it, he could see that it had just been extremely well cared for: cleaned and oiled, and the teeth individually sharpened.

"Boy," he heard himself say, "that's something."

"What?" Danny asked.

"The chainsaw. Mine's busted to hell. Shot."

"You want it? We got room. Take it."

"Nah."

"Hell, man," Danny said. He lifted the chainsaw himself and slid it into the burlap sack. He crisscrossed the bungee cords over the load on the sled, strapped it tight, and they started back up the path on fresh snow, the flurries now blowing into their faces.

The second thing was the scratching at the back of the woodshed after they'd reattached the sled to the snowmobile and were about to leave. They stepped around a box of kindling and saw the source of the sound: a ground squirrel caught in a trap by its right hind leg. It lay on its side pawing weakly in the sawdust, its mouth yawning slowly, a trickle of blood coming from its ear. Tim's eyes and the small, marble-like, black ones of the ground squirrel met. He knelt down next to it.

"Let's go," Danny said, "Damn thing probably has rabies." He pulled on his helmet, climbed on the snowmobile, started it on the first try, and backed it out of the shed. "Come on, soldier. Time to hit the trail."

Tim stood up and pulled on his own helmet. He looked back at the ground squirrel, then at Danny. "Maybe we should put it out of its misery. Bury it somewhere."

"Not in this life," Danny told him and throttled the engine. "Come on."

It couldn't have been much past two o'clock and already the light was beginning to fall. The snowmobile idled two-stroke oil exhaust into the white snow. The wind had lessened, but the dizzy canopy of fat, slow flakes still tumbled everywhere. Tim glanced at the squirrel a last time, got on, and they left.

Back at his truck, Danny first started its engine and heater. Then they secured the snowmobile on the trailer and put the sled with its load in the back under the shell. When they climbed into the cab, it was already warm. Danny took off his coat, gloves, and hat, cranked up the music, and sang with it while they drove back to where Tim had left his own truck. Danny pulled in behind it and left the engine idling, but lowered the music's volume. He put his right arm over the back of the seat and turned Tim's way.

"Well," he said nodding, "that was sweet."

Tim nodded back, he hoped, without obvious reluctance.

Danny asked, "So, how do you want to play this?"

Tim shrugged. "I don't know. You're the expert."

"Well, we could do it several ways. Seems to me fifty-fifty's pretty fair. You found the gig, but it's my old man's snowmobile. You're taking a bigger chance living up here, but I've got the contacts to run this stuff."

"That's fine," Tim said.

"All right. I guess we're on the same page so far. So, we can just split the cash and I can send you a money order or something for half of whatever I get in Yakima. Or you can come down and help with those transactions if you want."

"No." Tim shook his head. "I'm not interested in making that trip."

"Course you could just take the cash we got, and I could sell the rest for whatever I can get. But I'd be lying to you if I didn't say it'll probably be more than a few hundred smacks. Maybe considerably more."

"That sounds all right," Tim said. "That'd be fine by me."

"And that chainsaw's yours, of course. I'm thinking of heading down to Palm Springs for a while, get out of the lousy weather. Not much use for a chainsaw there."

"That's true."

Danny grinned and stuck out his hand. Tim shook it. Danny took out the roll of cash and gave it to him. Then they climbed out of the cab and walked to the back of the truck. Tim wrapped the chainsaw in the green garbage sack, and Danny followed him with it to his truck. Tim slid the chainsaw behind the seat, climbed up into the cab, and started his own engine and heater. Danny stood in his long-sleeved jersey and ski pants in the falling snow holding open the driver-side door.

He said, "Well, I'll call you after I run all this. Tell you how things turned out."

Tim shook my head. "You'd better not. My wife might get suspicious."

"Okay." Danny shrugged. "And I suppose we'd better not think about pulling another stunt like this around here anytime soon."

"No."

"So, you know how to get in touch with me."

"Sure."

"Give me a call . . . we'll go get a beer."

"Maybe. Don't get down that way much."

Danny kept nodding. He looked up the road, then slowly back. "You ever hear from Drexel or Bannister?"

Tim shook his head.

"Me neither. Peterson get married?"

"I guess. Last I heard, that was the plan."

"He still in?"

"As far as I know."

"Those were good times," Danny said.

"Yes," Tim lied. "They were."

"Damn right." Danny slapped him on the thigh. "Listen, you take care." He stepped back and grabbed the top of the door. "Drive safe in this mess."

"You, too."

Danny shoved the door closed, and Tim watched him in the rearview mirror walk back through the snow to his truck. They both backed out. Danny went south paralleling the river, and Tim turned up the frontage road towards home. He flipped the headlights on. He wished he could turn on the radio, too, but it was broken.

He stopped at the mini-mart about halfway to the trailer for gas. He chose a family comedy to rent from the DVD rack and bought a frozen pound cake, a package of microwave popcorn, and two sixteen-ounce cans of beer. He talked with the cashier, a guy he'd played junior varsity football with in high school, about the snow for a few minutes, then walked back outside into the early-twilight that was wild again with blowing flurries.

He drove slowly, watching the snowflakes swirl in the headlights and finished both beers before he reached the trailer. When he got there, he shut off the engine and sat for a moment looking at his wife and son through the front window. They were taking down Christmas tree ornaments, the television flickering behind them. He thought he'd wait until his wife was at work on Monday to move the chainsaw into the shed. He tried not to think about the man who had owned and cared for it. The beers helped a little in that regard. He thought he'd keep the cash in the shoebox with his military memorabilia. He was pretty sure that would be a safe place, but felt lousy about keeping it there and hadn't had enough beer to dull that; he had more in the trailer. Tim was sorry to see the Christmas decorations coming down. In fact, he felt close to tears. But the cab's warmth was long gone, so he climbed out of the truck and walked inside.

Austin ran to greet him with a hug, but his wife ignored his entrance. Tim was able to convince her to leave the lights up on the tree. But soon after that, they got in another fight because he hadn't realized the movie he'd rented was one they'd already seen and he'd forgotten to buy dishwashing soap like he'd told her he would. He tried to make things better by volunteering to heat up some leftover chili for dinner, but they ate in silence except for

Austin's sporadic chattering on the stool between them.

Afterwards, they watched the movie he'd rented anyway, and he had a couple more beers. For a while, he managed to forget about things and distract himself with the movie's silly drivel. When it was over, he lay next to Austin in his bed like usual and read to him before tucking him in. But that reminded Tim of his father who'd always done those same things with him, and then he was in trouble. Because that led him to thinking about how his father had always cared for his tools, as well as how quiet and strong he'd remained throughout his most recent hospitalization. And then there was the fact that his father had been a fly fisherman who was strictly catch and release. Tim found himself thinking of the time a big trout he'd caught when he was about ten had swallowed the hook, then got itself tangled in submerged tree roots, and by the time his father was able to unsnag it, the fish had fought the life out of itself. Tim couldn't forget how grim and silent his father had become afterwards. The memory of the dying squirrel came quickly next and settled in his mind uninvited.

If not for those things, maybe he could have gotten away inside with what he'd done. Instead, standing against Austin's bedroom wall before turning out his overhead light and noticing for the first time that the ears of his sleeping son were his own and those of his father, he knew that he'd try somehow to undo things. He didn't know how, but there was no question in his mind that he would try.

Tim stayed where he was after Austin's bedroom went dark and listened to the boy's slow, even breathing. Not too long afterward, he heard his wife turn off the TV, heard her heavy footsteps pass in the hallway, heard their mattress sag, heard her begin to snore softly herself. In spite of the alcohol, in spite of the things he'd try to do to calm and distract himself, in spite of the perfect stillness, he knew that for him, sleep would be a long time coming.

☙☙☙

The next morning before dawn, Tim rose, dressed, put the roll of cash in his pocket, and went out to the shed. The snow had lightened, but was still falling. It was dark and very quiet. He found his old pair of cross-country skis and a knapsack, stored them in the truck, and drove out to where Danny had parked above the river the day before. He strapped on the skis and wrestled the chainsaw into the knapsack, its weight awkward but manageable.

It had been years since he'd used the skis, and they weren't properly waxed. Tim took a couple of tentative slides and could do little more than lurch and scoot a bit. But it was better than walking. He figured it was a little less than a mile to the cabins. So much snow had fallen that there was no indication he could see that the snowmobile had ever been there. The sky above the ridge was just beginning to lighten like a splash of cream in black coffee. A small breeze tossed around the snowflakes. He started down the road.

It was slow going, and he was badly out of shape. Tim grew hot inside his parka, so kept it only partly zipped. A few times, one of his skis sunk nearly knee-deep in snow. It was a production to free himself, and his breath came in heaves, but he plodded on.

Just after Cougar Creek, the first glimpse of the river greeted him, gray at that hour but as loud as ever. He skied on and saw no one. He was alone with just his labored breathing, the tumble of the river, wisps of snow, and the growing early-morning light until he reached the long drive to the cabins.

Tim skied down first to the final cabin and replaced the chainsaw carefully where he'd found it. Then he continued along and just divided the money up randomly, setting a portion inside each doorway where they'd been the day before, working his way back hastily to the first log cabin with the green shutters. He didn't try to figure out what had been taken where; he simply portioned out the money as fairly as he could. He rarely even got out of the skis and didn't study the damage he and Danny had caused. He just wanted to be done with the whole thing as soon as possible.

On his way out, he did pause at the woodshed where they'd parked the snow machine. Snow had drifted over all but the squirrel's head. It was dead now and stiff, its black eyes still open, the trickle of blood dried and darkened. Tim brushed away the snow and released its leg from the trap, then used the hard toe of his ski boot to scoop out a depression in the pine needles and dirt, nudged the squirrel into it, and covered it as best he could.

He waited before getting back into his skis and looked over the tops of the cabins at the wide, fast-flowing river. He stood regarding its splendor for several moments until he finally said, "That's it, then."

Tim couldn't tell if he felt better or not. He wished he could do something about the ruined doorways and the other things they'd taken, but he couldn't. And if Danny got caught somehow, Tim could only hope it wouldn't lead to him. A chill crept down his neck. He thought, stop it. He thought, that's all you can do. He blew out a fog of breath and started back up the long drive on his skis.

He moved steadily, getting into a kind of clumsy rhythm without the weight of the chainsaw. He'd crossed both creeks and was most of the way down the road to his truck when he first heard what sounded like a motorcycle approaching from the direction he'd come. Another deeper chill spread through him. He stopped and turned around. Tim willed his heaving breath to slow as a single headlight approached and he recognized the Colonel on his four-wheeler spraying feathers of snow behind him. He swallowed.

The Colonel was wearing one of those layered jumpsuits the old-timers at the mill favored in winter and a woolen, flop-eared cap. He stopped the four-wheeler beside Tim's skis and pushed his goggles up over the front of the cap.

He squinted and said, "That you, Timmy?"

Tim nodded.

"What the hell you doing? Out exercising?"

"Getting some fresh air," he heard himself say. "Cooped up with all this snow, you know. How you doing, Colonel?"

The old man just nodded, then said, "Drive all the way over here to ski? That's a lot of trouble, isn't it?"

Tim raised a pole in the direction he'd come. "Pretty over here. Quiet."

"It is that," the Colonel said.

"My dad and I used to ski along here sometimes when I was young."

The Colonel nodded some more. Tim looked back up the road beyond the four-wheeler. He couldn't tell to what extent the falling snow had covered his tracks. And it was impossible to determine at what point the Colonel had noticed them. Chances were pretty good that he'd been concentrating on where he was heading and had not been aware of where they led down to the cabins. He wasn't sure how long it would take for those to be covered again. He wished it was snowing like the day before, but it wasn't.

The Colonel asked, "How is your dad? How's he feeling?"

"Fine. Better."

"I haven't seen him for a while. I'm glad he's improving. He's a good man, your dad."

Tim nodded. "Yes, he is."

"And you used to ski together over here back in the day?"

"Never went too far. Maybe down to that incline by Roaring Creek."

"That's a pretty good fishing spot," the Colonel said. "You can still catch some there, but too many people know about it now."

"That's true."

"Good memories, though," the old man said. "All right, then. I saw the tracks back there and wondered, what the hell?"

Tim didn't know what to say; he just nodded himself and stamped snow from his skis. He looked at the Colonel again and thought about all the time they'd spent working together when he was just an ornery kid who didn't know squat. The old man looked nearly the same as he had then, grizzled and sharp. The snow had begun to lighten a bit further, and streaks of blue were visible to the east.

The Colonel asked, "Where you parked?"

"Up by the Y."

The old man grinned. "You almost got her licked."

Tim waited for him to ask more about the skiing, but he didn't. Instead, he said, "Any word about the mill rehiring?"

"Not that I've heard."

"Might get some news soon."

Tim shrugged and said, "Maybe. Probably have to wait till spring, though."

The Colonel nodded and looked him over. With the snow lessening, the temperature had dropped.

The Colonel smiled and asked, "Don't suppose you want a ride the rest of the way."

Tim shook his head. "No, I'm fine."

The Colonel nodded some more and throttled the engine a little. "Okay, say hello to your dad for me."

Tim nodded, too, and lifted a pole in farewell. It seemed to him a feeble gesture. He watched the four-wheeler go off up the road and grow smaller, the sound of dissipating until it passed the Y and disappeared towards the bridge.

Tim thought the Colonel might be going over to the lodge for breakfast. Or maybe he was just out for a ride or would be heading back home soon. And perhaps on the way back, he'd fly right past where Tim had turned down to the cabins. There was no way to tell for sure. But standing there alone looking up that empty road, he knew it didn't really matter. What was done was done. You broke a glass on the floor, then you swept it up, but it was still broken. Even if you never got caught, you'd broken it. That wouldn't go away. Whatever you did yesterday was done, and whatever you did today would be history tomorrow. He felt so cold.

Tim whispered, "You make your own bed." That was something his father often used to tell him. "You made yours," he said to himself. "Now go sleep in it."

SURPRISE

The cabin phone rang just as my wife, Molly, and her parents were heading up the path for their morning walk along Lake Almanor's eastern shore. I answered it and called to my father-in-law. I heard Ralph stop and retrace his steps. He looked in the window.

"It's your sister," I told him.

He made a face and came back inside. I handed him the phone. He walked into the kitchen with it after saying, "Yes?" I turned the stereo down; he'd put on a Mozart CD before they'd left. I heard him say, "When?" Then, "Shucks."

I walked up the hall to look in on Ben. He was asleep in his crib, his feed almost finished. The pump made its soft whir on the pole. I checked the connection at his G-tube and it was fine. Molly had left the parts to his nebulizer scattered about again, so I put them away.

When I came back to the front room, Ralph was just putting the phone back in its cradle. We stood and looked at each other. Finally, he said, "Well, my Aunt Rita just passed away. She was eighty-something. Sometime in the middle of the night when she was sleeping. Down near Bakersfield or Barstow somewhere. Where she's lived just about forever."

"That's too bad," I said.

Ralph looked out at the lake. The sun had just touched the tips of the tall trees across it. "Well, she's the last one of that bunch. That generation is gone now." We were quiet again. Then he raised his eyebrows and said, "I'm going to try to catch the girls."

I watched him pass the window with his tall walking stick and listened to his footsteps go off up the path. I increased the music's volume again, but not as loud as it had been. I poured another cup of coffee and took it out on the front porch. A woodpecker skittered along the side of a thick fir tree. I could smell the dusty pine needles, not yet sun warmed.

After breakfast, Molly stayed with Ben while the rest of us went up the hill to the garage they'd had built that spring to continue our project of staining and sealing it. I resumed my spot up on the ladder under the eaves with Ralph below me while Marilyn concentrated again on the trim. Ralph played a mix of old folk music on his boombox while we worked.

We didn't last much more than a few hours because the day had heated up plenty by then. We were all wet with sweat, so Ralph called things off for the day. We sat in freckled shadows on the tailgate of Ralph's truck in the driveway and passed around a thermos of ice water Marilyn had brought along. We looked out over the two wide portions of the lake below bisected by its peninsula and the dark range of mountains that led off to snow-capped Mt. Lassen and the distant reaches of northeastern California. A few white clouds high in the sky on our side of the mountain left shadows on the surface of the lake that otherwise shimmered in the sunlight.

"Maybe it will rain," Marilyn said.

Ralph looked up at the clouds, then off beyond them. He shook his head. "That would be nice," he said, "but I doubt it."

Afterwards, Ralph and Marilyn went back down to the cabin while I got on the stationary bike they'd set up in a corner of the garage and rode that for a while. It approximated the sort of workout I might have gotten back in San Jose. I didn't like to run on the narrow roads at the lake because of the logging trucks, and I wasn't much of a swimmer. I was good and tired by the time I'd finished.

On my way back down the hill, I glanced at the *As You Wish* sign Molly had painted and Ralph had nailed above the garage door, the name she'd anointed the cabin. It was a line from Ralph's favorite movie. She'd given it to her parents as a gift when they bought the place just before her father retired from PG&E and they sold their little pretend farm outside Davis. Now they split their time between the lake and a furnished apartment they rented by the month near our house in San Jose. Molly and I both worked at separate colleges—her in admissions and me in financial aid—and they helped with Ben's care during the day, as well as getting him to all his appointments with the neurologist, pulmonologist, dysmorphologist, and other specialists and therapists.

After my turn on the stationary bike, I jumped in the lake, showered, and then we all had lunch on the front porch. A small breeze had come up, and with it, little waves that Ralph called "sheep running" when they got large enough to crest white. Ben was asleep again. I asked Molly if she was able to do his range of motion exercises with him before he went down.

"Yes," she said. "And he took care of business on his own. Ex-nay on the enema."

I said, "Touché." I reached out my glass of ice tea to toast with her, but she'd already turned away.

After lunch, Ralph took a nap while the rest of us sat in the shade on the porch. Molly answered some work emails on her laptop and Marilyn did her cross stitch. I read a book. There weren't many motorboats out on the water because of the chop, so it was quiet unless a logging truck went by up on the road.

A couple of hours later, Ralph came out on the porch carrying Ben and handed him to me. He said, "Either I woke him with my snoring, or he woke me with his squawking."

"Hi," I said to Ben snuggling him close. "How's my buddy?" I rubbed the flat back of his head. Ben moaned happily, burrowing into my chest like he did.

Ralph and Marilyn took their daily drive into Chester for the mail, and I got Ben's breathing treatment going. After he was finished, I put him in his backpack carrier and Molly and I walked up the trail towards the dam. We took along the coffee can pails in case we saw any blackberries, only to add small purpose to the outing. It had been a light August for berry picking, and except way over towards Seneca, they were still mostly red buds. But it was a pretty hike up through the pines and firs and clearings that had been logged years before and were now full of daisies, lupine, and fireweed. The breeze had cooled things a bit, especially when the sun hid behind the clouds.

We didn't find any berries, but on the way back down, Ben began to cry and had a small seizure. We sat on a log and waited for it to pass. I held him close and said "Shh" into his ear. It only lasted a minute, but afterwards he was wide eyed, as always, and had that frightened look.

Molly dried the bottoms of his feet and his palms with a bandana. "That wasn't too bad," she said. We smiled at each other, but in her eyes, I could see the same pallor that had hung over everything since his birth and, we both knew, always would. A long sigh escaped her. We sat up straight, startled as an egret lifted out of a treetop and flew out towards the lake.

When we got back to the cabin, Ralph was coming down the path holding a flat box. Marilyn walked behind him.

Ralph waved to us and said, "Hey, we have a little surprise."

They stopped in front of us at the bottom of the path, and Ralph opened the box. There were homemade brownies inside.

He said, "Linda sent these from Sacramento for my birthday. She's the daughter who loves me."

Molly made a mock pout, then smiled. I thought about early in our courtship when she told me how she and her sister had been treated like princesses growing up, like they could do no wrong.

We went inside. Ben had fallen into his usual postictal sleep, so I laid him down in his crib. Then we all had drinks, chips, and guacamole on the front porch. The end-of-summer shadows had lengthened, and a few more clouds had joined together to the northwest, tinged gray-black underneath.

After a while, Ralph went off for a sail in his little dinghy. The rest of us began his favorite meal for dinner. I barbecued chicken slathered with extra-spicy sauce. Molly and her mother made warm German potato salad and baked beans. Ben awoke momentarily when I started his last feed of the day, but then fell asleep again right away, still listless from the seizure.

After dinner, we went down on the dock while the sun hung reluctantly below the bloated clouds. We sat and watched it dip quietly off beyond Ruffa Ridge. The sky there was all purple and pink, and those same colors were spread lightly across that side of the lake. Molly sat next to Marilyn on the edge of the dock and watched her try to get Ben to kick his feet in the water. Ralph and I were on chaise lounges facing the setting sun.

He said, "Aunt Rita died early this morning. She's the one who lived in the Central Valley."

Molly and Marilyn turned and looked at him. His face was still with the sunset on it. Molly said, "Are you going down for the funeral?"

He frowned. After a few seconds, he said, "Nah. I didn't know her well."

Molly nodded slowly, then we were all quiet. A pontoon boat motored slowly out in the lake. It went off past the tip of the peninsula towards the western shore.

"He'd better trot along before it rains," I said,

"Let it rain, God," said Ralph. "I love a good summer storm."

Some more clouds had gathered from the north over the lake, but were still fairly high in the sky. I said, "It just might."

The light fell another shade as the sun crept behind the mountains for good. The air suddenly had that lick of coolness that was different from what it had been.

Molly said, "Can we please go up now and open presents?"

We had Ralph sit at the head of the table with his gifts in front of him. The rest of us sat around him. There was a flash outside and the first roll of thunder tumbled down from the north as he was opening our card. Inside was a gift certificate from the hardware store in Chester for sixty-eight dollars.

"One for each year," Molly told him.

He smirked and said, "Gee, thanks."

But I could tell he was pleased. Next, he unwrapped an elaborate utility tool knife that Linda had included in the brownie box. He opened Marilyn's gift last, which was a pair of binoculars he'd picked out himself during the spring when she'd chosen a salmon-colored cardigan that would be from him for her birthday. The second flash and roll of thunder tumbled much closer up the lake. Leaves on the black oak twirled outside.

We turned out the lights, and Ben squawked when we lit candles on a brownie and sang. Ralph blew out the candles and darkness surrounded us. Lightning lit the nearest ridge once, then again brightly enough so that the lake momentarily turned white. Just after it, came a loud clap of thunder and its roll that jiggled the plates on the table.

Ralph said, "My."

The first rain fell suddenly and lightly. We knew then that it would only be a quick-moving shower. We sat in the dark listening as the rain intensified briefly for a few minutes, then passed. Molly let me take her hand, but didn't return my thumb's caress. Another scratch of lightning lit the sky, and the thunder that followed it had moved south towards Butte Meadows. The next combination was further off still towards Chico.

Marilyn turned the lights back on and clapped her hands in applause. I did the same with Ben's. His head had begun to bob and his eyes were closing, so Molly took him off to bed. Ralph smiled, fingering his gifts. The air had turned much cooler, a coolness that was at once gentle and relieving.

When Molly returned, we ate brownies with vanilla ice cream. Then Ralph went down on the dock with his new binoculars, and I helped Marilyn clean up and do the dishes. Molly told us she was going off to bed to read; I watched the back of her go off down the hall.

After the dishes were dried and put away, Marilyn went into the front room to watch television, and I took a bag of trash out to the root cellar. Ralph was sitting in the old webbed lawn chair we kept near the barbecue, the binoculars in his lap. He had his head back looking up at the stars. I had never seen him sit there before during the day or night.

He glanced at me and said, "Hey."

I stored away the trash and stood on the river-rock patio we'd laid together the summer after Molly and I were married there four years before. I looked up through the treetops in the direction he was.

I asked, "Looking for constellations?"

"I don't know any constellations," he said. "I was going to learn about them, though, when I retired, as you probably remember. I got that astronomy book a few birthdays ago. I was going to do that sort of like I was going to learn to throw pots and lift dumbbells." He laughed once through his nose. "Oh, I guess I'm really just sitting here thinking about my own mortality."

I looked at him then. He was a handsome man with salt and pepper hair. I'd always been very fond of him. I said, "I suppose you're entitled to do that."

He was still looking up through the trees. A few stars were back out after the storm's passing. He said, "I had a few surprises today. Most of them were pretty nice. That one about my aunt wasn't. Life's full of surprises, I guess."

I thought about that. I thought about the spouses of two of our neighbors who had died suddenly during the last year; they were both in their mid-fifties. I was forty-three. I thought about Ben and his future, and felt my stomach fall, as it always did when I thought about that.

"Life is full of surprises," he said again. It came out quietly. "I suppose you embrace the good ones and do the best you can with the ones that aren't so hot."

I nodded, though I knew he wasn't looking at me. I said, "That makes sense." Of course, I couldn't know then that Ben would have all those pneumonias and hospitalizations upcoming, the tracheostomy and other surgeries, the wheelchair problems, and the need for round-the-clock care. And nothing could have prepared me for the day a few years later when Molly would tell me that she'd become involved with a professor at her school, that she was leaving, that she was done settling, done being a martyr.

I heard Marilyn laugh inside at something on the television. I'm sure Ralph had, too. There was a faint rumble of thunder, but it was far away now. The lake lapped at the shore. Otherwise, it was quiet. Nighttime there had a special stillness. It made sleep run deep. It was something I'd experience for only two more summers, but I didn't know that then either.

Ralph sighed. "Another day gone. All in all, it's been a pretty wonderful one."

"Yes," I agreed. "It has."

WOUNDS

Stuart started as a patient in the hyperbaric oxygen chamber about a week after I did. We were both part of the early afternoon treatment group, which meant we had to be changed into our hospital-issued scrubs and waiting for our vitals to be taken by 12:15 each day. He always got there before me, his motorized scooter stored off to the side, leaning on his fold-up walker and chatting with one of the staff. He couldn't have been taller than five-and-a-half feet; even the smallest of the scrub pants they issued us dangled over his blue tissue booties. His wounds involved acute circulation problems in his toes, and for some reason, he wore the booties over his bare feet instead of his socks or shoes like most other patients; the sight of his smaller toes through the tissue reminded me of dried cranberries, and his big toes of prunes.

The wound clinic and chamber were in the basement of Sharp Grossmont Hospital just up the freeway from San Diego State University. Along with an alternating staff member serving as our "tender," there were usually one or two other patients with Stuart and me on our chamber "dives," although those others changed fairly frequently. Stuart and I were the only patients that I was aware of who'd been authorized for forty dives, each of which lasted an hour-and-a-half and consisted of three thirty-minute sessions while "submerged" with a five-minute break in between. The chamber itself resembled a small submarine that had benches along one side with bed pillows for seats and back supports. Once the patients were settled inside and the chamber was sealed, it took about seven minutes for it to be pressurized to a depth of forty-five feet. Then the tender secured clear plastic hoods over our heads that snapped onto snug rubberized rings around our necks, and the flow of concentrated oxygen was started inside of them. The theory was that the oxygen would promote blood flow to wounds that otherwise hadn't healed naturally. While Stuart's were in his toes, my own wound was internal and involved the cavity that had formed where a cancerous tumor had been located in one of the lymph nodes in my neck. As a result, secretions that collected in it flooded my mouth, often mixed with phlegm, which I usually had to spit out every few minutes. Consistent throat pain and swallowing issues were additional side effects, necessitating the insertion of a feeding tube. It was a struggle for me to make it through a half-hour chamber session without being overwhelmed by accumulated secretions as I waited anxiously for the tender to remove my hood so I could spit into a small paper cup. Stuart's only accommodation in the chamber was a stool with an additional pillow on it so he could keep his feet somewhat elevated. The remaining patients had a variety of other wounds for which they were seeking relief. It wasn't uncommon for them to also need ambulatory assistance or be in wheelchairs; all told, we formed a pretty motley crew.

I guessed that Stuart was about my age, mid-sixties or so, with a bald dome of a head ringed with a rim of thin, graying hair that made him appear almost monkish. He was as talkative as I was restrained, engaging the tenders regularly with questions about the chamber's features or sharing stories with them about his own long career designing prosthetics, which it seemed to me, he deemed related in some way. Once hooded in the chamber, it was difficult to communicate easily, so Stuart mostly conversed with the dive's tender while descending, ascending, or during those short breaks. He never read or slept during the sessions, so when his hood came off, it seemed as if he'd been considering for the prior thirty minutes what would next come out of his mouth. He'd ask about the saturation of gasses in the chamber, its various valves and equipment, why the enriched oxygen knew to seek specific wounds in the body, the application of Boyle's law to the dives, why it was impossible to whistle at low register at maximum depth. He'd also talk about himself by comparing challenges he'd encountered in prosthetic design to ones he noticed in the chamber, commenting on unusual ebbs and flows he'd faced regarding the supply and demand of various limbs, and elaborating on some of his most difficult and unusual design requests.

"I once worked on a prosthetic nose," he told one of our tenders. "That was tricky. Getting the mucous membranes and tiny tissues just right."

The tender, I remember, looked at him blankly, and said, "I bet."

"It was," Stuart told him. "First, a mold of the person's original nose had to be taken and sprayed with a polymer scaffold. Then bone marrow cells were added to the nose shape, which, believe it or not, eventually grew over it. It's all about aligning the minute elements involved, the science of it." He waved his hand at the chamber's intricate interior. "Just like this finely crafted vessel."

One young man named Randy, whose long hair could have been used in a shampoo commercial, was most frequently the tender on our dives. Stuart's conversations with him sometimes extended to other topics. For example, I heard him tell Randy that he'd always lived alone with his mother out in the eastern part of the county, had recently retired, and had taken up baking as a hobby. While these discourses went on, I pretended to read whatever book I'd brought, spitting periodically into my cup, until it was time for our hoods to be reattached.

After his first few mornings as a fellow chamber patient, Stuart also engaged me in occasional cursory conversations. When those brief exchanges took place while we were seated next to each other in the chamber, they mostly had to do with our wounds and the related healing process. He claimed to have noticed a bit of improvement after his first couple of weeks; I told him I didn't feel any real difference at all at that point, even though I'd completed more sessions in it than him by then.

"Shucks," he said once after I'd repeated the same report. He shook his bald head. "And all that spitting you have to do. Must get old."

I nodded.

"You know, you're never going to get any better unless you truly believe." He tapped his forehead, then his chest above his heart. "That's what counts. Otherwise, you're just wasting your breath. Time to raise those spirits!"

I felt color creep up my neck.

"Say, how about if I bring you some fresh-baked raisin bread or lemon bars?" His eyes widened happily. "That'll pep you up. Which do you like better?"

"Thanks, but I can't eat by mouth." I lifted the bottom of my scrub top so my feeding tube button was exposed. "Still have to take all my nutrition and hydration through this."

"Shucks," he said again, but the curious way he studied my button seemed almost clinical and tinged with technical admiration.

The unfortunate truth was that Stuart wasn't far off about my diminished spirits. My treatment plan had called for two months of daily radiation and once weekly chemo. The first couple weeks of that weren't too bad, but the accumulating toll afterwards gradually began to wipe me out. I was told I should start feeling better a few weeks after treatments ended, but that never really happened due to the ongoing issues with my tumor site. When tests several months after treatment confirmed I was cancer-free, the docs decided to give the hyperbaric oxygen sessions a go to see if that would help heal it. At that point, I was up for trying anything, although after over half a year of basically feeling awful, I guess my demeanor must not have been a picture of hopefulness.

Stuart, on the other hand, always seemed buoyant. Sometimes, he even did a silly little soft-shoe dance, leaning on the tender's arm for support before entering the chamber. And he frequently hummed . . . mostly popular Broadway show tunes. I'm not sure when someone's smile becomes a grin, but he seemed to wear one more often than not, displaying a set of nearly perfect front teeth except for a slight gap between his two middle incisors on top. His eyes had a sparkle to them.

One morning when we were waiting next to each other for the staff to stretch our neck rings over our heads, he looked up at me with that twinkle in his eye and said, "You must have played basketball, am I right?"

"I did, yeah."

"High school, college?"

"Both, but only small-time college . . . Division III."

"How tall are you?"

I spat away some secretions, then mumbled, "Just south of six-three."

"Just? I'd kill to be anywhere near that. I'd be a rich man if I had a nickel for every time someone told me I looked like Danny DeVito."

I chuckled.

"See," he said, his eyebrows shooting up. "That laugh didn't hurt too much, did it?"

I shook my head.

Stuart grinned some more, then stuck a foot out and wriggled the darkened toes under his bootie. He looked up at me again and said, "Getting better every day. You?"

I shrugged and spat again into my cup.

⟡

The daily chamber treatments plodded on. It took me about twenty-five minutes to get to the hospital from my place near the coast, so along with the prep beforehand, changing clothes afterwards and using the stall's privacy to give myself a scheduled med through my feeding tube, then making the required co-pay on my way out, the whole ordeal took close to four hours door-to-door. But I didn't really mind too much; it filled the time. I lived alone and had recently taken a golden handshake myself from the consulting firm where I'd worked, so had long hours each day without many responsibilities to speak of anyway. I spent some time giving watercolor painting a try, played pickle ball a couple times a week once I started getting some strength back, watched sports on television and went to the occasional movie, but otherwise had nothing and no one special to attend to.

Stuart began bringing baked goods for the chamber's staff once or twice each week. I could hear them thanking him and fussing over the treats while I was having my vitals taken or waiting to enter the chamber. They had a little break room off to the side of the big control panel manipulated by staff while we were on our dives, and I could see the things Stuart brought through the open doorway on its tiny table, always arranged neatly under cellophane on paper plates adorned with festive prints. Sometimes, I could smell their sweet aromas: cardamon, powdered sugar, nutmeg, vanilla, ground mace. I'd basically pushed the idea of eating food out of my consciousness, but I admit those smells made my mouth water. They did.

❧❧ ❦ ❧❧

It wasn't until after my sixth week that I happened upon Stuart as he was leaving the hospital's parking garage in his little sedan with a handicap placard dangling from the rearview mirror. His motorized scooter was held aloft on the back in a wrought-iron lift contraption. The wave he gave me as I pulled towards him in my own vehicle was full of animated surprise, his head barely higher than the dashboard. I stopped my car and gestured for him to pull out of his parking space in front of me. He saluted with a big grin, a motion I marginally returned, then I stayed behind him down the circular ramp, through the turnstile, and out towards the traffic light that led onto the main thoroughfare fronting the hospital. We both turned left there and stayed in the far-right lane; I figured he was probably heading for the same set of freeway on-ramps I was, where he'd go east while I went west.

But we didn't make it that far because just past the next intersection, a loud thump came from the front of his car, it tilted left, then limped hissing into the adjacent mall parking lot. I felt a grimace deepen and cursed once, but followed him into side-by-side parking spaces serving a popular Mexican chain restaurant that anchored one end of the mall. It was an area without many other parked vehicles at 3 P.M. on a Friday afternoon. I climbed out of my car and walked around the front of his hood, watching him shove his door ajar, grab his fold-up walker from the passenger seat, and snap it open as I approached. By the time I'd come up beside him, he'd hoisted himself into a standing position. He rubbed the dome of his head, looked from his flat tire up at me with big eyes, and said, "Well, shit. Shit, shit, shit."

I managed what I intended as an understanding smile and said, "Yeah, not the best way to start your weekend, but if you have a spare, I can get it changed for you."

"Only have one of those damn donuts." His exasperated scowl tempered. "But it'd get me home until I can bring it to the dealership tomorrow for a real replacement."

"Okay," I said. "Pop the trunk, and I'll get started."

"Don't want to bother you. My insurance probably includes roadside assistance. I can give them a call."

"No need. I used to work in my dad's service station growing up. Changed these all the time."

He tilted his head, then shrugged. "Well, okay, if you're sure. Would do it myself, but . . . " He pointed at his feet, which were secured in thick socks inside rubber sandals with Velcro straps.

"No problem," I told him. "Go ahead, pop your trunk."

He pushed a button under the dash while I walked to the back of the car. The trunk lid lifted just free of the suspended scooter, and I found the things I needed under its floor. I carried them around to the front where Stuart had closed his door and flipped his walker around so he was facing it.

"I think the notch for the jack is on the frame just under the door there. I can get the manual out of the glove box if you want."

"Shouldn't need it."

I stretched out on the blacktop along the front side of the car, felt with my fingertips, found the notch, and raised the jack up to it until it met the frame. Then I loosened the lug nuts on the flat tire and finished raising the chassis off the ground. While I worked, I could hear Stuart humming softly a song from *West Side Story,* the name of which I couldn't recall. It was a warm day for mid-November, and I was already sweating a bit in my jeans and light fleece, but it didn't matter much because, aside from a few spits under the car, I had the donut secured and the flat with the other tools back in his trunk in less than fifteen minutes.

I returned to where Stuart stood and said, "All set. You're good to go."

He took a wallet out the pocket of his rumpled khakis and folded open the section that held cash. I put my hand over his and said, "Forget it. Not necessary."

"I mean to repay . . . "

I shook my head. "Nope. Won't take it. Piece of cake."

"Listen, I would have been up a creek without your help. I want to do something to show my appreciation." He searched around him, it seemed to me, a little desperately. "Look, that Mexican restaurant has neon beer signs in the windows. Means they have a bar. Let me at least buy you a quick drink."

I frowned to cover my smile. "You do remember about my feeding tube . . . ."

"Sure, but you take liquids through that . . . water, medications, what-not. Hydration, you said. So, you can also have a beer that way . . . or whatever you want to drink."

I huffed a little laugh. It was a thought that had never even crossed my mind. But he'd already started shuffling to the back of his car on his walker. He hit a button on the lift, and I watched it whir and lower, rocking a little, until it was flush to the ground. Stuart opened a short gate on its front, yanked the scooter's front wheel onto the blacktop, and said, "Let's go. Not taking no for an answer."

I stayed where I was. The sun had already begun its late-fall descent. Stuart wasn't looking at me, but I supposed that was intentional. I noticed that his cream-colored sweater had a geometric pattern on it and the turtleneck peeking up through its collar appeared to be a dickey; I hadn't seen one of those since junior high school. I watched him snap his walker closed, stash it in a slot on the back of his scooter, climb aboard, and turn its key. It made a whirring sound not unlike the lift as he zipped around the back of the car up next to me. His eyes met mine, and there was something almost imploring in them.

I said, "It's getting late."

"Twenty minutes." He glanced at his watch. "I have to get home and give my mom her insulin shot anyway. So, twenty minutes, tops. A quick drink. To say thank you. I insist."

He didn't wait for an answer, but whirled past me towards the restaurant bar's open door. I stood for a moment shaking my head. Then I heaved a sigh, returned to my car, got my daypack with my feeding tube supplies, and followed him inside.

The bar seemed dark after the glare outside. A sound system played quiet Mariachi music, and the walls were adorned with Mexican memorabilia. Stuart had already slid away a chair from a table near the door and settled his scooter in its place. I sat down next to him with my daypack in my lap. There were only a handful of other patrons in the place.

I watched Stuart's eyes travel around the interior until they met mine and he offered his gap-toothed grin. "Not bad, huh?" he said. "This place I mean. Nice enough."

I nodded.

"You ever been in one of these before?"

"No."

"Food's not bad. There's one not far from our house. I've brought home take-out from it a few times for my mom and me. A little cheesy for my taste . . . melted cheese over everything no matter what you order, but all in all, not bad."

I kept nodding until the bartender came up to us carrying a basket of tortilla chips and a little bowl of salsa. He was blonde-haired and blue-eyed, but wore a wide colorful sash that intersected his white shirt and black pants and a red bandana tied jauntily to the side around his neck. He set the chips and salsa down, then said, "So, what'll it be, fellas? You need menus?"

Stuart jockeyed the scooter a bit in his direction before saying, "Just drinks."

"Well, happy hour already started, so you're in luck there. Pitchers of margaritas are half-price."

Stuart looked over at me with raised eyebrows, his grin widening. I shrugged, which I guess was answer enough for him.

"Sounds good," he told the bartender. "On the rocks will probably work better than blended for my friend here. I'll have salt on the rim of my glass. Don't think he'll need one."

The bartender turned to me, his own eyes perplexed. "You don't want a glass?"

"No," I told him. "I'm good."

The confusion still hadn't left his face, but he turned and left. Stuart shook his cloth napkin free from its silverware and tucked it into the gap between his sweater's collar and the dickey. He scooped up a glob of salsa with a tortilla chip, then paused with it midway to his mouth, looked at me, and asked, "You mind?"

"Go for it." I jockeyed my tongue to keep my secretions at bay, then mumbled, "Doesn't bother me a bit."

He munched away while I unfolded my own napkin and unzipped my daypack. I took out my biggest syringe, my extension tube, a bottle of water, and the travel coffee mug with a snap-on lid; I'd previously used the last item while commuting to work, but had chosen it for its disguised purpose to get rid of secretions in public. I popped off the mug's lid, turned my head to the side, shielded my mouth with my hand, and spat as surreptitiously as possible into the mug. I dropped my daypack at my feet, then set the lid loosely on top of the mug before clenching it between my legs; the edge of the table came level with my belt, just high enough to hide the mug. I saw Stuart watching me.

"Sorry," I told him.

"Don't worry about it." He made a waving motion with another chip before dipping it in the salsa. "Do what you have to do. We're all dealing with our own shit here." He popped the chip in his mouth, chewed, swallowed, then said, "So, I'm guessing you had a type of oral cancer or something like that, am I right?"

I nodded and gave him a truncated summary of my related history between spits into the mug. When I finished, Stuart said, "That's some rotten luck."

I shrugged again and opened my palms.

"But I guess it's all pretty arbitrary in the end," he said. "Hell, I had no circulation problems until I turned sixty, then, boom . . . nothing but trouble. My mother has been battling diabetes since she was in her teens, and she's skinny as a rail. People deal with unexplained birth defects every day, or get born into famine and strife. It's all relative, arbitrary, isn't it? Misery, misfortune, bad luck, good luck, the color of your eyes, how tall you are or aren't . . . ."

I answered with another shrug and spat again. He ate a couple more chips, then the bartender came back to our table with a full pitcher and an empty, salt-rimmed glass, which he set in front of Stuart. He poured margarita into the glass up to where the salt began, then said, "Well, enjoy, fellas. Can I get you anything else?"

"No, we're good, thanks," Stuart told him.

We both watched him until he'd returned behind the bar. Then Stuart lifted his glass in my direction. "Go on and get busy now," he told me. "So we can toast properly."

I picked up the extension tube and the syringe. But before securing the tube, I glanced around the bar at the other patrons. An older, well-dressed couple sat a few tables away sharing a carafe of red wine and a huge plate of nachos. And a trio of guys sitting with their backs to us at the bar nursed draft beers, construction workers of some sort by the looks of their dress and hard hats perched on the bar.

"Don't worry about them," I heard Stuart say. "Gear up and let's go."

So, I lifted the bottom of my fleece up under my armpits, snapped the extension tube into my button, and twisted it back and forth to be sure it was secure. As I repositioned in the chair, some of the med I'd given myself back at the hospital crept up the extension tube. It wasn't a pretty thing to see, but it retreated once I sat straighter. I screwed the syringe into the tubing's fat end, made sure that was clamped shut, and picked up the pitcher. I looked over at Stuart, but he just gave me a short, expectant nod. I answered with an equally short shrug and tipped the pitcher so that margarita poured into the syringe, careful to avoid ice spilling after it. I only filled it about three-quarters of the way to start, the equivalent, maybe, of a couple of sips.

"There you go," Stuart said with his gap-toothed grin and sparkling eyes. He reached over, and I tipped the top of the syringe slightly so he could tap it with his glass. "Here's to you fixing that tire."

"Here's to it."

He tapped my syringe with his glass a second time. "And here's to wound healing and you kicking cancer's ass."

I said, "I'll drink to that."

"Darn right, you will."

Stuart gave another nod and took a swallow of his drink, licking away some of the salt. I spat again, took a breath, then released the clamp on the syringe. The margarita mixture was thinner than my regular formula and emptied more quickly out of the syringe. I watched it flow past the calibrated numbers etched on the side. It was cold entering my stomach, exposed and hairy like a dog's belly; otherwise, there was no sensation. I felt the woman at the table a few tables away staring at me. When I looked her way, the expression on her face was a mixture of astonishment and disgust. I gave her a nod, but she didn't return it; instead, she shook her head, then leaned towards her companion and whispered something to him. He quickly glanced over at me, shook his head, too, then looked away and squeezed the bridge of his nose. Her head kept shaking. They both took swallows from their glasses of wine.

"So, how'd it taste?" Stuart asked me and laughed.

I looked back at him and said, "Delicious."

"When's the last time you had a drink, anyway?"

I inclined my head, considering. "Oh, seven, eight months, I guess. Since before my cancer treatments started."

"Well, then, you're damn well due."

I shrugged, but felt my shoulders ease a bit.

He nodded several times, his expression gradually growing serious. He asked, "You have anyone at home to help you out?"

"No, never married." I paused. "Haven't really been involved with anyone . . . for a while now."

Stuart shrugged himself. "Me either."

We both nodded. I watched him drink from his glass again, licking at the salt as he did. The piped-in music changed from one song to another. A little burst of laughter rose from the guys at the bar, and a breeze from the open door lifted the napkin under Stuart's chin. He raised the margarita pitcher, topped off his glass, then extended it my way, and asked, "May I?"

I felt myself smile and tilted the open end of the syringe toward him. He took his time filling it. I hadn't set the clamp, so the liquid started descending right away, the same coldness spreading momentarily under my button. I felt the eyes of the woman from the table on me again, and from the corner of my own, I could see that hers had folded into squints of revulsion. She'd become quite stiff. She whispered something to her companion again, and he raised a hand to call for the bartender who draped a towel over his shoulder and headed their way.

Stuart drank, licked, then shook his head and said, "I can't imagine what I would have done without my mom's help through my ordeal. You know, having someone there who cared." He brushed some flakes of salt away from his lower lip. "I mean, she's old, real old, near ninety, but she's helped me plenty over the years. More than I can say. She's a scruffy old bird, but she's my scruffy old bird."

"Here's to your mother." I tipped the top of my syringe his way again. It was empty, but he tapped his glass against it and swallowed off more of his drink. His smile had softened somehow. I imagined him as a little boy and his mother as a young woman. I pictured her taking him to his first live musical at a theater, his eyes and gap-toothed smile expanding as the curtain opened, her hand on his wrist.

The bartender interrupted those thoughts when he appeared suddenly at our table, his mouth in a thin, tight line. He looked back and forth between us, then settled on me, and said, "I'm afraid that couple over there . . . ." He gave a quick, sheepish glance their way. "Well, the woman, to be specific . . . well, she's offended by the way you're drinking." He fixed his uncomfortable gaze on me again. "That tube into your stomach and all, the syringe. And also your spitting. Unsightly, she called it, in a restaurant. Says it's ruining their meal."

I looked up at him, growing warm, as Stuart said, "Oh, she does, does she?"

He backed out quickly from our table, then whirled past the bartender on his scooter over to the couple, the napkin fluttering under his chin. He pulled up between the pair as easily as if he was joining them for a get-together, and they both stared at him with darting eyes.

"I understand you feel my friend over there is disturbing your meal." I watched Stuart gesture with his chin. It wasn't hard to hear him; his voice was plenty loud. He rolled his shoulders and asked, "Is that accurate?"

The man and woman looked at each other, then back at Stuart. The man nodded.

"Well, that's too bad," Stuart said. "That's really awful, seeing as it's the only way my friend can hydrate. So, I'm wondering how we're going to rectify this situation." His face was at an angle where I could see him look back and forth between the two of them, it seemed to me, almost serenely. "Oh, wait a minute," he said. "I have an idea." He reached across their table, lifted the plate of nachos, and dumped its contents on the floor. He replaced the plate, centered it on the table, brushed his hands together, and said, "There you go. Problem solved. He won't be disturbing your meal any longer."

As quickly as he'd arrived, he zipped back to our table, took three twenty dollar bills out of his wallet, and handed them to the bartender. "This ought to cover both tabs," he told him. Then he swallowed off what was left in his margarita glass, and said to me, "Not what I had in mind when I asked to buy you that drink. Sorry."

He dropped his napkin on the table, made a punctuated turn with his scooter, and whirled away out through the open door. I sat still for a moment, blinking rapidly, then began breaking down my things as quickly as I could. Unfortunately, it took a while because I had to flush the syringe with water several times due to the stickiness of the margarita, unsnap the extension tube, shake it free of moisture onto the napkin, then store everything back into my daypack. At first, the bartender and the couple at the table did nothing as I hurried through those movements except watch me, the woman's mouth like a fish's out of water. Eventually, the bartender shifted the towel from one shoulder to another, and walked past the mess on the floor back behind the bar. When I finally stood up slinging on my daypack, I avoided looking at any of them and left through the same open door. By the time I got back outside, though, Stuart's car was just leaving the parking lot. I raised my hand to wave, but if he saw it, he gave no indication of it. He turned towards the freeway on-ramps, his head just visible above the steering wheel, while I stood alone in the clean, white light of the dwindling afternoon.

Stuart wasn't there after I'd finished my prep at the chamber before the next treatment on Monday afternoon. I thought he might just be delayed, but when the staff started loading a couple of new patients into the chamber, I asked Randy about him.

The look Randy gave me wasn't a happy one. "Yeah," he said. "I'm afraid he's not coming."

I felt my eyebrows knit. "He's never missed a session, that I can remember. What's up?"

Randy shrugged. "I can't really say. Patient confidentiality, you know."

"Is he okay? Can you at least tell me that?"

"It's not him." Randy eyes flitted furtively around him; no one else was nearby. He lowered his voice and said, "It's his mother."

I felt my fingertips raise to my mouth and said, "Oh, no. Is she all right?"

Randy just looked at me.

"Will he be back?"

"Not for a while, that's for sure. Maybe someday." He shrugged again, then said, "Let's get you loaded on. We're already running late."

I finished my chamber treatments a couple of weeks later. When they concluded, my secretions had improved a bit, to the extent that they didn't overwhelm my mouth as frequently as before. And I could also speak a little more clearly. The throat pain and swallowing issues remained unchanged. My oncologist asked me if I wanted her to see if my insurance would authorize another round of chamber treatments, but I told her, no, not yet. I said I wanted to think about it for a while. What I didn't tell her was that I'd grown pretty accustomed to the spitting and tube feeding. And the meds continued to control my throat pain to a manageable level; if I wasn't eating by mouth, then the issues with swallowing food also became a moot point. I was sixty-seven years old. I didn't know how many years I had left, but I lived alone, and there were worse things I could imagine than continuing on my own with those inconveniences for whatever time I had remaining. After all, I'd beaten cancer, that was the important thing.

Stuart never returned to the chamber during my last two weeks there. On my final day, I thought about asking for his contact information, but knew that regulations would prohibit that disclosure. However, I did think about him quite often afterwards. Him and his mother. I wasn't religious, but in my own way, I suppose I sort of prayed for them. Whatever that might mean.

Winter came on, and with it, the shorter days, the longer hours of darkness. Something about those changes troubled me more than in the past. Years passing by, time dwindling, chances squandered. But then I'd think about what Stuart had said while we sat next to each other in the chamber, and that helped. When those memories of him crossed my mind, I'd pause and smile. I hoped his toes were okay and that he didn't have to use his scooter or walker anymore. But even if he did, I hoped he was still humming, still grinning, still baking, and that his eyes still had that sparkle. I sure wanted that to be the case. In fact, there were few things I could have wished for more.

SUNSHINE IN A BOWL

1.

Ruth sat on the edge of the waiting room chair. She hadn't really moved from that spot since arriving at the hospital with Carl at 6:30am, an hour early for his outpatient surgery. A thin woman with white hair twisted into a tight bun at the back of her neck, Ruth had just turned seventy-one; Carl was a few months older. While she waited, she glanced often up at the wall clock and unconsciously shifted her weight. At eleven, an hour-and-a-half after Carl was supposed to be moved to recovery, she left for a few minutes to use the restroom. When she returned, she sat in the same spot, watched a square of sun inch closer across the carpet, and bit at a thumbnail.

A little before two, a nurse finally approached and startled her from her daze.

Ruth looked up at her, then said, "Yes?"

"I'm afraid they've run into some complications with your husband. Having to do with his procedure." The nurse paused. "That's the reason for the delay."

"Is he all right? Carl?"

The nurse offered a hopeful smile. "They should know soon. It shouldn't be long now."

Ruth lowered her eyes and stared off at the opposite wall. The waiting room, nearly empty, was almost silent. She said, "Thank you."

The nurse gave another encouraging smile, but Ruth didn't see it. She continued to stare straight ahead and only heard the retreating footsteps and click of the door. She began folding and unfolding her hands in her lap.

2.

The surgeon finally came into the waiting room in his scrubs just after three-thirty and perched on the edge of the seat next to Ruth. He was an older man, whose eyes, she had decided during their initial consultation, were caring.

He said, "I'm sorry this has taken so long."

"What's wrong?" she asked. Her lower lip had begun to tremble. "Tell me."

"Well, we're not sure. Nothing, perhaps." His bushy eyebrows raised and lowered. "The surgery went fine. No problems there. But your husband . . . Carl . . . hasn't come out from under the anesthesia as he ought to have. In the typical fashion or timeframe. In short, he hasn't woken up yet."

"Like he should have."

"That's right." The surgeon nodded. "Some time ago. Several hours, actually."

Ruth felt her forehead knit. "Is he in a coma?"

"We're not calling it that," he said. "Not yet. Not at this point, anyway. We're not there yet."

Ruth's eyes widened; she felt a burning behind them. The surgeon put his hand on hers in her lap. She began to cry silently, her shoulders shaking almost imperceptibly. His hand closed over hers.

"It could be nothing." His voice had softened. "At his age, it could just be taking a while."

Ruth's head jerked up. "Five hours?"

"Well, we just don't know at this point. At present, we're just monitoring things very closely. His vital signs are good. They're stable. So, to be honest, we're as perplexed as you right now."

"Can I see him?"

The surgeon hesitated a moment, then said. "Well, I suppose it couldn't hurt. He's still in a recovery bay, although we may admit him upstairs. If things don't change, you know, don't come around here pretty soon."

"I want to sit with him," Ruth said. "I want to be with him."

The surgeon nodded slowly and gave her hand a pat. "I understand," he said. "Follow me."

3.

Carl's recovery bay was enclosed on two sides by curtains. He lay on his back, his head and shoulders inclined slightly. He was sleeping, or whatever it was that they couldn't yet name, his breaths coming in the short gasps Ruth was very familiar with. She held his fingertips through the guard rail with her own. He was a large man with wisps of white hair above each ear and a wide belly that stretched his covers.

Ruth stroked the calluses inside his hand, keeping her eyes on his face and the rise and fall of his big chest. A sat monitor on a pole hooked to wires and probes leading to various places on his upper torso beeped regularly. Numbers and wavy lines moved across its face that she didn't understand. Now and then, a nurse came by and pushed some buttons on it, checked his probes, typed something into his chart, gave Ruth another hopeful smile like the first nurse had, then went away.

Ruth studied Carl as he slept. Every so often, she whispered, "Wake up. Please. Wake up, Carl."

4.

When the surgeon stopped by again a little after five, Carl still hadn't awakened. Most of the other bays had emptied out, and only a few staff remained at the central work station. Ruth watched him as he reviewed the computer monitor's chart.

He frowned before turning to her and saying, "Well, as you can see, there's been no change. That's unfortunate and frankly, distressing. So, we're moving him upstairs. They're getting a bed ready for him now. He'll be in good hands there. Dr. Killion will be the attending for the next few days. She's a longtime colleague of mine, and she's great. I think you'll really like her."

Ruth looked at him, blinking rapidly again. A good portion of the hair in her bun had come undone.

"Listen, why don't you go home and get some rest?" the surgeon said. "Not much more is likely to happen tonight. They'll call you if something does."

Ruth looked from him to Carl and said, "I want to stay."

"It's been a long day. You need to take care of yourself, too." The surgeon paused. "No telling how long this might last."

Ruth's head jerked back, her eyes narrowed. "What?"

"Well, we just don't know," the surgeon said. "That's all I meant. There's just no way of knowing. And you've got to keep up your own strength."

"I'll stay," Ruth told him. "I'm going to stay."

The surgeon watched her turn slowly back to her husband. He knew from their consultation that they lived on a farm well beyond the city limits. He knew that Carl had worked the place himself and had also repaired farm equipment on the side for a long time until he'd finally leased out the fields and sold the animals a half-dozen years before. Ruth had baked pies for a nearby coffee shop. They had no children, probably not much, the surgeon thought, in the way of extended family left, if any. He watched Ruth pull the covers up under Carl's chin.

"Well," he said. "Get some rest when you go upstairs then. The rooms there have recliners they can turn down into a sort of bed for you."

Ruth didn't turn back his way, but she nodded.

"You hang in there then," the surgeon said.

He watched her nod again once, then compressed his lips and headed towards the stairwell.

❦

5.

The upstairs room Carl was moved to was a double, but the other bed was unoccupied. After the new staff got him settled, Ruth pulled the curtain closed between the beds and turned off the lights on the other side of the room. She slid the recliner over to Carl's bedside, sat down, and studied Carl's face for a while. Finally, she shook her head and turned towards the tall window next to her with its slatted blinds collected in an uneven bunch. Ruth stared outside where snow blew in the glare of a parking lot streetlamp. She became aware of her own reflection in the window's glass and was startled, as had grown commonplace, by how bent she'd become. And how frail.

Ruth sat very still and listened to voices and movements outside on the unit. When things grew quiet, she could hear wind blowing the snow in gusts and Carl's short, gasp-like breaths. She looked at him with his closed eyes, laid her hand on his wrist, and thought about their empty farmhouse where they hadn't even considered turning on a light or opening a tap against the chance of freezing pipes. She began to weep again.

❦

6.

About ten, the nurse assigned to Carl came in and asked Ruth if she wanted the recliner turned down. Ruth nodded, took her hand away from Carl's wrist, and moved out of the way. The nurse slid and folded the recliner until it was flat and made it up with sheets, a blanket, and a pillow. Then she flipped switches on the wall that turned off the overhead light and left just the muted glow of a small fixture on the wall above Carl's head.

"There," the nurse told her. "That should help you sleep. And we're right outside if you need anything." She glanced at Carl, then back to Ruth. "Don't worry about him. I'll be monitoring his numbers regularly out there and checking on him frequently, too."

Ruth nodded and fought back more tears. The nurse looked like she was barely beyond her teens. So young, Ruth thought. About the age their great grandchildren would be if they'd had any. About the age she and Carl had been when they met at that grange hall dance.

"Can I get you anything else?" the nurse asked.

"No," Ruth looked at the full name on the badge clipped to a pocket on the nurse's smock. "Thank you, Cheryl."

"You're welcome." Another small, hopeful smile followed. "Good night."

Ruth watched her leave. She sat perfectly still for several minutes before closing the blinds and taking off her plaid Mackinaw jacket and shoes. She smoothed the hair above Carl's ears and kissed his forehead. Then Ruth crawled under the covers and lay on her back. She stared up at the dimly-lit ceiling tiles listening to the beep of the sat monitor, the murmur of voices outside the room, the soft, even rasp of Carl's breaths, and realized that it was the first night they had not slept in the same bed together in a long, long time. In fact, she couldn't remember the last time.

Ruth turned onto her side and reached over to Carl's bed. She was too far away to hold his hand, so she rested the side of hers against his elbow, wrinkled with age but comforting to her touch.

7.

Ruth rose often during the night to check on Carl, to readjust his covers, to wipe spittle from the corner of his mouth. She got up for good, like usual, just after dawn, folded and stored away her bedding, and restored the recliner to its original position. She kissed Carl's forehead again, letting her lips linger there, then held his hand some more, concentrating on his breathing, until Cheryl came in and gave her a small plastic bag that contained a new toothbrush, comb, travel-sized toothpaste, soap, and shampoo.

"There's a designated restroom just down the hall for patients' families," she told Ruth. "Even has a shower stall if you'd like to use it. We have towels."

Ruth recognized the same quality in Cheryl's eyes that she had in the surgeon's.

"And there's a cafeteria downstairs if you want breakfast."

"Thank you," Ruth said. She tugged at a corner of Carl's pillow. "I think I'll stick around in case he wakes up."

Cheryl nodded slowly and watched Ruth return her troubled gaze towards her husband. "Okay," she said. "Well, we change shifts at seven, so I'll bring your day nurse in to meet you then. And Dr. Killion usually rounds about nine."

"Good." Ruth looked at this young woman who was just starting out in life and was about to go home to whatever awaited her there. She said, "You've been very thoughtful."

Cheryl's cheeks colored. She glanced once more at Carl. "I hope he wakes up soon. I really do."

Ruth stayed standing while Cheryl went through the steps to take Carl's vitals and record them into his chart. Then they exchanged small smiles and Cheryl left.

Wan light crept into the room when Ruth opened the blinds. The snow had stopped, but the parking lot and grounds below lay still in a carpet several inches thick, pristine and unspoiled at that early hour. It was lovely, but she worried about making it up their long driveway to the house. It wouldn't have been an issue if they'd returned home early yesterday afternoon as planned. But now, if it snowed more, she'd have to call their nearest neighbor who lived a half mile away and ask him to clear it for them.

Ruth looked over at Carl. Before she'd left, Cheryl had repositioned him on his side with a pillow wedged under his hips and buttocks as she had several times overnight. She'd told Ruth it was to prevent bedsores from forming. How long, Ruth wondered, did it take for those to become a likelihood?

"Wake up," Ruth whispered to Carl. "So we don't have to worry about things like that or the driveway. So we can get on with our lives." She stepped over to the bed and put her palm on his chest. It rose and fell slightly with his breathing. "Hear me, now?" she said. "Go on and wake up, you old coot."

8.

Cheryl's replacement was a middle-aged Filipina woman named Grace whose movements were efficient but grim. Beyond a narrow lap table at the end of the bed, the wall clock's big hand seemed to jerk from one minute to the next.

Dr. Killion came by briefly a little before nine. She was short, copper-haired, and had no new insights to share. She did a thorough examination of Carl and added notations to his chart while she told Ruth that she'd ordered some routine labs. Then she called for Grace and directed her to put Carl on a low flow of oxygen.

"What's that for?" Ruth felt her hands clench together in her lap.

"Oh, just comfort mostly," Dr. Killion said. "He doesn't really require it, but this will keep him comfortable, just in case. So he won't have to work so hard."

Ruth's eyes danced as she watched Grace uncoil clear plastic tubing from a cannister on the wall behind the bed, wrap it around Carl's ears, and insert its nasal cannula into his nostrils. When Grace started the oxygen, it made a soft hiss. She adjusted the dial on the canister and they all watched the O2 number on Carl's sat monitor trickle up into the high nineties.

"There," Dr. Killion said. "Better." She gave a nod of reassurance and said, "I'll be back later."

Ruth watched both women leave. It was quiet again in the room. She stood up from the recliner. One of the cannula prongs had slid down a bit, and Ruth reinserted it into Carl's nostril. His skin remained warm to her touch, which was somehow encouraging. If they were at home, she supposed he'd be out in the barn tinkering with a piece of machinery, the space heater glowing nearby. He still took on a few farm equipment repair projects from old customers from time to time. It kept him busy, he said. By that, he meant he loved it. By that, he meant he didn't know what he'd do with his time without it. Like her, with her baking. Or their walks together after supper, down the long, gravel driveway, then east along their fence line. Or the way they still kissed each other whenever one or the other left or returned to the house.

9.

The technician came to draw Carl's blood shortly afterwards, then nothing much of note happened during the rest of the day. When she wasn't fussing over Carl, she dozed or stared through the window down into the parking lot. But mostly, she just sat, watched him breathe, and let her thoughts tumble over themselves in random fits and starts. She thought about their move halfway across country after they were married to work on the farm that was owned by a buddy he'd served with during the Vietnam War, a quiet, solitary man who knew he was in failing health but kept that to himself, and then left the place to them when he died. She thought about watching Carl out on the tractor or walking the fields, the slow, methodical way he moved, and the downturned outside edges of his eyes that always seemed to suggest tenderness in spite of his size. She thought about how he liked to surprise her at the kitchen sink by coming up behind her and wrapping his arms around her, enveloping her, and his good smell of sweat and livestock and soil as he nuzzled her neck. She thought about the many long nights they'd spent birthing calves or foals in the barn and the time he sat crying quietly on a hay bale when he'd had to put a cow down that he couldn't rescue from an unsuccessful breech birth. She thought about him making her breakfast sometimes on Sunday mornings while he let her sleep late. She thought about the silent way they'd accepted things when a pregnancy just never happened. She thought about him humming off-key while he showered. She thought about his hands so large and rough and soft on her in bed with the lights off. From time to time, she shook her head.

In the late afternoon, Dr. Killion made another visit almost identical to her first and told Ruth that at least there had been no decline in Carl's condition and that his labs had come back normal. Ruth resisted the urge to probe further, deciding that no news was better than bad. After the doctor left, Ruth sat staring at where she'd stood, an emptiness there like the one she felt inside. Light fell. Every now and then, a few sparse snowflakes blew by the window.

10.

Shortly before shift change that evening, Ruth hurried down in the elevator, bought soup and a paper cup of tea, and was back at Carl's room in less than ten minutes. She exchanged smiles with Cheryl, who was conferring with Grace just outside the door, glad that the young nurse was on night shift again.

She'd finished her meal and was sipping the last of her tea when Cheryl first entered the room a little later. Cheryl set a paper sack she held on the edge of the bed, went through her regular routine of vital signs, charting, and repositioning with Carl, then reached the sack out towards Ruth.

"Here," she said. "I brought you some things."

Ruth felt her forehead wrinkle as she took the sack and opened it on her lap.

"They're a few clothes of mine I don't need anymore," Cheryl said. "I washed them all. They're clean."

Ruth looked from the sack's contents up at Cheryl's face, her mouth open. "I don't know what to say."

"I think they'll fit," Cheryl said. "The underwear has actually never even been worn."

Ruth pulled the sack close and mumbled, "So nice of you."

Cheryl shrugged. "Might feel good to take a shower and get into something else. Eventually, I mean. Whenever you're ready . . . whenever you like. Refresh you a little."

Ruth managed a nod.

"Didn't seem likely that you'd be leaving on your own, I mean, running home to do that. Wherever that is."

"Our farm."

"Well, then, that's probably a bit of a drive."

"It is, yes."

Cheryl nodded, then let her eyes run over Carl's chart. She said, "Not much change with him, I guess."

"No, none."

"Sometimes these sorts of things just take a while."

Ruth straightened. "Have you seen this happen before?"

Cheryl's lips closed for a moment before she said, "Not really, no."

They both turned their gaze from one another to the big figure of Carl lying still in the bed. The sat monitor made its slow, steady beep. A gust of wind whistled by outside. Ruth blew out a long breath.

Cheryl watched the old woman's shoulders drop, lowered her voice, and asked, "You doing okay?"

Ruth looked up at her with moist eyes. She said, "I don't know what to think, to be honest. It's hard not to imagine the worst."

"Don't do that." Cheryl said quickly. She reached over and put her hand on Ruth's shoulder. "Don't."

"I want you to tell me that things will be just fine. That's what I want you to say."

"I think they will." Cheryl gave her shoulder a gentle rub. "That's what I'm betting on, anyway."

Ruth nodded without enthusiasm. Cheryl left her hand on the bony shoulder and they both watched Carl breathing in bed again. Someone from another room called for a nurse. Ruth nodded as Cheryl gave her shoulder a last small rub. After she left, Ruth twisted down the flap on the paper sack and set it next to the recliner. She tried to piece together an old church tune her mother had taught her, one she often sang to herself while working in the kitchen, but couldn't muster the strength or the concentration or whatever it was that was missing just then.

❧❧ ❦ ❧❧

11.

That overnight went much the same as the first, although Ruth slept even less. After her last check on Carl, she stood beside the bed watching him sleep where he lay turned on his side away from her. Except for the low beep from the sat monitor and soft hiss of oxygen, it was completely silent, no wind outside, no conversation from the nurses' station, no footsteps in the hall, still dark. Ruth looked up at the clock on the wall: a couple of hours before they'd normally be rising at home, about the time Carl usually made his final trip of the night to the toilet. When he got back into bed, they always adjusted themselves so they were spooning, even if she was half asleep, with him up against her back, his knees closed into the cavity her own made, his arm over her chest, his hand sometimes cupping her breast.

Ruth lowered the bedrail closest to the recliner and crawled into Carl's bed next to him, careful to avoid wires and probes, in the opposite position to the one they occupied at home. When Cheryl came in to check on him shortly before dawn, that's the way she found them, both in the depths of separate slumber. The young nurse raised her palm to her cheek and bit her lower lip. She decided to delay that round of Carl's vital signs; those, she told herself, could wait a bit. Instead, she took the blanket from the recliner and laid it gently over Ruth, then left the room as quietly as she could.

12.

Somehow, Ruth slept through shift change, and as she climbed out of Carl's bed, she recoiled at the rank smell of her body. It wasn't yet 7:30, so she chanced a quick shower, but when she returned to the room, she was told that she'd missed Dr. Killion, who'd rounded early. The new day nurse, Regina, an older Filipina, said that the doctor had ordered a CT scan for Carl.

Ruth felt a jolt. "What's that for?"

"It's like an X-ray of the brain," Regina told her. "It can show signs of hemorrhage, tumors, strokes, other conditions. And it can sometimes determine the cause of a coma."

"What?" Ruth's hand shot to her chest. "No one has told me he's in a coma. To my knowledge, that hasn't been confirmed by anyone."

"And it still hasn't," Regina assured her. "In fact, the doctor said that there's been no sign of stroke, seizures, or infection. No irregular breathing. Nothing. The CT scan may just help rule some things out, may provide some useful information."

"About what's going on," Ruth said, "with my husband."

"That's right." Regina nodded. "Nothing to get upset about. A completely normal and appropriate procedure under the circumstances. Doesn't take long at all."

Ruth looked down at Carl. He'd been repositioned onto his back with the head of the bed inclined a bit.

More quietly, Regina said, "You've had a shower. That's nice. Bet that feels better."

Ruth glanced down at the clothes from Cheryl she'd changed into; they hung loose on her small frame. She'd combed out her damp hair into thin strings that fell to just below her shoulders. She nodded.

"Good for you."

Ruth watched her smile, collect a pair of empty syringes from the lap table at the end of the bed, and leave. Sunlight from outside warmed the back of Ruth's neck. She twisted her hair into its customary bun and heard a snow plow's blade drop and scrape along in the parking lot below. Carl's chest rose and fell. She touched the center of it and said, "You're going to have a scan done, sweetheart. It's nothing to be concerned about. You'll leave for a bit and then be right back. And I'll be here waiting for you. I won't be going anywhere. Don't you even give that another thought."

True to Regina's word, he was gone and back later that morning in a half-hour. The afternoon passed much the same as the previous one. Ruth sat thinking and waiting while the room grew progressively darker in the early winter's steady decline until the phone on Carl's bedside table startled her. She answered it and said, "Hello?"

"Ruth, this is Dr. Killion. I just wanted to check in with you before I left to let you know that the CT scan results showed nothing noteworthy, nothing revealing."

"What does that mean?"

"They were inconclusive."

Ruth closed her eyes, then opened them again. "Is he in a coma? Can you tell me that?"

"If he is, it certainly doesn't display like others we've seen. The markers just aren't there. So, we're still not sure what's going on. Why he hasn't woken up, why he hasn't roused."

"It's been going on sixty hours."

"I know." Rose heard her breathe out through her nose. "But all his vital signs continue to be fine. And he's getting plenty of nourishment through his IV."

"So, what do we do?"

"Well, for now, we continue to wait."

"Wait," Ruth repeated.

"Wait and hope for the best."

Ruth shook her head. Another gust of wind rattled the window. With her free hand spread wide, she pinched her temples, then rubbed her forehead.

"Try to remain optimistic and not get preoccupied with worrisome possibilities," Dr. Killion said. "Perhaps we'll know more tomorrow. If there are still no changes by the time I round in the morning, I may order an EKG."

Ruth sucked in her own breath. "That sounds serious."

"It's just the next step. Standard procedure and nothing more." She paused. "So, don't concern yourself with that, Ruth, okay? All right, then. I'll see you first thing in the morning."

Before the doctor hung up, Ruth heard herself say, "Good night."

Carl's sat monitor continued to make its slow, steady beep, so familiar now that it had become almost like that of his own breathing. A bigger gust outside rattled the window. In that cold, dark, early-winter evening, her heart felt like a stone. CT scans, EKGs, continuous oxygen, something that lingered on and on that they wouldn't yet confirm as a coma. Three evenings ago, they were just sitting down at the kitchen table at that hour to beef stew she'd put up during the morning in the crock pot. What had transpired since hardly seemed possible or real. It all seemed like a bad dream, an awful aberration. Except that it wasn't.

❦

13.
    Cheryl was on again that night, her last, she told Ruth, of what she called "three twelves." She was pleased when she noticed Ruth in her old clothes, but she said nothing about it as she began her regular routine with Carl. Ruth found herself admiring again the careful and respectful way Cheryl treated him, even though he was unresponsive, and decided to ask her about herself. She told Ruth she was unmarried and lived in a small apartment alone, a granny flat over someone's garage. She said her own grandparents had lived on a farm an hour or so away; she'd been very close with them, and they'd both passed on several years earlier. She said that for fun she sang in a community choir and enjoyed canning vegetables from her family's garden.

    "Us, too," Ruth said, brightening. She gestured towards Carl with her forehead. "He loves to help." Her lips folded into a tiny smile. "He likes to wear an apron . . . you should see him in it."

    Cheryl smiled in return. "He's a big guy."

    "He is." Ruth reached across from the recliner and covered his hand with the blankets. "And when we put up tomatoes and cucumbers, he always cuts up a couple fresh-picked and still warm from the garden into a kind of salad with just a drizzle of olive oil and salt and pepper." She smoothed the blanket over his hand. "It's a favorite of his . . . a favorite thing."

    Cheryl had been repositioning Carl towards Ruth and paused. "Sounds delicious."

    Ruth nodded. "It's really good. He calls it "sunshine in a bowl.""

    "My," Cheryl said softly. "I'd like to try that."

    "You should."

    They nodded together for a moment, then Cheryl resumed her remaining duties with Carl. When she left to care for other patients, the room became quiet again, dark and lonesome and still. Ruth checked the wall clock. It wasn't even 8:15 yet, but she took off her jacket and shoes anyway and climbed in bed next to her husband. She didn't bother lowering the recliner and getting it ready to sleep in later on. Instead, she pulled part of his blankets over her, scooted close to him, wrapped an arm across his chest, and closed her eyes.

❦

14.

Sometime in the depths of the night, a voice woke her. Ruth opened her eyes in the near darkness to find Carl's looking at her with curiosity. He said, "Where are we?"

Ruth went stiff beside him, her eyes slowly widening. She heard herself say, "Oh."

Carl frowned. His arm was draped over her and his hand slid down her back. "I asked, where are we?" His voice was hoarse, but clear.

Ruth drew him into an embrace, then released him so she could continue to look into his wakened eyes, to be sure they remained open. In that room's dark canopy, a light bloomed inside her. She tried to call for Cheryl, but her own voice wouldn't work right; it came out as hardly more than a whisper.

Carl searched her face, his frown deepening. He said, "What's going on?"

"You're here," Ruth told him. She gave him a little shake. "That's what's going on. You're here."

❦

15.

A few weeks later, after breakfast, Ruth waited for Carl to head out to the barn to work on someone's old hay baler, then addressed a manilla envelope to Cheryl. She used the hospital's address with the floor that Carl had been admitted to noted after it. Inside, she put a photograph of the two of them and a couple packages of seeds, one for tomatoes and the other for cucumbers. On the back of the photo, she wrote "Thanks" and signed their names. She licked the envelope sealed, stamped it, and pulled on her Mackinaw jacket.

It was a sunless morning, frigid, but without wind. Ruth turned the jacket's collar up against the chill and left the house through the kitchen door. She buried her hands into the pockets, one of which held the envelope. It was a long way down their gravel drive to the mailbox, but she walked slowly, enjoying the sight of late-to-migrate birds as they flew off towards the cottonwoods across the road, the empty, fallow fields on either side of her, the vast stillness. The space heater's red glow was just visible inside the dimly lit barn when she passed it; she knew Carl stood hidden within the ring of its warmth selecting tools for his morning's work. One of the birds soared higher and the others followed. A small smile creased her lips watching them disappear into the gray distance. Ruth breathed deeply, her exhales in short, white clouds. She wasn't in any hurry, so she moved gratefully and without haste, savoring every step.

THE HAY IS IN THE BARN

I'm sixty-two years old. Like most my age, I suppose, there are a number of things I regret. For some reason, one occupies a particular place for me. It's not the most significant or memorable in my life, or even very notable in and of itself. But, when I think of it, something different falls in me, something irrevocable.

It occurred between my junior and senior years of college at UC Santa Cruz. I shared a rambling old rental house downtown with five other guys who played with me on the school's basketball team. One was my best friend, Eric. We'd been high school teammates over the hill in San Jose, and then were happy to keep playing together in college. The house had four bedrooms; Eric and I each had our own and the other guys shared. We all became pretty close spending that much time together. We kept the place over the summer, but except for Eric and me, the rest of our housemates left during the break for jobs at home or to travel. He and I stayed to keep up the yard service business we'd started when we were sophomores. It wasn't much, but it helped pay the rent, and we could build a flexible work schedule to accommodate classes and practices.

One of our housemates, Drew, grew up over the hill, too, in Menlo Park. Our high schools had been in the same league, so we'd played against each other before becoming college teammates. He was a nice, easy-going guy who'd had the same girlfriend, Claire, since middle school. She'd just transferred to UC Santa Cruz the semester before so they could be together, and she rented a room in a house around the corner with some other female students from school. Drew was spending the summer at home working for his dad, as he had for years during school breaks, painting houses. But he was about to take his annual July trip to Montana to help bring in the hay on his aunt and uncle's farm. He asked me if I wanted to come with him to help, and I said sure. Eric was fine with handling the yard business alone for the week or so that I'd be gone.

We were scheduled to leave early on a Saturday. I was going to drive over the hill, pick up Drew, and then we'd make the trip in my old Volkswagen Beetle. I went to a party the night before and came home late. The light was on under Eric's bedroom door when I passed it, and I could hear voices laughing quietly inside. One was a woman's. That surprised me because of Eric's shyness; to my knowledge, he'd never had a girlfriend or even been intimate with a woman before.

Later that night, I heard a rustling in the kitchen and got up to see what it was. Eric and Claire were standing with their arms around each other and their backs to me looking into the refrigerator. They were both naked. Their heads turned when I came into the room, but they made no movement to cover themselves.

"We're looking for something to eat," Eric said.

I stood frozen in place. The white light from the refrigerator's interior was like a beacon across them in the darkness. Claire pointed to the refrigerator.

"We were hungry," she added.

I nodded, then returned to my bedroom and shut the door.

❧❧ ❦ ❧❧

I left in the morning before they were up. Drew was waiting on his front step with a rucksack and sleeping bag at his feet as I pulled into the driveway. When he climbed in the car, he gave me one of his big, goofy grins and tossed his stuff in the seat behind him.

"Ready for this?" he asked.

"You bet."

He pointed up the road and said, "Tally ho."

His brown eyes were clear and, like always, full of hope. He'd told me often before how much he looked forward each year to this trip. He'd been making it since he was thirteen when he'd become big enough to help.

"Wait until you see those mountains," he said. "The Beartooths. They look like they're biting right into the sky. Unbelievable."

He kicked off his sandals, leaned his mop of dirty-blonde curls back against the headrest, and put his feet up on the dashboard. I watched him close his eyes. I was glad because I didn't want to engage in more conversation with him; I didn't know what, if anything, to say to him about the night before, and I was afraid my words or expression would indicate that something was amiss. By the time I got on the freeway, he was sound asleep.

We spent that night in a cheap hotel outside of Wells, Nevada. It began raining the next morning as soon as we crossed into Idaho. The big canopy of sky was solid gray in all directions.

"Well, there you go," Drew said. "My uncle told me they've been battling this on and off for weeks. Wettest summer in as long as he can remember."

"Can they hay in this?"

"They've been cutting and baling in little windows when it stops and the sun dries things out. They staggered field planting in the spring so they don't have a single window when they have to bring it all in, but he says timing things has been a real challenge. They started on it earlier than usual because of that, even before some of it was full height."

It kept raining most of that day. We stopped for lunch at a lookout along the western edge of Yellowstone National Park. We were planning on camping there on our way back, so stayed steady afterwards until Bozeman where we had dinner. It was already getting dark and the rain had stopped as we came upon the outskirts of Livingston.

Suddenly, Drew said, "There they are."

I looked into the distance where he pointed. The dark gray sky had cleared a bit, and snaggy tips of mountains that did resemble teeth emerged as we rounded a bend, still snowcapped on the highest peaks and expanding off towards the southeast. They seemed impossibly high.

I whistled.

"Yeah," he said softly. "I know."

We followed the Yellowstone River for the next couple of hours, then headed south at the town of Joliet through endless fields and finally entered the one main street of Red Lodge at the base of the mountains. His aunt and uncle's farm was ten miles further on, heading towards Billings, and down a long gravel track. It was well past ten when we arrived, and the farmhouse was dark, the barn was dark, all the outbuildings were dark and still. I parked off the turnaround under a maple tree. We stepped outside where light rain had resumed. I followed Drew between the house and a barnyard with its sweet-sour stink of manure and the sound of cows' tails swishing from inside the barn. He led us to a little silver tag-along trailer where the back yard met the fields alongside a big mounded vegetable garden. We ducked inside the trailer and both had to stay a little stooped to avoid the ceiling. Drew switched on a light over a small kitchenette sink. All the little windows had been slid open, but the cramped space smelled moldy.

"Here we are." He grinned. "Home sweet home."

🙠🙠🙠🙠

Drew was up early before me the next morning. The rain had stopped, but the sky was still a sheet of gray. I headed towards the barn where I could hear Drew's voice along with an older man's. They were walking toward me together in the dim light when I came inside, each carrying a tall pail of milk thicker and more yellow than what was sold in the store. They set their pails down when they got to me. The air was already warm, the air thick with humidity.

Drew said, "Uncle Onni, this is my friend, Adam."

"Pleased to meet you," he said and stuck out his hand. I shook it. He was a small man in his late-sixties with a dusting of white hair. He wore wire-rimmed spectacles stretched over his ears, coveralls, and black rubber boots. He smiled and said, "You got up at the right time. We just finished. Elli should have breakfast ready."

I recognized the faint Finnish accent that Drew had told me about and that he said neither his aunt or uncle had completely lost even after forty-five years. A few minutes later, the three of us were seated around a table in the farmhouse's dining room eating from plates heaped with scrambled eggs, pork chops topped with brown sauce and scallions, rutabaga casserole, and rye toast. Elli didn't sit with us, but busied herself back and forth from the kitchen bringing more food, refilling coffee cups from a percolator, and clearing dishes. She was the same slight size as her husband, her gray hair tight in a braid, and wore a faded, flowered housedress. She moved quickly and with purpose.

"This is delicious," I told her.

She gave me a small smile.

"Those rutabagas came from her garden." Onni waved his folk towards the back yard. "And the pork chops were running around the barnyard last fall. We harvested the rye, too. She bakes new bread every morning."

I chewed appreciatively and nodded to them both.

"But you wouldn't often have eggs for breakfast in Finland," Onni said.

"We've adapted. Maybe piirakka or cranberry pudding instead."

His wife kissed his cheek and scurried back into the kitchen. A rumble of thunder came from the near distance. Onni turned in its direction and shook his head. Drew and I turned and looked, too, until he resumed eating and we followed his lead. A few minutes later, the first raindrops splattered outside, and soon after, a soft downpour began.

"Shucks," Drew said.

The corners of his uncle's mouth had turned down.

Drew asked, "How much have you been able to bring in?"

"Well, all the timothy." He spoke quietly. "There was a little dry spell at the end of June when we got that. And most of the rye a couple weeks later. But the big fields of alfalfa are still uncut. And that's where most of the money is. We've sold it all, if we can get to it." He set his fork down and gazed outside the window. "We aren't going to do any today, that's for sure. So, why don't the two of you get Leo to take you fishing up in the mountains and bring us home dinner?"

As if on cue, the front door opened, and a man about thirty and a head taller than Onni came inside. He closed the door and stomped his work boots on the mat. He wore jeans, a short-sleeved chambray shirt, a well-worn ball cap with a John Deere insignia on the front, and several days of stubble across his cheeks and chin. He had the same blue eyes as Elli and Onni's small smudge of mouth.

"Leo," Drew said. A big grin had spread across his face as he stood. The two of them embraced, clapping each other on the back.

"Son," Onni said. "I was just saying that you ought to take Drew and his friend fishing today. It's supposed to rain again steady, so we won't be seeing the fields."

"But I was going to help you with that machinery."

Onni made a face and waved him off. "Nothing I can't do myself."

Leo's own grin grew. "Well, you don't have to convince me." He looked my way. "So, you're Adam."

I nodded and we shook hands.

"Take them up West Fork Road to Wild Bill Lake," Onni said. "I heard they're biting there or any of those tributaries along that stretch."

His son nodded and said, "Sounds good." His eyebrows lifted. "Fellas?"

"Sure," Drew said, and I nodded, too.

"I'll go get the gear ready." Leo gave Drew a last clap on the shoulder and walked out the way he'd come.

The three of us returned to our breakfasts. After we finished, Drew asked if he could make a collect phone call. His uncle said sure and pointed to the phone on the wall just inside the doorframe that joined the dining room and kitchen. Onni and I sipped our coffee while he dialed. Drew stood just behind my shoulder, close enough that I could hear the operator say that she had a collect call for Claire Douglass. I heard a young woman's voice respond that Claire wasn't there and decline the charges. Drew hung up, and I watched him frown.

"That's funny," he said. "It's hardly past seven. She's never up this early."

I looked away, sipping at my coffee cup.

❦ ❦ 🪷 ❦ ❦

Two hours later, Drew, Leo, and I were spaced out on a stretch of champagne-clear stream that was bracketed on both sides by boulders and tall pines. We all wore chest waders and ponchos that Leo had provided and were casting with small lures against a dark, deep bank littered here and there with fallen trees. The hoods of our ponchos were up against the light rain.

We worked our way upstream as the morning went on. Leo got the first hit a little before ten. He set the hook with a little yelp, and we saw his rod bend into a quivering arch. Drew and I brought our own lines in and watched him fight the fish for a few minutes, backing it up to a short, pebbly sandbar. Drew netted it when it was almost to shore. After Leo dislodged the lure, he lifted the fish by a gill. It was fifteen-inch rainbow, its firm belly glistening with color even in the rain.

"That's a nice fish," Drew said.

"It'll do," his cousin replied, but the look on his face showed pride.

Drew asked, "Just rainbows here, then?"

"Mostly. But they're getting some brownies, too."

He bent down, whacked the trout's head with a palm-sized rock, and the fish went still. He dropped it in the creel that was strapped around his waist, closed its flap, and we waded back out into the cold, fast-moving water.

❦ ❦ 🪷 ❦ ❦

By one, the rain had stopped and a corner of sun had peeked around the jumble of clouds. We'd each caught fish by then and had accumulated a handful of rainbows and one fat brown trout in the creel.

For lunch, we sat leaning against flattened boulders at a spot where the stream entered a wide meadow fronting a wall of mountains that climbed almost vertically into the sky. The meadow's ankle-high grass was deep green and sprinkled with wildflowers, shimmering wet and wafting a fresh scent in the brightening sunlight. The stream narrowed through the center of it, flat, quiet, and gentle-flowing. Several birds lifted from the grass and flew off towards the mountains disappearing into the mass of granite. I couldn't remember seeing anything lovelier. We ate the thick sandwiches, sipped the ice tea that Elli had packed, and looked out over the expanse in silence.

"Well," I finally said to Leo, "you live in quite a place."

He nodded. "Yeah, we're lucky."

"I told you," Drew said to me.

"You were right." I nodded slowly, gazing back and forth. "You were definitely right."

We were quiet again as the early afternoon continued to warm. We'd taken off our ponchos. A little steam had begun to lift off the meadow.

Drew pointed towards the sun that had emerged fully between clouds. "You think this will last?"

Leo shrugged. "Not supposed to, but you never know." He balled up the wax paper his sandwich had been in. "What say we walk back and head up to Wild Bill Lake? Try our luck at the intake. We've done okay there before."

"I remember," Drew said, his hopeful eyes widening.

❧❧

We only caught another couple of fish at the lake before calling it a day when it began raining again mid-afternoon. We packed the fish in a cooler of ice in the back of Leo's pickup and drove into Red Lodge where he stopped at one its handful of bars. All of them along that lone street looked the same: narrow, long, with open doors dark against the daylight and heat. We drank beer while Drew and Leo caught up on family news. Drew's father had followed Onni over a couple of years after he and Elli immigrated; he'd helped on the farm for a short time before marrying Drew's mother and moving to the Bay Area where her friend's husband had the house painting business.

At one point, Leo asked Drew about Claire. I knew she'd come with him there on a few of his trips over the years.

"She's good," Drew said. "Taking summer classes right now. She transferred to our school."

"That's what I heard." Leo took a sip of beer. "So how long have you two been together now?"

Drew moved his fingers counting. "Seven years. No, eight."

"Hell, that's longer than most marriages."

They both chuckled and clinked bottles. We were sitting together on stools at the bar, Drew in the middle. Leo leaned forward to look over at me. "Adam," he said, "you know Claire?"

"Sure."

"What do you think?"

I nodded a couple of times, then said, "She's great. Terrific."

"Too good for this big lunk."

Leo cuffed his cousin on the arm. The two of them laughed some more. I swallowed off the rest my beer and signaled the bartender for another round.

⟡

We got back to the farm a little after five. Leo pulled his truck up in front of his mobile home that I hadn't noticed when we drove in the night before. It was tucked back onto a little patch of grass next to a tall rectangular stack of hay the size of an eighteen-wheeler. The stack stood just up the gravel track from the barn with tarps across the top that were cinched down with a collection of ropes and bungee cords.

Leo's wife, Debbie, came out to meet us with their baby boy on a hip. She was big-boned and dressed in shorts and a tank top. She clapped her hands when she saw the fish we'd caught, and the boy did the same. Leo lifted his son into the air and nuzzled his tummy with the tip of his nose; the boy squealed with delight. The rain had become a drizzle, but hadn't stopped since we'd left the lake.

The three of them joined us at the farmhouse for dinner. Along with the fish, Elli prepared beetroot salad and boiled potatoes from the garden. After dinner, the men all headed to the sauna that was built against the far side of the barn. Even at eight o'clock, the temperature was still in the mid-seventies, but Drew had told me that it was a nightly tradition. Onni ladled water liberally and often over the heated rocks inside the close, cedar-paneled room where we all sat sweating on benches with towels draped across our thighs. He told me that in the winter, they'd sometimes go back and forth outside to jump in the snow.

Afterwards, we took turns showering in the two stalls that adjoined the sauna, changed into clean clothes, and gathered in the living room again for rhubarb pie and cold, fresh milk. It was a little past nine when Leo and his family left. Before we went to our trailer, Drew asked if he could use the phone again.

"Sure," Onni said. "But don't worry about reversing the charges. Just go ahead and make your call. Say hi to Claire for us."

We all said goodnight and the two of them climbed the stairs to their bedroom. I walked out through the kitchen door leaving Drew alone inside. It was still drizzling, but there was a sprinkling of stars in the wide, wide sky off to the east. I hadn't even completely undressed before Drew came into the trailer.

"Hell," he said. "Not there again. Another housemate answered this time."

He sat down on the edge of his own bed. He lowered his head and clasped his hands between his knees. I thought again then of telling him something about what I'd seen in our kitchen the night before we left. But I was hoping that it would be over by the time we got back, that he and Claire would be together again, and that he'd never have to know anything had happened. My reasoning, as faulty as it may have been, was that it would be better not to upset him with something he might not ever have to know about.

He looked up at me. I just shrugged, continued undressing down to my boxers, and climbed under the sheet. I left the light for him to turn off. The rain falling on the tin roof sounded like tiny grains of sand.

❧❦❧

Except for the twitter of birds and the rustle of a stiff breeze, I awoke the next morning to stillness. When I opened my eyes, I could see milky-blue sky above the line of pink dawn through the window above my bed. I sat up, rubbed my eyes, and smiled.

As I came into the farmhouse kitchen, the radio on the counter was playing low. I joined Onni and Drew at the dining room table. They were already eating breakfast; Leo was there, too, drinking coffee. There was excitement on Onni's face as well as his son's. Elli put a plate of food down in front of me and poured me coffee. I thanked her and said, "So, the weather .

. . it's good, right?"

"Damn right, it is," Leo said. His grin showed crooked teeth. "Radio report says it should keep up like this for about three days before we get more rain. That's not much of a window, but it's supposed to stay hot and this breeze will help a lot."

"Let's finish eating and get all the machinery checked over," Onni said between chews. "Grease up what I didn't get to yesterday. I finished the mower, all the cutter bar parts. But we need to do the rake and the baler. And the big conveyer. Drew, you and Adam walk up to our neighbor, Hank's. He's done bringing in the little bit of acreage he keeps for hay and is just waiting on his wheat. He can't help us because he busted his wrist, but he's lending us a tractor with a hay wagon. That will speed up our operation. The two of you bring it over. Called him earlier and he's expecting you."

"The Culbert twins ready like last year?" Leo asked.

His father nodded and took his last bite. "I called their dad, too. They'll work the conveyer here and build the big stacks again; Deb can help when she's not tending to the baby. Drew and Adam will be on the hay wagons; Elli will shuttle those back and forth with my pickup. If all goes well and the fields dry out enough, you and I can try cutting a few acres around noon, rake before dinner, and see what we've got. If it's dry enough, then you'll run the baler tomorrow morning while I cut and rake ahead of you. Providing the weather holds, that is." He looked out the window. The curtains there blew inside the room on the warm, sunlit breeze.

Elli's voice came from the kitchen. We heard her say, "God willing, it does."

🙠 🌼 🙢

When we got back to the farm later that morning with the loaned tractor and hay wagon, Onni sent Drew and me out in his truck to repair some barbed wire fencing that the cows had damaged. That was something Drew had done before, so I just held wire taut or fence poles in place while he did the rest. We got back to the farmhouse about the same time as Onni and Leo returned from cutting their trial acres.

After lunch, we helped Elli weed the garden and harvest a few vegetables, then drove into Red Lodge to the hardware store to pick up baling wire and a few other supplies. The heat had stayed intense with a dry, furnace-like breeze all day, so Drew made a turn on the way back on an empty side track where we stopped, stripped off our clothes, and took a dip in one of the irrigation ditches.

A little before five, Onni and Leo chugged off in their tractor with the rake hitched behind them. I helped Drew with the evening milking, though I wasn't much assistance because I could rarely get the right tension pulling the teats. The cows quickly became restless with me, so I mostly lugged the pails Drew filled to the holding tank, tossed new hay into the feeding troughs, and fed the pigs and chickens.

As we were finishing about an hour and a half later, we heard the tractor returning. We walked out in front of the barn and watched Onni and Leo approach. Onni drove, and Leo stood on the running board next to him holding on to the back of his father's seat. Their faces were in shadow, but both gave us a thumb's up; Onni shook his.

❧ ❦ ❧

Drew took the first shower after the sauna that night so he could try calling Claire again. We were all heading off to bed right away because of the early start we had planned for the next morning. But Drew was already in the trailer after I finished showering, sitting against the wall on his bed writing in a notebook. He looked up at me as I closed the screen door.

I asked, "Any luck?"

He shook his head. "No, same as the last two calls. I know she has midterm papers due, so she's probably spending all her time up at the university library. She likes to do her studying there."

I nodded and said, "Sure.

"So I'm writing her a letter instead." He showed me his open notebook page. Even glancing at it quickly, I could see the words "miss" and "love" written several times.

I nodded again, then undressed, and got in bed under the sheet. I turned away from him and could hear the scratch of his pen on the paper.

"That light bother you?" he asked.

"Don't worry about it."

I heard him resume writing and pulled the pillow up over the side of my face.

❧ ❦ ❧

By eleven that next morning, we'd finished baling most of the trial acres. Once Drew and I finished stacking and filling a wagon, Leo stopped the tractor and used a yoke stand they'd welded together under the wagon arm to exchange the full one with the empty on the back of the big pickup that Elli drove. Then she shuttled the load back to the farm where the teenaged twins and Debbie were building the first big stack, and an hour or so later, we'd do the same thing over again. We could hear Onni cutting in another field not far away, but couldn't see him.

The day was even hotter than the previous one. The rectangular bales were just short of completely dry, so were heavier than normal, sixty or seventy pounds each. They gave off a musty, dank odor. The work was hard, but had a steady rhythm to it. The cut and raked alfalfa lay in neat, straight rows about two feet wide, and those rows lay the width of the mower apart in the stubble. Leo kept the tractor crawling forward over the center of the row, and the baler behind him collected the hay, compressed it into a rectangular block, wrapped and secured it in baling wire, and then pushed it onto the teeth of a short conveyer belt that inched it along to the where it met the hay wagon. Drew and I took turns meeting the bales there, swinging our baling hooks into the middle of their two short sides and lugging them back to the next spot on the hay wagon. From field to its place on the wagon, a bale took about twenty seconds to finish, which, except for an occasional pull off the water cooler Elli kept refilling for us, kept Drew and me in constant, plodding motion. We built crisscrossed rows with gaps of an inch or so between each bale to allow for air flow and further drying because of the extra moisture. The stack reached as high as the rear framing and then descended by a row each like stairs as the stack approached the front of the wagon. I'd sweated through my T-shirt before we filled the first wagon and the sun hadn't even reached the tops of the sycamore trees in the distance.

We stopped for the lunch Elli brought out about noon. She, Onni, and Leo went off in the truck to check on the how dry the hay was in the first field that had been cut and raked that morning. Drew and I found a little spot of shade on the side of the tractor and huddled together in it sitting against the running board to eat. Before he lowered himself beside me, Drew poured ice water over the back of his head, shuddered, and shook it.

We ate slowly, looking out over the field's remaining unbaled rows in the stubble. The mountains loomed off in the distance, craggy, stretching up into a cloudless blue sky. Neither of us spoke until we'd finished our sandwiches when Drew said, "You know, I really love her."

I glanced his way. He was looking straight out at the fields and mountains. He nodded a few times, then said, "This spring and summer have really cemented things for me. First, being together at school, then apart when I went home to work and she stayed in Santa Cruz." Without warning, he cupped his hands around his mouth and shouted, "Claire, I miss you so damn much!"

There was no echo afterwards, just the soft, hot breeze and the sound of him blowing out a long breath. He turned and looked at me. "I'm going to propose to her." He said it evenly. "I am. As soon as we get back. I bought a ring just before the term ended. It's in my bedroom bureau in Santa Cruz."

I felt myself staring and my eyebrows beginning to knit together. I turned away, shook my head, and mumbled, "Wow."

"It's time," he said quickly. "Hell, you heard Leo in the bar . . . we've been together longer than most people stay married. We both graduate in June, so then we'll be ready for our next chapter."

A feeling of dread had spread up through me. I heard myself ask, "Do you really think you're ready? I mean, you're barely twenty-one."

"We're older than our parents were when they got engaged."

I looked over at him. The usual hopefulness was in his eyes, but there was certainty there, too. I said, "You're sure about this."

He nodded. "Never been surer about anything."

I was vaguely aware of Onni's truck emerging then and approaching over a rise in the track, a long ribbon of dust trailing behind it.

❧❧❧

We didn't quit that day until the sun was beginning to set behind the mountains. Onni said he wanted to squeeze every dry minute we had out of the window in the weather. I'd never been more bone tired. It was after eight when we sat down to dinner. Elli told us that the last weather report on the radio said rain might be returning sooner than first thought, so we skipped the sauna because Onni wanted to start even earlier in the morning. Drew and I showered in the stalls next to the sauna, and I headed straight to bed, while he went into the farmhouse to try to make another call to Claire. He came into the trailer shortly afterwards, too quickly for the call to have been successful. I was glad to already be in bed and turned away. I kept my breathing slow and deep, feigning sleep.

From our spots on the hay wagon, Drew and I watched clouds slowly gather way off towards Bozeman throughout the next afternoon, but didn't hear the first distant tumble of thunder until after seven o'clock. By that time, we'd finished baling more than three-quarters of the remaining fields. All the cutting and raking was done, and Onni had joined us to help on the hay wagon. He looked briefly in the direction of the sound, then lowered his head and went back to work.

Perhaps forty-five minutes later, we were changing hay wagons, and a flash of lightning split the sky over the westernmost mountains. We all saw it except for Leo, who was fastening the clap on the ball of the pickup truck's hitch.

Elli stood with her hands on her hips and began counting quietly after the lightning flash. She got to eight before the next round of thunder tumbled. The clouds over the mountains had darkened, and several of the larger ones were heavy-bellied.

"Getting closer," Onni said. "We might have another hour. With the mountains, maybe a little more." He looked at Drew and me. "You boys okay with a late dinner? Even later, I mean."

We nodded.

"The twins and Deb are keeping pace," Elli said. "They're ahead, actually. I'll have them take turns eating when I get back."

She left, and we kept at it. The sunset hadn't been visible because the storm was coming from the west, but the clouds there briefly streaked reddish-purple against the mountains giving them the appearance of a bruise. They quickly darkened again. A few stars had begun to dot the moonless eastern sky. The temperature continued to inch lower.

Elli brought a camping lantern with her when she came for her next exchange. Onni turned it on and hung it from the side of the wagon's framing. A flock of birds flew off low over the fields on the cool breeze that had risen from the west. Another streak of lightening lit the sky, followed shortly by the roll of thunder. The clouds now obscured most of the mountains and seemed to be funneling around them where I imagined Joliet to be.

Once the wagons had been exchanged, Onni turned to Elli and said, "Don't bother coming out again. We'll get what we can for a little longer, then bring what we have back with the tractor."

"Be safe," she said, "Don't push it."

We all followed Onni's eyes over the remaining fields. There were perhaps a dozen acres left, their neat, straight rows of cut alfalfa silent and still in the gathering darkness.

He turned back to his wife and said, "Pull that load into the barn, cover the big stack, and then run the twins home. We'll be along."

Elli's truck wobbled away, the full wagon rocking in the stubble, and we continued baling and stacking. Leo had turned on the tractor's headlights. We weren't even able to finish another full acre before the next round of lightning and thunder came, closer still. Onni shouted and called Leo's name. His son's head swiveled, and Onni made a slashing motion across his throat and pointed towards the farmhouse.

We started our slow way back. The three of us sat on the last row of bales we'd fashioned, while Leo rumbled us along. It was almost completely dark, just a milky streak on the horizon above the sycamores. The lantern jangled and threw a dim, bouncing globe of light over the side of the wagon. We felt the first raindrops splat when we could just make out the farmhouse's lamplit windows a few hundred yards away.

It was after ten-thirty by the time we'd finished eating and showering, too late for Drew to try another phone call. We both hit the sack right away. Each time I awoke during the night, the rain was a strong, steady clatter on the trailer's roof.

❧ ❧ ❧

Neither of us got up to help with the early morning milking or feeding. By the time we came into the farmhouse for breakfast, Elli told us Onni and Leo had headed out to the fields in an empty pickup truck; they had pitchforks and a tarp with them and wanted to see if they could find hay dry enough underneath the remaining cut rows to use for feeding the cows that day. It was still raining, but more lightly. The forecast, Elli told us, was for it to continue without interruption for at least the next few days.

After breakfast, Drew made another fruitless call trying to reach Claire, then we headed back to the trailer. We both stretched out on our backs on the beds.

I said, "I hurt all over. I hurt in places I never even knew I had."

I heard Drew chuckle. Then he sat up suddenly and said, "Look, why don't we start driving home? I know it's a few days earlier than we planned, but there's nothing special left here that we can help with, and I'm not interested in camping in the rain." He set his jaw and looked at me with those eyes. "That way I'll have time to go over to Santa Cruz with you and surprise Claire. Do the deed."

My stomach sank. I looked at him as evenly as possible and tried to think of a way to object. But I couldn't come up with anything, so I just said, "Fine with me."

🙾 🌺 🙾

So that's what we did. We packed and waited until Onni and Leo got back, then exchanged hugs and goodbyes with all of them under the maple tree out of the rain. They made a special fuss out of thanking me and inviting me back. Elli gave us a big lunch she'd packed. It was about eleven when we made a last wave to them from the end of the turnaround and headed up the track towards the highway.

It rained all the rest of the day. We finally left it behind for good towards dusk in Pocatello, where we stopped for dinner. Then it was mostly fields, high desert, and small towns across Idaho and Nevada throughout that next section of the night. We took turns driving and reclined the passenger seat as far as it would go to sleep. We didn't talk much. I kept chasing away the dim sense of dread that never completely left me. I tried to stay hopeful that things had somehow resolved themselves and ended with Clare and Eric back home while we'd been gone. I didn't know what else to do.

We entered the Sierra Nevada mountains a little before midnight, made good time over the pass, and were in Sacramento by three. We were early enough to beat most of the morning commuter traffic through the Bay Area, and got on Highway 17 at Los Gatos for the last stretch over the hill around seven just as the sun was coming up.

We were both awake then, Drew in the passenger seat. We watched the familiar stretches of dense trees and other markers on both sides of the car. When we were going over the summit, Drew asked, "What do you think about us keeping our own last names? Lots of couples do that now when they get married."

I gave him a quick glance. "Never gave it much thought, I guess."

"Well, I'm pretty sure that's what Clare will want to do. Or maybe we'll do that hyphenated thing and use both."

I nodded and kept my eyes on the road. A few more minutes passed before he said, "The ring just has a tiny diamond. That's all I could afford."

I paused, then said, "I don't think the size of it matters."

"You don't?"

"Nah." I shook my head, but still didn't look over at him.

The commute going the other direction towards San Jose had already begun, the cars there crawling along. I almost wished we were in it so something would slow us down. But we drove uninhibited past Scotts Valley and into Santa Cruz where I got off the freeway and onto Chestnut Street. It wasn't quite seven-thirty and there were few people out downtown. I turned onto Locust and saw our house midway up the block. "There it is," I thought to myself. "Here we go."

I pulled up in an open spot at the curb a few cars down from our house, but kept the engine idling. Drew had already turned in his seat and was stuffing things in his rucksack. As he did, I looked through the side window of our house and saw the back of Claire go by. She was carrying two steaming mugs and was wearing Eric's basketball practice jersey. I knew it was his because of his uniform number. The bottom of it didn't quite cover her bare buttocks. Through the living room window, I could see the glow of the television and the lower part of Eric, naked, too, on the couch where she was heading. The couch faced the front door. I knew the sound of the television would cover Drew's footsteps on the porch, and the door was cracked ajar. There was nothing to interrupt the encounter that they were about to have. I swallowed and shook my head.

Drew yanked his rucksack and sleeping bag over the seat onto his lap. He glanced once at the house, then back at me, his eyes happy and expectant. "So, turn off the car," he told me. "Let's head in."

I hesitated, then said, "I think I'll run and get gas first. Almost on empty."

He shrugged, then opened the door. He gave me one of his grins and said, "Suit yourself, big guy."

Then he was out of the car, and the door closed behind him. I waited just long enough to see him get to the front steps and then accelerated up the street. My heart thudded away as I sped through the neighborhood. I ground my teeth and swore out loud. I didn't know where I would go or what I would do except that I was sure I didn't want to be back in that house for a long time. I thought about going down to the beach, diving in the ocean, and then heading up to the university gym to shower and change clothes. Maybe get breakfast at the cafeteria up there and then take a hike on one of the fire roads through the woods behind campus. I wasn't sure. The only thing I was certain of was that I'd let my friend walk into that house unprepared in any way. And unlike the previous days, I'd made that decision knowing without doubt what awaited him when he pushed through that front door. I'd let him do that. I'd done nothing to prevent it.

🦅🌸🦅

As I said, I'm sixty-two, and I've had my share of regrets. Some involve acts of commission and others of omission. This was one of the latter kind, and I still think of it from time to time. I can't quite understand why it holds such a special place inside me, but it does. I wish I could do it over, make a different decision. But I can't. That hay, as the expression goes, is in barn. It's been there a long time now. It's never going back into the field. It can't be undone.

THE COW JUMPED OVER THE MOON

I'd just celebrated my fifty-ninth birthday by selling my graphic arts and website design business in Seattle to a competitor across town. With what I got from the sale and that of my house, I was able to downsize to a little condo outside of Reno and sock the rest away. It had been 1976, almost four decades earlier, since I'd last been there doing volunteer work after college and developed a fondness for the area. The nicer weather certainly figured in my decision. As did the fact that it didn't really matter where I lived because I'd begun doing almost all my work remotely. But I'd be lying if I didn't admit that getting away from things was also a major factor; while almost fifteen years had passed since my wife and our daughter had died in their rafting accident, that painful memory still lingered never far away.

So, I retained a dozen or so of my most longstanding clients, drove down to Reno to meet the movers, and left most of the boxes unpacked inside my new home. Then I flew back to Seattle to finalize the transfer of the business, make a last visit to the cemetery, and sell my office furniture. I'd just finished that final task when I got a call from Nick Phillips.

Nick was one of those few longtime clients I was holding onto, and I'd grown to know him pretty well over the years. On a kind of whim, he'd started his fishing lodge on a little island about four hundred miles up the British Columbian coast from Vancouver. He and his wife had previously run a successful government lobbying firm in Olympia, and he told me he'd gotten tired of dealing with all the political shenanigans and maneuvering day in and day out. He said he just asked himself one sleepless night how he could make a living doing something he loved and the fishing idea put itself together.

He looked around and found that remote spot advertised on the internet. It had begun as an Irish potato farm, had later become a kind of hippie commune, and had finally sat empty for a number of years. His plan was to create a combination fishing and first-class dining/lodging experience largely designed for corporate outings of several days at a time. He thought that equation would lend itself to a steady stream of primarily repeat customers who could foot an expensive bill without blinking. His idea had worked out even better than he imagined.

The place started as a group of old buildings on a hill above the water. He turned the main farmhouse into a dining area with some spaces for relaxing and recreation, built a cluster of small log cabins that were rustic but well appointed, repaired an old stone and mortar sauna, and added a couple of hot tubs and decks. Then he bought a few secondhand boats set-up for fishing, extended the dock, hired a few locals as guides and college kids from Port McNeil on summer break for staff, brought up a chef from San Francisco for the season, and opened for business. He had some established contacts from his past work associations to get started, and things went much as he'd planned from there. He'd added a new wrinkle here and there and had maintained a mostly full calendar of visits for up to fifteen guests at a time from late April to mid-September ever since. I figured that after expenses, he cleared a couple hundred thousand a season.

Nick was a big one for working trades for business. He exchanged all his wine and liquor for portions of trips and did the same thing to reduce costs with the floatplane company he used out of Seattle. He'd been trying to swing a deal with me for years. Finally, shortly before I sold out, I agreed to do some last-minute changes on his brochure and website on the promise of a fishing trip at his lodge anytime I wanted. The truth was I'd spent a couple of summers many years before working on commercial fishing boats in Alaska to help pay for college, so I'd pretty much caught all the fish I was interested in for a lifetime.

I'd forgotten about our deal entirely until the morning the furniture had been removed from my Seattle office. My cell phone rang as I was locking the door behind me; it was Nick.

"Listen, buddy," he said. "I've got a couple of open spots on my last trip of the season and I want you to come up on that freebie. Quick three-day. We're killing the chinooks right now."

"Nick, I'm leaving for Reno tomorrow." I rubbed the back of my neck. "All my stuff is there. Just finished taking care of the last few things here in Seattle for the move."

"Perfect. You be standing tall with my other guests on the float plane dock in Renton tomorrow afternoon at two. I'll even pay for your flight; my account's still outstanding, isn't it? Bill me."

"Jesus, Nick," I said. However, the idea wasn't without some appeal. Over the last several days, I'd felt a strange loneliness about the move and starting over in Reno. I looked out the office hallway window where the familiar layer of low, gray clouds drifted over the city.

Nick said, "We've been working together a lot of years, partner. You don't jump on this, you might never come. What the hell you got waiting for you down in Reno that's so urgent?"

I said, "I guess nothing."

"You're damn right. I'll lend you whatever gear and clothes you need and see you tomorrow then. I'll be sure they have a drink waiting for you at the float plane dock. Send me that bill." He hung up before I could respond.

So, shortly before two that next afternoon I found myself in a little waiting room off the floatplane hangar next to Boeing Field. I was standing with about ten employees of a Midwest beer distributorship and a few of their top clients, as well as a surgeon from Medina. The beer folks were all drinking cocktails from red plastic travelers and laughing together near the counter. I stood off to the side trying to make conversation with the surgeon, a stern, well-dressed man who was going along comp, too, in exchange for shearing the alpacas that were Nick's newest addition to the lodge. The surgeon told me he'd grown up on a sheep farm in New Zealand, though I could detect no accent. Apparently, he'd gotten to know Nick after doing some repairs on his shoulder. For all I knew, Nick might have been paying off part of a medical bill by having him join the trip, as well; I wouldn't have put it past him.

Three hours later, we were climbing out of floatplanes onto the Phillips Lodge dock in late afternoon sunshine where a pretty college-aged girl distributed lodge caps from a basket as we disembarked and Nick met us with a hearty greeting. He was about ten years younger than me, a big bear of a man.

When I stepped onto the dock, Nick gave me one of his customary claps on the shoulder and growled, "I'm glad you made it. About damn time. This is great." Then he moved on to his paying guests.

I looked over the vista I'd seen many times before on his brochure and website. The lodge and surrounding cabins sat forty or so yards up the sloping, grassy hillside that was dotted with oak and pine trees. Dense spruce forest stood behind it. A wide garden of raised beds in front of the lodge held vegetables and flowers, adding color against the green and weathered gray wood. A small corral enclosed by a new split rail fence ran along one side of the property in which several alpacas grazed on the grass; it led to an open barn and some outbuildings that looked like they'd been retrofitted into staff quarters. A scattering of old farm equipment had been left to rust for effect and had grown over here and there with ivy.

A couple of smiling young men dressed in chinos and lodge sweatshirts, who we would later get to know as fishing guides, begun shuttling our bags to the cabins. We followed the hostess past potted geraniums on the sides of the dock up the hill to the wide deck that surrounded the lodge. Nick caught up to me on the way and gave me another squeeze on the shoulder. He told me he looked forward to seeing me but knew I'd understand that he had to spend most of his time his customers. I told him not to worry and that I appreciated his hospitality.

Nick gathered us together on the deck while one of the college girls passed out flumes of champagne from a tray. He welcomed us with a rousing toast to a good catch and then went on to explain which cabins we'd been assigned to, a little about the lodge, the surrounding area, and our trip's itinerary. He told us the immediate plan was to socialize a bit, get unpacked and then return for dinner at seven.

After I finished my champagne, I went and settled into my cabin. It was top-notch inside. From its window, I could see Nick and a couple of guides readying the fishing boats at the dock for the morning. Their movements and expressions had a punctuation to them that seemed to border on practiced choreography.

A little after seven, I was seated at a large round table in the lodge's dining room with the others. Nick gave us the weather and fishing report for the next morning and told us they'd be providing us with wake-up calls at 5:00 a.m.. Next, he had the college girls hold up the bottles of white and red wine that were going to be served with dinner and gave a description of each. Finally, he led us in applause after he introduced the chef who came bounding up the stairs to explain each course for the night's fare. It was about then that I realized that fishing was not necessarily the primary ingredient in the trip's experience, but that Nick intended pleasant and memorable moments for the guests regardless of how successful the sport might be. It seemed to me on his part both contrived and inspired.

After dinner, most of the party moved into the adjacent game room for billiards, cigars, and cognac. I walked down the hill to the shore. The tide was out, the beach full of kelp and large, barnacle-encrusted rocks. The water moving among them made the sound of children's blocks knocking together. The sky was stained purple over the mountains and black above, full of stars. I looked at things and thought about my life, the longer part behind me and the shorter one ahead. I watched the red traveling light of a boat out in the channel heading across the water toward Port McNeil. I looked up at the sky and hoped it might turn cold enough for the Northern Lights, though I thought it unlikely. I hadn't seen them since I'd been in Alaska. A few minutes later, I turned and headed up to bed.

That next morning before full dawn, we were trolling slowly along the shoreline of an area known as Mitchell Bay, four of us to a boat, everyone wearing a lodge poncho and cap adorned with the logo I'd designed. A guide on each boat worked the trolling motor and tended the lines and outriggers. The early morning's air was cool and damp. As the mountains to the west on Vancouver Island emerged in the muffled light, big bloated clouds hung against them.

I was on an open boat with the surgeon and two area managers from the distributorship. The three of them sat drinking coffee together on the bow seats up front while I leaned against the stern with the guide. We motored almost imperceptibly about two hundred feet from a long narrow shore of crushed rock and driftwood; the other boats had moved off in their own directions. Stands of straight pines behind the beach led up the hillside towards the top of the island. Except for the soft burbling of the trolling motor and the mumble of voices from the front of the boat, it was quiet, still.

Our guide's name was Jim. I didn't remember seeing him the evening before. I figured him for about my age. Like me, he had moist, weary eyes and a stubble beard. His cap was the only one on the boat not advertising the lodge and sat crooked and worn on his head. He wore faded jeans, an old brown twill shirt, and high black rubber boots.

"So," he said to me. "You're Nick's advertising guy."

I told him all I did was design his brochure and website. We bobbed along for a while watching the lines. I asked him how long he'd been on the island.

In his quiet voice he told me, "Pretty near forty years now. I did some commercial fishing up on the outside for a while."

"You from here?"

He looked at me evenly for a moment. His eyes were as blue-green as my own and crinkled a bit at the edges. He said, "No."

"Been guiding for Nick long?"

He nodded. "Since he started. What's that, seventeen years, I guess? Got tired of fishing for myself. Pretty much phasing out of guiding now, too. Only go out anymore when he's short. I'm his handyman mostly, and caretaker after the season."

"What's involved with that?"

"Not a hell of a lot." He laughed. "Now with the new alpacas, there'll be a little something more, I guess." He stopped, studied the tip of one pole, then jumped to it. He pulled it from its holder, jerking in one motion, and shouted, "Fish on! Get those other lines up!"

We all scrambled into the drill Jim had rehearsed with us before leaving. We'd drawn numbers and the surgeon had the first fish, so the rest of us got the other lines out of the way and huddled off to watch him bring it in. Jim stood next to him and said things like, "Perfect . . . keep the tip up . . . easy . . . let it run."

With the way Jim had set the hook and the first long deep dive of the fish, I was pretty sure the surgeon could do just about anything and not lose it. The beer guys cheered him on, and as I watched him grunting in his pressed jeans and alligator boots, I decided that I'd forget how ludicrous the whole thing was and just try to enjoy myself.

After a bit, Jim was able to net the surgeon's salmon and lift it into the boat. We all whooped and hollered while the surgeon beamed. Jim took his picture holding the fish with the surgeon's cell phone.

The tide had already turned and none of us caught anything more that morning. We headed back to the lodge for lunch. All the boats arrived at the dock at about the same time. Nick met us there and led us in a fish weighing ceremony. Seven fish total had been caught. We all clapped for the biggest fish, which turned out to be the surgeon's.

After lunch, most of the group headed back out on the boats to deeper water to try jigging for halibut and bottom fish. A couple returned to their cabins to rest; a few headed to the sauna and hot tubs. I changed into my own poncho and went for a walk. I wandered along a path through the back of the property and came out on a gravel road that followed the coastline to the north along a bluff. It had begun to rain very lightly. Aside from the forest, the only things I passed were a couple of abandoned spots that looked like they were once small attempts at farming. One building had an undulating roofline that seemed like it had been built that way intentionally; a rusted iron half-moon with a cow leaping over it was nailed above the door. The road was empty. I thought that perhaps it circled the island. The only sound was of the water in the channel, the soft fall of the rain, and my footsteps in the gravel.

I turned around after a half hour or so and retraced my steps. I came back on the far side of Nick's property and entered through a gate near the open barn. Jim was inside spreading hay into a narrow feeding trough while the alpacas pranced in the small dirt area next to it. He glanced up as I came over and said hello. I watched him finish filling the trough, then step away and click to the alpacas. The animals followed one another to the trough, three cream-colored and one brown whose fur was so thick it looked like a saddle around its middle. The brown butted one of the others out of the way and began eating in its place. Chewing, it craned its neck, looked at us, then dipped for more hay.

Jim laughed and said, "You don't want to mess with her. She's testy."

I asked, "The brown?"

He nodded.

"Why are they here anyway?"

Jim shrugged. "You know Nick. Always working an angle. Course, the guests like the curiosity, and the fur will bring three, four hundred bucks each. But Nick's mostly interested in the money they can generate breeding. A healthy yearling goes for about fifteen grand."

I whistled and said, "No kidding."

Jim nodded again. "The brown's due to give birth in the spring. That'll be our first."

"Where'd you learn to care for them?"

Jim shrugged again. "Not much to it, really. Been reading things online. Worked on a farm or two back when." He scratched the brown's head as she ate, the fur there dusty and flaked with bits of straw. He said, "I've always liked animals."

The light in the barn was dim. I heard the distant sound of a motor and turned to see the first of the lodge's boats returning from around the headland.

⪜ ⩊ ⪜

Dinner that night was a little later than the evening before. While the salad was being served, I looked out the big picture windows across the channel. There was no sunset, though the rain had stopped and the ceiling of clouds had lifted a bit. Nick came over and stood next to my chair to talk for a while. He told me a little more about a new business venture in Tucson he and his wife were pursuing; she was down there now, and he'd join her there right after this trip. The concept he explained was essentially a winter equivalent of the lodge except it was built around a southwestern theme and would cater to trail rides and customized golf packages.

By the time dinner ended, it was nearly dark. Most of the guests headed into the little nearby village to the local tavern. Nick went off with his two yellow labs to his house at the rear of the property, a larger, two-storied version of our cabins. I walked back to my cabin and stood a while against the porch railing. I watched the lights at Nick's house blink off one by one. The tide was going out again, and across the channel I could see the glow of Port McNeil like a rudely tossed string of Christmas lights in the distance. Other than that, it was nothing but water, trees, and mountains in all directions. Lovely.

Down at the entrance to the barn, I saw Jim brushing the back of the big brown alpaca. Even at fifty yards away, I could hear the slow, course pull of the brush. I took my wallet out and looked at the photo of my wife and daughter. Then I replaced it, went inside, and called it a night.

⪜ ⩊ ⪜

The next morning, we motored north along the island's curving coastline for better than an hour before putting our lines in. I got my fish not twenty minutes afterwards: a small late-season king, skinny but long, not even twenty pounds. Our guide was named Geoff, a lanky kid with bad teeth and earnest eyes. It was just after sunrise and the tide had begun to turn. The sun hadn't yet peeked over the mountains on the mainland, but it promised to be a nice day.

Geoff told me he'd lived on the island since he was three. He helped his dad and uncle at their gas station in the village during the off-season. I asked him what it was like to grow up there, and he shrugged.

"All right, I guess. I liked it. Suppose it gets kind of slow for some kids."

"Did hippies really used to live on Nick's property?"

"So the story goes. That was before my time. Ask Jim. He was around then."

A little before noon, we brought in the lines and motored around to a small cove where lunch had been set up for us on the beach. The scene looked a little like a reception area for a fancy outdoor wedding. A canopy had been raised over folding tables and chairs and chamber music was playing from a boom box. The chef was lifting live crabs into a big iron pot suspended over a smoldering fire dug into the pebbly sand, and the college girls were seating people and pouring chilled white wine. Nick shuttled folks from the anchored fishing boats to the shore in a dinghy with a small outboard that looked brand new.

We were the last boat in. I could see the surgeon waiting in the back of a skiff with no fishing gear, and I assumed it was what Nick had come out on himself. When he came for our boat, I asked Nick about it, and he said he was taking the surgeon back to do the shearing. I asked if I could go with them.

"Suit yourself," Nick said. "But you'll miss this spread. All we have is sandwiches and sodas in a cooler on board."

I told him that was fine. On the way back, I ate and listened to the surgeon and Nick discuss plans for the shearing. The surgeon did most of the talking. I supposed his confident tone must have been a lot like the one he used in his profession before operating. It seemed to be sufficient for Nick, who mostly nodded and maneuvered the skiff to avoid the chop.

When we got to the lodge, I asked if they needed any help. The surgeon shook his head and said they'd be fine. Nick told me to come around to watch if I wanted. I saw Jim down by the barn leading the last of the alpacas into the corral and could hear him clicking to it softly.

I went up to my cabin and laid down for what I planned to be a fifteen-minute nap, but I didn't open my eyes again until I heard someone shout, "We gotta show this one who's goddamn boss!" I glanced at my watch and saw that I'd been asleep for almost an hour.

I looked out the window toward the corral. The three cream-colored alpacas were already shorn, prancing along the reaches of it. Strange-looking to begin with, they now appeared even odder: completely bald except for their heads and the portion of the ankles above the hooves. A boy Nick used as a deckhand was filling a burlap sack with the last of their fur; a dozen or so sacks like it leaned against the barn wall. Jim was slowly circling the big brown alpaca in the middle of the corral while the surgeon gestured angrily with what looked like a barber's electric clippers. Nick stood off a little ways outside the corral leaning against the fence. I could see him smiling. Dark clouds had rolled in from the north.

I roused myself, went down the hill, and stood next to Nick. He gave me a clap on the shoulder and said, "Well, you missed most of the fun, pal. The job's just about done."

"How's it gone so far?"

"Piece of cake." He nodded toward the corral. "Our gal here is putting up a bit of a fight. No surprise there."

Jim was walking the big brown alpaca towards the corner of the corral where it met the barn. The surgeon was already waiting there with belts. "Just grab her and hold her against the fence!" he shouted. "We'll have to strap this one in!"

I wasn't sure what I was seeing in Jim's eyes, but it wasn't happy. He shuffled the brown into the corner.

"Jim wants to go easy with her because she's pregnant," Nick said quietly to me. "He treats them like they're his pets. Just like he treats the dogs."

The surgeon stepped up behind the big animal, wrapped his arms around the middle, and began wrestling her against the fence. The alpaca made a strange bleating noise; the first sound I'd heard from any of them, bared her yellow teeth, and turned her head toward the surgeon.

"Grab her goddamn neck!" the surgeon shouted.

Jim did as he was told, it seemed to me, reluctantly. He tried to keep his face in her line of sight and whispered, "Shh, girl, shh."

The surgeon slipped once on the wet grass, swore, steadied himself, and managed to strap her middle to the fence with one of the belts before cinching it tight. He did the same with her neck. The alpaca kicked at him once hard, and he jumped out of the way.

"Ride 'em, cowboy," Nick called, laughing, but the surgeon wasn't smiling.

I heard Jim say, "Do you need to do that? We didn't with the others."

"This one's pissing me off," the surgeon said. "Not taking any chances. Hold her rump against the fence."

Jim moved to the rear of the alpaca, held her haunches, and turned his head away. The surgeon wasted no time starting the clippers, running them first over the lower part of the alpaca's long neck. As he did, she continued to squirm and thrash. The thick fur fell in clumps onto the grass. There was nothing technical about the clipping itself; the surgeon just moved methodically up and down with studied focus. He moved next to the hind end and worked back towards the front of the animal. When he got to the brown's middle, she began bucking her head so desperately that the fence shook and wood splintered.

The surgeon finished quickly, turned off the clippers and knocked them against the heel of his hand shaking the excess fur loose.

"Move up and hold her around the middle," he told Jim. "Until I get these belts loose."

Jim nodded, shifted his grip forward, but kept his head down.

The surgeon set the clippers on a fencepost, loosened the belt around the heavy, low middle of the alpaca, and pulled it free. Her legs wobbled. When he got to the belt on the neck, he said, "Easy now." I wasn't sure if he was talking to the animal or Jim.

He pulled off the final belt and stepped back. "All right," he told Jim. "Let her go."

Jim took his hands away and for a second the big animal swayed, then the legs buckled towards the fence and the rest of her fell over in the opposite direction into her own carpet of fur. She made a short thud when she landed. She lay completely still there in the low light.

I heard Nick say, "Jesus H. Christ."

He straightened next to me. For a moment, no one else moved. Then Jim knelt next to the alpaca and ran his hand gently from the base of the skull down to the top of the back. He turned and looked from the surgeon to Nick and said simply, "Broke her neck."

He looked back down at the brown, his shoulders fell, he shook his head. Nick ducked under the railing of the fence and I followed him up to the animal. The deckhand stood in the barn's opening, the sack dangling from his fingers.

The surgeon had knelt next to the alpaca. We watched his hands make the same trip down the animal's neck, then over her middle. He looked up at Nick and asked, "How far along was she?"

Nick's shrug was slight. "Maybe a few months."

The surgeon nodded slowly, stood up, wiped his hands together. "That's that, then," he said. "We lost them both."

I heard a motor faintly approaching on the water followed by the sound of distant laughter. I turned and saw one of the lodge fishing boats coming around the point in the distance.

"Well," Nick said evenly, "it won't do to have her lying here when the guests return. Let's get her in the back of the truck and bury her off in the woods somewhere."

He went around the barn where the vehicles were parked. No one said anything. The deckhand just stood there. The surgeon wound the belts into coils. Jim stayed kneeling, shaking his head back and forth. I turned away and watched the boat make its slow, distant approach towards the dock.

Nick came around the corner of the barn in one of the pickup trucks. The deckhand opened the wide corral gate, and Nick drove up alongside the alpaca. He jumped out, came back to us, and let down the tailgate. He'd already put a shovel and pickaxe into the back. He said, "Let's all just take a spot and lift. See how that works."

We did that and began lifting when he'd counted to three. The animal was heavy, stubby-haired, awkward, but we managed to slide her into the truck's bed. Her eyes were still open, pointing upward. It had begun to drizzle.

"I'll take her," Jim said.

Nick nodded and said, "Fine." He turned to the deckhand and told him, "Get the rest of that fur bagged before the boats come in."

The surgeon said, "If we'd had a proper shearing pen and equipment, that wouldn't have happened."

I watched Nick narrow his eyes and regard him. I suppose he was weighing the options of how to reply. After a long moment, he looked at the surgeon and me and said, "The two of you head up to the lodge and get a drink. I'll go meet the boats and join you later."

"That sounds good to me," the surgeon huffed. "I could use a drink."

I said, "I'll give Jim a hand."

Nick looked towards the water and shrugged again. I don't think he really cared what we did as long as the mess was cleared away before the rest of the guests came back up the hill from fishing. I watched him climb back through the fence and head down to the dock. Jim was already in the cab behind the wheel. I climbed in the other side and he drove away slowly, the wipers whacking. I didn't look back.

We drove in silence along the same road I'd walked on the day before. I looked over once, but Jim's face was blank. We drove along the bluff until we came to the spot with what had looked like old abandoned farm buildings to me; Jim pulled into a field there and stopped the truck. He got out and immediately started swinging the pickaxe in the earth. He didn't say a word. I waited for him to clear himself some space, then started digging with the shovel behind him. He'd chosen a good place; the dirt was soft and loamy.

After a half hour, I was sweating and breathing hard. My palms had begun to blister, but Jim didn't slow down and neither did I. We continued until we had a hole that I assumed Jim thought was big enough because he tossed away the pickaxe and pushed the cap back on his head. He took a bandana from his jeans pocket and blew his nose once loud. He didn't look at me, but I could see he'd been crying.

"Well," he said, "let's get it done."

He backed the truck up against the hole and we slid the alpaca into it. Jim closed her eyes. Then we covered her, Jim using the side of the pickaxe, me the shovel. It only took a few minutes. I realized that it had stopped raining. We tossed the tools in the back of the truck and Jim slammed the tailgate. He stood looking over the clearing.

I said, "That digging could have been worse."

"We used to grow poppies here," he said. "Good spot. Compost pile was right about where the front bumper is."

"You raised around here?"

"He shook his head. "San Francisco."

I frowned thinking about that and watched him go around his side of the truck. I did some quick mental math, counting backwards by the decade. Jim climbed in the cab.

We didn't talk on the way back until we were almost to the lodge. Then Jim said, "The son of a bitch never even said he was sorry. He never uttered a word of apology, did he?"

I shook my head. "Not that I remember."

❦

Dinner that night was essentially more of the same: cocktails and appetizers, Nick's positive spin on the day and plan for our last one, the wine descriptions, the chef's culinary preview. The clouds had lifted and the evening was like our first: quiet, full of wide, dappled light. A few wispy clouds hung over the charcoal-shaded mountains across the channel and tinted to the color of cranberries as the sun settled among them. Looking out the window while I ate, the light seemed to fall like a long sigh.

I excused myself during dessert and took a nearly full bottle of Cabernet off the buffet. I went downstairs with it and out the screen door there toward the barn. Cicadas called in the weeds. The tide was creeping in, running along the shore, crackling in the rocks.

I didn't know which of the staff's quarters may have been Jim's, but as it turned out, I didn't need to. I stopped at the entrance to the barn and found him sitting against a creosote-soaked post inside scratching one of the smaller alpacas behind the ears. Its head was on his lap. The other two were eating hay from troughs nearby. Jim held a dented metal mug in his non-scratching hand. I took a couple of steps inside the barn, and he looked up. The light was low, and the smell of manure twanged the back of my nose.

"Brought this," I said and held the wine bottle out towards him. "In case you wanted some."

Jim shook his head, lifted the mug, and said, "Way ahead of you."

I walked over and sat on a hay bale. I took a swallow from the bottle and said, "They look like something out of a Dr. Seuss book, don't they?"

Jim gave a small chuckle and nodded, but didn't respond. One of the eating alpacas snorted. A few late sunbeams crept almost horizontal through the barn's slats.

"So," I said. "I guess you came up here about '71, '72?"

His hand stopped scratching, but he kept his eyes on it. He mumbled, "Thereabouts."

I nodded, though he couldn't see it, then said, "You come to beat the system or beat the draft?"

Jim looked at me quickly, considering, I suppose. He took a sip before he said, "Both, I guess. Mostly the latter. I tried going Conscientious Objector, but was denied. My dad was an ex-Marine, wanted me in the officer-training route." He paused, studying me, his almond-shaped eyes damp at the edges. He said, "You're old enough to know."

I nodded again. "Got a high draft number is all. Dumb luck."

He said, "Well, I didn't get so lucky. Tell the truth, I was flat out scared. A friend of mine in the same situation was coming up, so I just went with him. We crossed together by Hope, Canada, at the Montana state line. He went to Toronto; I came north and west. Heard about this place, the farm, from a guy in Prince Rupert. Been here, really, ever since."

I nodded some more, then looked up at the rafters in the shadows, curved like the bottom of a canoe.

"I hung those," Jim said, following my gaze. "Made the cow and moon too, up where we buried the brown. Stoned most of the time, if I remember correctly."

We both laughed. Afterwards, we were quiet for a while. Jim went back to scratching, sipping from his mug. Music came from the lodge, as well as the sound of laughter and chairs sliding. I listened to that, to the water in the rocks, to the alpacas breathing.

Finally, Jim said, "Talk about dumb luck. Day before I left, I was protesting about the bombing raids in Cambodia with a big group of people in Oakland. Buddy I was with, same one I came up with, got a crooked hair and set off some kind of explosive against a corner of the post office." He shook his head. "I had no idea what he was doing. I was in some bushes next to him taking a leak. But he grabbed me afterwards and we ran." Jim stopped scratching, put his head back, took a sip from his mug. He said, "Drove straight through the night. I read about myself and him in the newspaper the next morning before we crossed over. Fair amount of damage from the explosion, but no one hurt. Federal offense, though."

I sat looking at him. I asked, "So, the Ford amnesty didn't help you? The Carter pardon?"

He shook his head. "Moot point with my felony warrant outstanding."

I shook mine, too, and said, "You got to be kidding."

He held up his mug as if to toast, took a sip, said, "Wish I was."

Someone had turned the music up in the lodge and changed it to swing. I heard happy shouting and the pounding of dancing feet. It was warm in the barn. I took a couple more swallows of wine, then just sat still.

A minute or two passed before I asked, "You in touch with anyone from home?"

He said quietly, "A sister."

"You ever think of trying to go back anyway?"

He shrugged. "Hell, I'm sixty. Too old to chance prison. My brother's a Vietnam War vet, an angry one. Dad was career military; he's never forgiven me either. Only he's in a home now with Alzheimer's." He spit into the dirt. "My mom's on her last legs. Hooked up to a bunch of tubes in a hospital."

I looked at him sitting there. I wondered if we might have become friends when we were younger. I wasn't sure. I took another swallow from the bottle; he did the same from his mug.

He looked up at me. "And then there's the fact that I think I'm a father. Truth is, there's really no doubt. My sister let me know that the woman I'd been seeing at the time had a baby not long after I left. A little girl."

A pit had opened in my gut. The light in the barn had fallen; it was musty, quiet. After a while, I could hear Jim drink, but could barely see him. A few frogs began to groan outside. At some point afterwards, I said goodnight, found my way up to my cabin, got in bed, and thought. It was that last thing he said that really got to me. I didn't fall asleep for a long time.

⟡⟡ ⟠ ⟡⟡

I skipped the morning wake-up call. I rolled over, tried to go back to sleep, but couldn't, so just thought some more. I waited until I heard the boats depart, then dressed and headed to the lodge. I ate a muffin and drank coffee on the deck while I waited for the horizon to brighten and the lights to come on up at Nick's house. When they did, I waited a decent amount of time, then walked up there and knocked on the door. He met me in his bathrobe, one of the same plush kind that hung in each cabin, and asked me in. He was toweling his hair, fresh from the shower.

We sat down and I told him my idea. He listened, holding the towel still in his hands. Once I'd finished, he looked over my shoulder towards the water, then back at me and said, "Go ahead. Do what you want. But if you get into trouble, don't turn to me. I need someone here to look after the place when I head south tomorrow, and it doesn't much matter whether it's him or you." To be honest, I'd expected some sort of opposition or, at least, disbelief from him, but he was customarily matter of fact.

I went down to the barn next. Jim wasn't inside and wasn't around the staff housing. I found him over by the garden, hosing out some plastic buckets. He had the cup end of a thermos steaming with coffee on the grass next to him. He turned off the hose, but left the coffee alone.

I told him the same version I'd given to Nick, except that I added that he was free to use my condo and car, stay as long as necessary; my new neighbors didn't know me anyway. My bank paid all my bills electronically. I kept a debit/credit card and gave Jim my others, my driver's license, passport, plane ticket to Reno, and the keys to my car and condo. He opened the passport and glanced at the photo. When he closed it and our eyes met, I knew he thought we looked enough alike, too; that it would work.

I said, "In Nanaimo on the way up in the float plane, they only radioed customs. No one even came down to the dock. I bet they're just as slack going back. Might stick a head inside, ask the purpose of the trip, stuff like that. You just take the last plane, sit in the back, shove a lodge hat over your head, act like any other asshole from Chicago. Guests ask, tell them you're going down for some end-of-the-season errands. They inquire about me, say I'm staying to spend some time with my old friend, Nick. They won't ask; won't happen."

He looked down at the items in his hand for a while as if weighing them. Finally, he said, "If I went, I'd just go long enough to say goodbye . . . you know, try to look up my daughter, take care of things like that."

I said, "There's no rush."

He said, "I can't guarantee there won't be problems."

I nodded and said, "I think you should try."

He looked out over the water, where or at what, I could only guess.

Then he asked, "Nick okay with this?"

I nodded again.

"God almighty," he muttered and shook his head. "This is a hell of a thing you're doing."

"We all get dealt cards," I told him. "Let's exchange money."

He gave me the Canadian cash he had. It wasn't much, but I was sure I wouldn't need more. Nick had accounts at the stores in the village he'd said I could use, as well as several more over on Vancouver Island. I had that card of my own I'd kept. What else did I need?

In the end, I sent Jim to shave his stubble, clean up, and get packed just as the boats were coming back in. They had finished their little run to pull crab and shrimp pots before the floatplanes arrived. That way everyone would go home with catch, even those who hadn't landed a fish; everyone would head back happy.

I didn't go down to the dock for the farewell. I watched from my cabin window as they took group photos and listened to their bursts of laughter. I heard Nick say something about the last trip of the season, what a great group they were, that he'd see them again next year. Then he had the staff pass out handsome tweed satchels as gifts, each with the lodge's name and my jumping fish logo stenciled on the side. I stayed long enough to see the planes fly off, Jim on the last one.

The rest of the staff took their leave over the course of the afternoon. The college girls all went on the late afternoon ferry over to Port McNeil. I guess a few of them saw me around, but no one said anything. I suppose Nick gave them the same explanation I'd suggested to Jim. Anyway, they were anxious to get on to the next step in their lives, that was plain to see.

Nick had me up to his place that evening. We barbecued hamburgers, ate on his wrap-around deck, and drank beer while the sun made its slow descent. He told me some more about how the Tucson idea was progressing and that he'd probably be needing my services soon on that, too. After dinner, he took me on a tour of his place, explained the circuit breakers, procedures with the animals, where the keys were kept, and the like. I slept in his guest room, which would quickly become my home for an uncertain amount of time.

Early the next morning before his floatplane came, I walked the grounds with Nick. We brought the boats up into a storage area behind the barn, but left the skiff in case I wanted to use it myself. I walked down to the dock with him before he left. He gave me a last shoulder clap and called me stupid this and stupid that. We made vague plans for me to drive down to Tucson from Reno to visit. Then he boarded and we waved as they motored away from the dock. I looked after the plane until it had lifted and disappeared from sight. It was another clear, clean day, warm, hardly a cloud in the sky. My heart had steadied a bit, but I still felt as if I was in a dream. It wasn't unpleasant.

❧❧ ❀ ❧❧

That was almost three months ago now. I still haven't heard from Jim, that's true. I don't actually know how to get in touch with him. He didn't own a cell phone, and I never even had the chance to install a landline in my new place, but it's unlikely he's there anyway. I suppose I could contact Nick, but I doubt he knows either. At any rate, I haven't been inclined to try, nor do I expect to feel a pending compulsion to do.

The fall was wonderful, more colors and drier than might be expected this far north. I took the skiff out quite a few times in early October and hit a good run of silvers, all legal. I'm still eating off the fillets I froze. I've recently tried my hand at fishing in some of the nearby streams and have gotten a couple nice early steelheads.

As for spending time, aside from keeping up with my few work accounts, I found the high-quality art materials Nick told me his wife never used and have put those to good use. I paint daily for several hours, which I haven't done since college; it's wonderful, like discovering an old friend. The lodge has a whole library of books that I've only begun to investigate. I've started some seedlings in the greenhouse next to the garden; that's a first for me. I go into the village on one of the bikes or in the truck when I need to, and have taken the ferry over to Port McNeil a few times.

I guess what I enjoy as much as anything is just sitting on Nick's deck studying the tides and watching the landscape change, watching the winter approach. I have the dogs and alpacas for company, who I've grown to love. We've recently had this little powdering of snow that has softened things, quieted them, added stillness. And with the colder weather, the Aurora Borealis is like a symphony. This is a beautiful place. I'm fine.

If you were to ask me, I'd still say I'm all but sure Jim is coming back. Perhaps his parents' illnesses have become prolonged. Or maybe he's established some sort of relationship with his daughter, and is spending time with her. I hope he has. Life takes its twists and turns. Forty years is a long time. There's really no hurry. Heck, if pressed, I could probably stay indefinitely without much trouble at all.

SAM

I live in Iowa, always have, in a place which is not a farm. There are lots of farms around me. Mostly corn, some dairy cattle. My place isn't a farm, but I have an old white house, a big field on one side, some tall trees, a vegetable garden, a chicken coop out back, and a little corral with a lean-to where my horse, Pronto, used to stay. Pronto up and died of old age twenty years ago, about the time I started getting old too, just before Sam and her mother rented the house next door.

I suppose Sam was about seven or eight then. She was a short little thing who mostly wore red sneakers, overalls, T-shirts when it was warm, and a gray hooded sweatshirt when it wasn't. Her mom told me that the thing with Sam's hair was that it had just never really grown in fully. She had a kind of coating of white, new-corn silk on her head, big blue eyes, little nose. Her face was mostly eyes, though.

Her mom was a nice lady. When the school year began, she started working days as a checker at a supermarket in town, but she was back when Sam came home on the bus. She also did alterations on her sewing machine for a clothing store. She was a quiet, thoughtful lady, but she was pretty busy working as much as she did, and I didn't ever know her too well. Anyway, it's Sam I mostly want to tell about. Sam and that late summer and fall, a summer that stayed plenty hot and a fall that was cool and short, before they moved down to Omaha.

I guess I first noticed Sam soon after they arrived on an early August afternoon sitting out in her back yard by their row of poplar trees looking up at the birds. Those were wrens up there who gathered on the high branches and telephone wires to wait for evening so that they could invade undisturbed the fields and vegetable gardens like the one I was tending that day. Sam sat cross-legged on the grass looking up at the birds and scratching Mrs.

Lemmink's mutt, Jeff, who'd come across the alley behind the trees.

I watched her do that for several days before I finally went over to the back fence. As softly as I could, so as not to startle her, I said, "Them's wrens. You like 'em?"

She looked up at me and nodded.

"Like birds and such?"

"Yes."

"I got some chickens. Want to help me feed 'em?"

"Sure."

"Run, ask your mom first."

She did. Her mom came to their back door, wiping her hands on her apron. She waved and smiled at me. It made me feel good. Sam ran through the hedge that separated their side yard from mine for the first of many times during those few short months, the sort of visitor every one of us deserves, but few get to have. I wish she were here to run through that hedge today.

Came so almost every afternoon she'd stop over to visit for a little while. Usually, I'd be sitting in the front yard under the maple tree in one of those metal, tulip-backed chairs that used to be green. She'd come tearing over, climb up in the other, and try to rock it back and forth. Her legs just stuck out straight, the chair was that big for her. If it was warm, I'd have maybe made a pitcher of lemonade for us and have it waiting on the little wooden bench between the chairs. If it was cool, sometimes I'd have out a plate of store-bought cookies. Sugar cookies were her favorites, with a dollop of dried jelly in the middle.

Then we'd sit and talk, watch the rye grass across the road sway if there was a breeze or wait to get turned under when the field got set to go fallow later on. Sometimes, we'd go poke in the garden or feed the chickens. On occasion, we played rummy or Chinese checkers. When it was raining, she'd come upstairs to my attic workroom and watch me tinker with my model ships. But mostly, we'd just sit and talk. There, in the front yard under the maple tree. Truth be told, I guess I did most of the talking, and her the listening. She was a good listener, Sam. That's a pretty rare thing for a person to be.

Turns out Sam and I had some things in common. For instance, my wife and her dad had died around the same time, about five years before Sam and her mom came to live there. I had no children, and she had no siblings. We both liked root beer, hated lima beans. Both of us liked to sleep with the window open, even in cold weather. Both liked fires in the fireplace. Both were unsettled by the sound the house made late at night when it was dark and the furnace kicked on. Neither of us was fond of television. Sam didn't really have any hair to speak of, and I didn't have the little finger on my left hand.

I liked Sam straight off when she went ahead and asked me about my hand that first afternoon when we were feeding the chickens. She stopped tossing feed when she noticed it and said, "You're missing one of your fingers."

I said, "That's right."

"Why?"

"Got chopped off in a machine at the factory where I used to work in town."

Sam screwed up her face then, like she did sometimes, crinkled up her nose like she was going to snort. "Does it hurt?"

"Not anymore."

She was quiet for a while. Then she threw some feed to the chickens and said, "I don't have much hair. It doesn't matter. Who cares?"

And that was the last we ever, either of us, brought it up.

❦❦ ❦ ❦❦

Sam had a few friends, I guess. She used to walk down the road sometimes to an older girl's house who had a big Appaloosa. And when her mother had to make trips to the clothing store, she left Sam with a lady from the supermarket who had two little boys. But mostly, Sam seemed to be alone. Not lonely, just alone. Watching things, singing to herself, reading, playing pretend, and making things that she never explained to me.

I could watch her from the window of my workroom down in her back yard, or off in the Hodges' pasture, or in the narrow, dirt alley behind our houses that led to the county road. For one solid week after they first got there, I watched her build a kind of fort down there in the alley between our sheds with boards, an old canvas tarp, and a tattered quilt on the dirt floor. Most of the front of it and part of the top were covered by the branches of a climbing rose bush that grew high off the ground. I could see her through the branches, but to walk past it without knowing it was there, you'd never suspect it was anything but a heap of scrap lumber and such.

That fort was a pretty sturdy little deal, the way she'd built it. When she was gone one day, I walked back and looked it over. It was safe. She'd arranged a couple of shelves with some books and things on them. And she'd hung an old, brown felt hat on a nail. I think it had probably been her dad's. Sometimes, she wore it in there.

Not many people used that alley. Every now and then, a car or truck from one of the houses would go down it to or from the county road. Sometimes, a person would walk out through a back yard behind a garage or shed to empty trash or toss away grass clippings. But the only other person I saw back there much was the new boy from the brick house up a ways and across the alley.

He was maybe a couple of years older than Sam and had moved in about a year before them. I'd see him back there racing his bicycle, cutting through yards, messing around. When his parents wanted him to come in, they shook a big cowbell outside the back door. I'm pretty sure he was the one who broke all the jack-o-lanterns on the front porches late on Halloween night the year before. I didn't think much of him.

I didn't know his name, but he was a tall stringbean of a boy with freckles and bright red hair. So I called him "Red." Watching him through my workroom window, I'd say to myself, "Red, you'd best not run that bicycle into those folks' fencepost," or, "Stop spitting over the Rogers' hedge, Red." One evening, I watched him blow up an anthill with a firecracker.

I guess he was away on vacation or something after Sam and her mom first moved in because I didn't see him back there afterwards until shortly before school started up again. So, for the first month or so that she was there, Sam had the place pretty much to herself. It wasn't until a gray, drizzly, late August afternoon that I first saw them in the alley at the same time.

She was lying on her back in the fort reading. Red came riding his bicycle up the alley from the county road. Halfway along, he began zigzagging back and forth pulling down garbage cans as he did. Sam knelt up in her fort at the sound and watched him pull down the rest of the garbage cans between her house and his own before he turned through his hedge and disappeared into his back yard.

She walked into the alley and looked up and down at the tipped-over cans and the little piles of trash they had left where they'd fallen. She just stood in the drizzle with her arms folded and that crinkled-up look on her face. The last train of the day blew its whistle beyond the cornfields across the county road. It went off through the hollow and along the river towards its stop in town. Sam stood in the alley like that until all of it had passed and you couldn't hear it anymore. Then she walked down the alley, and I watched her stand up each of the cans and put the trash back into them. By the time she'd finished, the drizzle had turned to rain.

Sometimes in Iowa, winter turns into spring, and summer into fall, overnight. This happened one night in mid-September of that year. If your window was open, you could taste fall on your tongue before you were fully awake, cool and fresh. Dew stood the grass firm, and some of the leaves on the maples and birches that had been green the last time you looked, had quietly gone and turned yellow and orange: splashes of color. When a breeze came up, the propellers from the maples, now dried, twirled to the ground. And there was usually a thin, crisp breeze. The breeze smelled nice, like fall.

That first afternoon of the change, I was sitting in my workroom. I know that Sam was happy to greet the fall, too, because we'd talked about it earlier over cookies in the front yard, and then she'd collected some of the fallen leaves, still damp, beneath the maple tree. Now she was down in her fort pressing those leaves between the pages of a thick book. I'd watched her for a few moments before I began working on the model I was making of a clipper ship.

Time passed. We must have heard the first small pop and plink at about the same moment because when I stood up and looked through my curtains, I could see Sam kneeling in her fort peeking between the branches of the rose bush. Red was kneeling, too, up the alley behind his house. A row of empty bottles was stacked together in a neat line across the alley about twenty-five feet away from him. The top half of the first bottle, tall and thin and green, lay shattered on the ground. Red lifted the BB gun he held, closed one eye, took aim, and blasted away at the next bottle. I blinked at the sound of the shot. I blinked another handful of times before all of the bottles were shattered in a long pile of broken glass across the alley.

My heart was beating pretty hard. I guess Sam's must have been, too. We watched Red stand up, blow the smoke that was not there from the end of the barrel of his gun, hitch up his jeans, and walk through the hedge into his back yard. It was quiet again. Then the screen door to the back of his house banged once, twice, three times shut. I blinked then, too.

This time when Sam came out of her fort, she didn't stand in the alley long and didn't make her snorting face. She went into her shed and came back out with a short-shafted, flat shovel. Then she walked up the alley, pulled out the garbage can from behind Red's shed, and shoveled the glass into it. The shovel scraped, the glass tinkled. After she was finished, she smoothed the dirt in the alley with the back of the shovel and pulled the can over where it had been. She leaned against it with her chin on the backs of her hands at the end of the shovel handle, thinking, I guess. Next, she went over to where Red had run into his back yard and looked through the opening in the hedge. The back of his house was dark, no lights.

After a while, Sam dragged the shovel back to her shed, and ran through her own back yard into her house. I could see her mother at the sink under the yellow ceiling light, steam billowing around her from hot water. I looked over the top of their house at the dwindling early-fall afternoon, not yet quite evening. There was enough of a breeze to toss the big, colored leaves slowly and crazily to the ground, and enough of the same colors low in the sky to wash the last of its blue to the shade of India ink that's been mixed with water. I knew that had the day turned out differently, it was the type of thing that Sam would have stopped to watch and enjoy.

I never went down there while Sam was in her fort. I felt like it was her own special place, a secret place, and it wouldn't be right for me to interfere with that. I'd check on her from time to time from my workroom window to be sure she was all right, but that was all.

Mostly, I saw her having fun by herself down there. Besides reading and building things, she liked to paint and draw. She also made things out of clay and liked to dig in the dirt around the front of the fort with large spoons. Sometimes, she brought her stuffed animals and played with them, house or school, I suppose, or something like that.

Once, I watched her line up some of those stuffed animals on short benches she'd fashioned on either side of the fort. Then she tied a rope around a stake at the back of my chicken coop and set a pail upside-down in front of the fort. She put that felt cap on backwards, sat on the pail, shook the rope with two hands, and bounced up and down on the pail like she was driving a stagecoach. I smiled, watching.

I remember another interesting time not too long after they moved in involving Mrs. Lemmink and the rack where she used to let her cakes cool. It was a little shelf her husband had built for her up on the back of her garage in the alley right behind Sam's house—like a mailbox but screened in to keep away the cats and dogs, with a little latch to fasten it that she could reach from the back gate. A big shoot of lilac grew over the back of their garage and kept it shady and cool, and if there was any breeze on a hot, still day, it would always come up the alley from the river across the county road.

Maybe it was the first occasion that Sam was in her fort when Mrs. Lemmink set out a cake to cool, I don't know. But I watched Sam come out of her fort after Mrs. Lemmink had set the latch and gone back inside. Sam stood and looked at the cake across the alley there. A little breeze was turning the leaves, and I knew she could smell that cake; maybe it was one of those lemon ones Mrs. Lemmink was famous for at the church bazaars.

After a few minutes, Sam walked over to the cooling rack, which was about as high as her forehead, stood on her tiptoes, and peeked inside. Then she looked up and down the alley, lifted the latch, and took out the cake. She held it on the plate in front of her, studying it. She bent over, smelled the cake, closed her eyes. No one was in the alley. She looked up and down it again, then through Mrs. Lemmink's hedge into her empty back yard. Somewhere across the fields, a dog barked.

Then, Sam wrinkled up her nose, put the cake back, and closed the latch. She went into her fort and put on her hat. She sat against the wall and began to sing to one of her stuffed animals.

≫≫ ⚜ ≫≫

There was one other thing about Sam and her fort that was always the same. That was the bread that she brought for the birds. She brought it with her every day. First, she'd check to see if the bread from the day before was gone. It always was, and she'd smile. Then she'd break it into little pieces on top of the fort, spread it out, and go inside it to play.

I guess it's the bread and the birds that made what happened next so difficult. I can still see her with that bread folded in her little hand coming to check the top of her fort. I can see it like it was yesterday. That, and her sitting cross-legged looking up at the birds. If I close my eyes, as I often do, I can see it. There she is: Sam.

I remember it was a late afternoon full of gray, solid clouds and muffled light, but no rain. The deepening fall had turned the air chilly. From up in my workroom window, I could see Red in his back yard with his slingshot shooting rocks at tin cans at the same time that Sam came around her shed and put out the bread on top of her fort. When Sam went into it and opened a book, Red was crouched in his hedge shooting rocks at old tires that were leaning up against the neighbor's garage. A rock went "ping" against one of the hubcaps. Sam dropped her book and knelt up in her fort. I sat forward, I remember, on the edge of my chair, the breeze through the open window lifting the curtains. We were both watching Red.

It was a cold afternoon, as I said. Not much more than a month later, our first snow would fall. In that hard, white-gray light you could see well a black rock fly. Red rolled over like a soldier into the alley, and from his knees took aim at three wrens on the telephone wire above him. He hit the first one pretty near the center of the breast. The bird fell straight down with the rock. They hit the ground at the same time with a small thump, and a tiny cloud of dust lifted around them in the middle of the alley. The other wrens called and flew away.

Sam had her hands over her mouth. Red got up and stood looking down at the bird with his fists on his hips. The bird was very still, dead. I began to lift the window but waited because I saw Sam walking fast up the alley. She stopped a few feet from the bird and Red. He looked at her without grief or insolence, just blankly.

I heard her small voice say, "Why'd you do that?"

Red said, "What do you care? It's just an old bird."

"You killed it," Sam said and began to cry.

"It's just a dumb bird. Go away."

"It was mean."

Red turned and faced her fully. "Go on, get lost."

For several long seconds, Sam just looked at him and he stared back. Then she walked past him to the side of the alley, picked up a broken piece of shingle, walked back, and knelt in front of the bird. She slid the shingle gently under it, lifted it with two hands, and carried it carefully down the alley into her back yard. Before I went down to her, I saw Red shoot the slingshot once more at the old tires, the rock skipping over them in the dirt, then spin and run through the hedge into his own back yard.

When I got down there, Sam was squatting under the row of poplars at the edge of the alley. She had already dug a small hole in the damp earth with her hands and was crying quietly. She looked up at me once, then went back to her digging. She didn't ask why I was there, but she let me help her finish digging the hole.

When we were done, she picked up the bird on the shingle and said,

"It's still warm."

I said, "It'll be cold in a few minutes, Sam."

I took the shingle from her. She sat down and stuck her hands into the pouch of her sweatshirt. I buried the bird quickly, smoothed the dirt, and put a few stones over the top. Then I sat down across from her and watched her stare at the little grave.

Mrs. Lemmink came up the alley in her car. Her headlights swept over us through the leaves. She stopped in the alley behind the poplars and left the car idling. I heard her garage door open, then the car pull in. The engine quit; the spring on the garage door groaned as it came down. There was a little thud and an echo after it closed. Then it was still again. A low fog was drifting up from the river.

After a while, Sam stopped crying and sniffed. She wiped her nose on the sleeve of her sweatshirt. Finally, she said, "A boy killed it. He shouldn't have. I don't know why he did."

I said, "It was a bad thing to do."

"Then why did he?" she demanded. She looked up at me.

I said, "I don't know. I don't think most folks are just plain mean. Some people don't know better, or they haven't been taught. Some don't think or are just ignorant. Maybe he didn't understand it was wrong. Thing is, you do. So it hurts you bad. That's okay. That sort of thing ought to make you feel bad. It's part of what makes you a good person."

She crinkled up her face at me like she was going to snort and said, "I don't know about that. I just wish that bird didn't die."

"Sure," I said. "But you did the right thing, the good thing. Seems to me you usually do. You got to rest with that."

She just looked at me: a small girl on a cold evening out near where the farmland begins with very little hair and big eyes who was learning about things with a grace that made me ache.

I said, "Say, I got me a few ears of late corn in the garden still haven't been picked. You ever had corn boiled fresh-picked? Tastes like candy."

"No," she said and smiled. "I'd like to."

"Well, I'll go put a pot on to boil. You run, ask your mom, then meet me in the garden. We got to be quick."

"Okay," she said and ran off.

Shucks, I would've liked to have done more to comfort her, you can be sure of that. I felt lucky to know her. Blessed that she'd moved in for a while next door and brought some joy to my life. Hope, too, I guess. I would have given the rest of my fingers to see her never have to try to make sense of something like that again. So, I just did the best I could and made my way home to heat water, hoping that fresh-picked sweet corn put to boil right away could make her forget the bad things and remember the good ones again for a while.

❧❧ ✿ ❧❧

Sam and Red had one more time together, about a week later, I think. It was only a little thing. No more than a moment, really. It was just something that happened and then was over. A small thing.

She was sitting outside her fort rubbing a stick in the dirt, and he came racing down the alley standing up on his bicycle pumping like crazy. He shot past her, his front tire hit a divot, and over the handlebars he flew. He landed in the gravel on the side of the alley and started howling, holding his knee.

Sam was out to him before I could stand up at my desk. He looked at her through that grimace of pain, and he recognized her; I could see that. He hesitated before he let her help him up. But he did. And he leaned against her through the hedge limping up to his backdoor. I think she might have knocked on the door for him. After his father had come and brought Red inside, she went back, wheeled his bike through the hedge, and set it against the side of his house.

That was all. A small thing. Not much more than a moment. She returned to her fort, and he didn't come out again that afternoon. I don't think they saw one another again, because the next week Sam's uncle came with a big flatbed truck and moved them down to Omaha where he lived.

The move made sense for them. It did. Sam's mom was going to manage a second restaurant he was opening. He was married, and there were a bunch of cousins down there for Sam. Omaha is nice place. Lots to do. Pretty park along the river, museums, even a zoo. I helped them load the truck. When they left, Sam leaned out the window and waved until they turned onto the county road. So did I.

❧❧ ✿ ❧❧

I wish I could say that Red straightened out and never did anything wrong again, but I can't. I still saw him riding down the alley on his bicycle with his BB gun from time to time, and I could hear him shooting over by the river. On a weekday morning in March, I saw him painting his back porch; Mrs. Lemmink told me he'd been suspended from school for something.

And one May night, when only my first shoots of butter lettuce and radishes were up, I was awakened by the sound of splintering wood in the garden. I opened the window, saw my scarecrow cracked at the waist, and shouted, "Hey!" I saw someone running out of my field, someone his height and shape. It was a waning moon, and although I couldn't be certain, I'm pretty sure his hair was red.

His family moved, too, soon thereafter. Mrs. Lemmink told me they'd gone to a bigger town nearby where his father had heard the schools were stricter.

As I said, nearly two decades have passed since then. About ten years ago, the climbing became too much for me, so I stopped using the upstairs. Then a while back, I closed off the downstairs bedrooms, too, to help with heating costs. Now, I have a cot I sleep on next to the dining room table. That's where I work on my model ships. The light is good. I can see the fire in the living room fireplace and feel it. I still keep a couple rows of beans, some tomatoes, a few ears of corn in the garden. Things are fine.

I exchanged Christmas cards with Sam and her mother for quite a few years, but eventually they stopped coming. I kept sending mine for a while longer, but they were returned because the address was incorrect. Then, last Christmas, here comes a box from someplace in Montana that's mostly woods, and what do you know, it's from Sam. Her card said she was sorry she'd misplaced my address for so long, but she hoped I was well, that she was happy, and what's more, was married now. Her husband was a forest ranger of some sort, and she was teaching school. They sent a picture. He was a nice looking fellow, tall, slender. She looked good, big eyes, short hair, kind smile.

Come April, they're expecting a baby. She said she doesn't care what it is, but I hope it's a girl. She said they're thinking of taking a trip though here after the school year is out and the baby is born, maybe visit her mom who's living down south now on the coast. If they do, she said they'll stop to see me. I hope they do. I'd like that a lot.

In the box was a birdhouse. Her card said she'd made it herself. It had a nice bow on it, which I took off and saved. At first, I hung it in the maple tree out front, so I could look at it from the picture window and my lawn chair when it got warm enough to sit there. But then I got to thinking, and I moved it.

The people who live next door don't bother with that shed out back, especially the side where the climbing rose has grown over the eaves. I hung it there. It looks good. I've started bringing bread back there in the afternoons. Every afternoon, when I go out, the bread from the day before is gone. It's a joy to see. Small, but joyful. Whether it's cold and gray or the kind of day you can taste on your tongue before you are fully awake, I know that feeding bread to the birds is a good and joyful thing.

ACKNOWLEDGMENTS

These stories originally appeared, some in slightly different form, in the following journals:

"Uncommon" in *The Write Launch*
"Something Like That" in *Clackamas Literary Review*
"Inconceivable" in *Superstition Review*
"If You Treat Them Right" in *High Desert Journal*
"Swap and Shop" in *Westchester Review* (Pushcart Prize nominee)
"Make Your Own Bed" in *Sunday Salon*
"Wounds" in *Green Hills Literary Lantern*
"Surprise" in *The Writing Disorder*
"The Hay is in the Barn" in *The Write Launch*
"The Cow Jumped Over the Moon" in *Sobotka Literary Magazine*

AUTHOR

William Cass has had over 280 short stories accepted for publication in a variety of literary magazines and anthologies such as *december, Briar Cliff Review,* and *Zone 3.* He has won writing contests at *Terrain.org* and *The Examined Life Journal,* been a nominee for both Best Small Fictions and Best of the Net anthologies, and has also received four Pushcart Prize nominations. His first short story collection, *Something Like Hope & Other Stories,* was published by Wising Up Press in 2020. He lives in San Diego, California.

SELECTED BOOKS FROM WISING UP PRESS

FICTION
My Name Is Your Name & Other Stories
Kerry Langan

Germs of Truth
Heather Tosteson

Not Native: Short Stories of Immigrant Life in an In-Between World
Murali Kamma

Something Like Hope & Other Stories
William Cass

Rowing Home
Sybil Terres Gilmar

MEMOIR
My Brother Speaks in Dreams
Catherine Anderson

Keys to the Kingdom: Reflections on Music and the Mind
Kathleen L. Housley

Last Flight Out: Living, Loving & Leaving
Phyllis A. Langton

POETRY
Source Notes: Seventh Decade
Heather Tosteson

A Little Book of Living Through the Day
David Breeden

A Mother Speaks, A Daughter Listens
Felicia Mitchell

A Hymn that Meanders
Maria Nazos

Epiphanies
Kathleen L. Housley

PLAYS
Trucker Rhapsody & Other Plays
Toni Press-Coffman

WISING UP ANTHOLOGIES

ILLNESS & GRACE: TERROR & TRANSFORMATION

FAMILIES: *The Frontline of Pluralism*

LOVE AFTER 70

DOUBLE LIVES, REINVENTION & THOSE WE LEAVE BEHIND

VIEW FROM THE BED: VIEW FROM THE BEDSIDE

SHIFTING BALANCE SHEETS:
Women's Stories of Naturalized Citizenship & Cultural Attachment

COMPLEX ALLEGIANCES:
Constellations of Immigration, Citizenship & Belonging

DARING TO REPAIR: *What Is It, Who Does It & Why?*

CONNECTED: *What Remains As We All Change*

CREATIVITY & CONSTRAINT

SIBLINGS: *Our First Macrocosm*

THE KINDNESS OF STRANGERS

SURPRISED BY JOY

CROSSING CLASS: *The Invisible Wall*

RE-CREATING OUR COMMON CHORD

GOODNESS

FLIP SIDES:
*Truth, Fair Play & Other Myths We Choose to Live By:
Spot Cleaning Our Dirty Laundry*

ADULT CHILDREN:
Being One, Having One & What Goes In-Between

THE POWER OF THE PAUSE
The Wonder of Our Here & Now

Lightning Source UK Ltd.
Milton Keynes UK
UKHW012050060223
416584UK00007B/146

9 781737 694069